The Parallel World

D. M. Henry

abbott press®

A DIVISION OF WRITER'S DIGEST

The Parallel World

Abbott Press books may be ordered through booksellers or by contacting:

Abbott Press
1663 Liberty Drive
Bloomington, IN 47403
www.abbottpress.com
Phone: 1-866-697-5310

ISBN: 978-1-4582-0213-0 (sc)
ISBN: 978-1-4582-0215-4 (hc)
ISBN: 978-1-4582-0214-7 (e)

Library of Congress Control Number: 2012902212

Printed in the United States of America

Abbott Press rev. date: 3/8/2012

To Jessica and Marcus
For showing me what my purpose in life is

Acknowledgements

I want to thank my parents, Maggie and Gus, for making me the person I am today. I also want to thank my family and friends for their unconditional love and support.

I especially want to share my gratitude and appreciation to my husband Marc, my brother Peter, and friends Tamara and Drummond for taking time out of their busy lives to read completed versions of The Parallel World and provide not only support, but also constructive criticism. You have helped to make my dream become a reality.

CHAPTER 1

Rain was pouring down unrelentingly in waves across the half empty parking lot diminishing any light reflecting from the grey light poles. A cold and heavy wind was forcing the rain to fall diagonally hitting Alex in the face as she ran to her car. Alex inserted the key in the car door, and quickly threw her gym bag in the passenger seat before collapsing in the driver's seat. She rested her head on the headrest and slowly wiped her face with the back of her wet hands. A sarcastic smile appeared on Alex's face. She had to admit that the weather fit her mood perfectly.

Alex turned left out of her gym's parking garage and headed home. She turned the radio on to her favorite evening talk show and decided to turn the volume up high. She only lived fifteen minutes away, but wanted to listen to the program especially tonight seeing how the topic centered on single career women. Alex was a practicing paralegal at one of the nation's top law firms, but found herself, after four years, of not only thinking about the next phase in her career, but also her life. She didn't want to give the wrong impression to anyone. She loved her profession and working at the law firm, but she also wanted to learn and grow professionally as a paralegal and in her personal life.

Alex had to admit that it would be better if she broadened her knowledge and skills by expanding into other fields of the law. She just didn't know how to go about it. Should she go back to school for a masters in law?

1

Alex had a pile of admission's brochures for the law schools in and around the Baltimore area, but wasn't sure if law school was the answer. She also kept toying with the idea of talking to her paralegal manager about the possibilities of progressing in the firm. Who knows, maybe she should even look at becoming a paralegal manager. The only problem was that this solution would take her away from her current law firm. Alex stopped at a red light and turned the blinker on.

If there was one thing for sure Alex knew that her real present obstacle in life was figuring out what she, a twenty-five year old single career woman, wanted to do for at least the next five years. She had always admired people that knew what they wanted to do early in life and wondered why she hadn't joined the club. How could it be so easy for them? Alex turned right at the corner and stopped in front of the Chinese food take out restaurant. She stepped out, happy that the rain had stopped, and walked inside. Alex had known that the food was ready seeing how she had called the order in just before beginning her exercise class at the gym.

The worker behind the counter knew Alex, which showed how often she ordered from them. This gave Alex the advantage of calling in orders and being able to set a pick-up time; something that she did often. Alex paid for the appetizers and two meals before walking out and climbing back into her car. Her best friend was coming over in an hour for dinner and Alex wanted to be there beforehand to freshen up and change into lounge clothes. Alex was beginning to become impatient about her current lifestyle, but was careful not to show it on the outside, not even to her friends. She knew that they wouldn't understand her and view her words as empty complaints.

Alex walked into her apartment after a short drive from the Chinese food restaurant, turned the stereo on and moved to the bedroom to freshen up before putting her grey sweats on. The doorbell rang cutting into a caller's question on the radio. Alex swept her hair up and pulled it back into a ponytail. She looked in the mirror and immediately felt more relaxed and comfortable. She sauntered towards the front door and found a smiling Melanie looking back at her.

Mel walked through the door and gave Alex a bear hug. "Hey sweetie, look what I have for dessert." She opened the bag she was carrying and Alex peered in to find Ben and Jerry's Cherry Garcia and Triple Caramel Chunk ice cream snuggled neatly in the bag.

Alex smiled. "You know just how to make a girl happy. Come on in. The food is getting cold. I ordered your favorite and no I didn't forget the chop sticks this time."

The two friends sat down on the couch with Mel immediately turning the television on. They fixed their plates each taking an egg roll along with the main course and then settled in to watch *Grey's Anatomy*. They had both moved onto the ice cream half way into the program with Alex picking up the Cherry Garcia and Mel going for the Triple Caramel Chunk. They waited for the end of *Grey's Anatomy* before daring to say anything. Neither wanted to miss a second of Mr. McDreamy. Alex walked into the kitchen to pick out a bottle of wine. She didn't dare drink alone, but used every opportunity to rob her wine rack when company was over.

She picked out a French red wine and returned to the living room with the bottle and two wine glasses. Alex filled the glasses and the girls made a quick toast before enjoying the first sips from a new bottle. Alex looked at Mel watching television. If she could talk with anyone, then it should be Mel. They had become friends back in middle school and had been inseparable ever since. There was only one thing between them and that was money. Mel came from a middle class family. Alex knew that Mel had a good family upbringing and knew Mel's family quite well. They were her second family. Mel was fortunate and given many things to help her grow into a well rounded person, but her parents weren't rich and therefore had to make sacrifices of their own to give Mel and Mel's brother and sister opportunities.

Mel was compassionate and sympathetic about many things that Alex thought were important, but she was doubtful that Mel would feel the same when it came to Alex's chances and money situation. Mel felt that she was being stared at and turned towards Alex only to find Alex staring back at her over a half empty wine glass.

"Are you okay?"

Alex contemplated her answer. If she answered yes, then she would have to be prepared for Mel's response and maybe she wasn't ready for whatever Mel was going to say in reply. She could only hope that it was compassionate and understanding. She also wouldn't mind an answer.

Alex took a sip of her wine before responding. "I'm tired, Mel."

"What?" said Mel as she flipped through the television channels. It seemed as if the networks were playing a joke on her by showing programs only others could be interested in. "Why is it that there's never anything on TV?" Mel said.

"Because you're too much of a snob to like anything that comes on anyway. Did you hear me? I told you that I'm tired!"

"Tired? What do you mean?" Mel asked.

"I mean that I'm tired of my life. I'm tired of a monotonous sixty hour work week. I'm tired of being underpaid and overworked. I'm tired of not being appreciated for the work that I do. I'm tired of not being able to use my brains. And I'm tired of being single and childless!"

"Humph, sounds like you have a problem there," Mel joked. "Meanwhile, is it weird that I'm finding *National Geographic* more exciting than *CBS*?" Mel asked.

"Come on, Mel," Alex said. "I'm serious here."

"Okay, then…" Mel said. "What do you want?"

"That's the problem," Alex confessed. "I want everything…" Alex stood up and walked over to the window looking out onto a Baltimore City street. It was night time, but the stars were impossible to see through the haze of city lights and tall dingy buildings. "For starters, I want a job where I can exercise my talents and knowledge and get paid for my worth. I want financial stability. I want to be able to buy something without checking the account balance first. I want to find a nice, gorgeous man that wants more than a one night stand or casual sex. I want to settle down one day, and actually be happy. Not just say that I'm happy, but actually feel happy and be content," Alex said looking dreamily out the window.

"Sounds peachy to me, but let's look at the bright side of things." Mel smiled. "Look, you have a paralegal job at the number one law firm in Maryland. May I also add that it's one of the largest and in the top ten nationwide? You have a beautiful apartment located on Charles Street and I don't think that your salary is that bad. I think that you're just bored and over exaggerating things. Oh, and can I add one more thing – your grandmother was also a founding partner in the law firm that you're working at!" Mel said with a roll of the eyes.

Alex looked over at Mel, but quickly returned to looking down below at the cars passing by. She forced back the urge to cry. Alex took a breath before speaking again. "You're right. Many people would love to stand in my shoes right now, but I want more challenges in my life. I'm currently working on condom in the hamburger and false claim cases. Call me a snob, but I've lost the purpose with these cases. I didn't obtain degrees just to process subpoenas. I need to find a purpose. Feel like I'm working on something that matters. And as for the money, I can always be paid more," Alex said. "Does it hurt to want more?" Alex said as she turned around. "By the way, I am completely independent, including financially, from my parents," Alex said. "It's the only way that I would take the job at the firm."

"Well," Mel sighed. "I see people at the library every day in worse situations than us. Look, every day I see kids where the library is their safe haven, a place where they can dream of a better life. So, forgive me for not joining in on the parade of tears. If you want to do something else, then look for something else – you have the smarts, the means, and you're not bad looking." Mel smiled.

"Maybe you're right. I feel lost. I need to find my own way. I just don't know what I can do or even where I can do it. All I know is that I want a normal life. I want to be taken seriously. I want to be liked and loved for who I am and not treated differently because I'm a Cayhill. Basically, I want to create my own milestones and rise up the ladder based on my hard work, because I deserve it." Alex shifted her weight from one foot to the other. "What my family has done shouldn't affect my life right? I own my life and I should be able to dictate how I want to live it."

Mel stood up slowly, walked towards Alex and gave her a bear hug. "You'll find it, Alex. Just remember that you have options. Do what will make you happy, not your family and definitely not for anyone else," Mel said.

------------------- CHAPTER 2 -------------------

At six fourteen on Tuesday morning, the African sun was bathing the plains with its glorious rays. The bare trees stretched out across the orange red sky while the animals grazed contentedly on their breakfast in the distance, their shadows the only shade for miles around. Mothers were already outside, embers burning ready for breakfast. Kilambèa was ready for a new day, a day filled with more choices to make and opportunities to seize. General Kimbala stood in his balcony door looking out across his land, breathing in the fresh morning air, and mentally recording every inch of the orange red sky.

"Another beautiful day for our homeland," General Kimbala commented to no one in particular.

General Kimbala woke every day at five-o'clock and this day was no exception. His morning routine was his church. He awoke every morning, worked out, took a shower, and completed the first phase of the day by taking in the sunrise while waiting for breakfast.

"Is breakfast ready yet, Simka?" General Kimbala asked his maid turning his back to the sun.

"Yes, sir," replied Simka.

"Then let us proceed to the dining room, Mr. Edwards," General Kimbala said.

Simka began to place an English style breakfast on the table as the gentlemen sat down. Edwards was always amazed during his visits to General Kimbala's residence. He couldn't even get a poached egg at his hotel. This was heaven. He wondered what it would take to receive a personal invite to stay at General Kimbala's residence on his next trip.

"How was your flight yesterday, Mr. Edwards?" General Kimbala asked.

Edwards didn't know where to begin, everything looked delicious. "The trip was the same as usual, General Kimbala, but breakfast at your residence is always the highlight of my trip."

"Well, then maybe you can return for dinner tonight. I am hosting a dinner for the political elite. You are more than welcome to attend." General Kimbala smiled.

This invite sounded better than the dry chicken and bread awaiting Edwards at the hotel. "I would be honored, Sir," Edwards said.

"Good. Now that that's settled, let's eat. I'm famished." The General sighed.

"Tell me, Mr. Edwards, why do I have the pleasure of your company this morning?" General Kimbala smiled at Mr. Edwards. Edwards returned the General's smile fleetingly.

"General Kimbala, I was hoping to evade this subject as long as possible, but the British government has its concerns about some of your government's activities," Edwards stated as he bit into a sausage.

"Which activities are you referring to, Mr. Edwards?" General Kimbala looked dismayed at the comment.

"General Kimbala, my government was hopeful that you would give a new face and clean slate to the Kilambèan Government. We both know that this hope was short lived. Your country is rife with corruption and nepotism…" Edwards talked quickly.

"I see that we've finished with the cordialities," General Kimbala sighed, wiping his mouth with the expensive red cloth napkin given as a present from the President of France.

"General Kimbala, I wish that I could be visiting under different circumstances, but truth is truth. My government has seen some very disturbing events unfolding in Kilambèa. Tensions are rising among the people. They are restless and want positive changes to come about. You were supposed to change things around in your government and give these people some hope. But, until now, we have seen a mirror version of the previous government, if not worse. We have been informed that the rebels have been gathering and will not wait long for matters to change course. What are you going to do about the situation?" Edwards replied blatantly.

General Kimbala looked over at Edwards and in a stern defiant voice stated, "Mr. Edwards, I understand your government's concerns and that you are a true ally of my government. You must also understand that I have everything under control. The rebels are no threat to me or the current government. You have nothing to fear."

"General Kimbala, if I speak truthfully, then I hope that you have nothing to fear. I'm leaving on tomorrow's flight, but we will keep track of your country's developments. I hope that my next visit is under different circumstances."

CHAPTER 3

Sanders Cayhill is a prestigious law firm with its main office on Charles Street in Baltimore. The building itself is impressive with thirty floors towering above Charles Street. The inside of the building was not only breath taking, but also intimidating. Opposing counsel hated walking through the corridors of Sanders Cayhill, while the staff was filled with a strong sense of power and invincibility. Alex walked through the large revolving doors into the lobby of the law firm. She walked towards the elevators as the guards greeted her with smiles.

The lobby never ceased to amaze her. The multiple brown colored floor to ceiling Italian white marble, black leather lounging sofas and chairs, beautiful dark green potted plants, and magnificent paintings hanging on each wall showed the wealth and success of Sanders Cayhill. Alex entered the elevator and went to the twelfth floor.

"Crap, where is my badge," Alex mumbled to herself ruffling through her bag.

"It's in there somewhere." Carter walked up behind Alex smiling. "Here, we'll use mine and then you can look for yours in your office," Carter said.

"Good morning, Carter," Alex smiled. "Hey, did you have a good dinner last night?" Alex asked.

"Humph, are you serious? Remember I told you that we were having dinner with my in-laws! They came, we had 'pleasant' conversation meaning dull, and they ate our food, drank our wine, and then left. Boring as usual." Carter stated. "Sometimes I wonder if Daniel was adopted. He couldn't have come from those two people. I keep studying them every time I have to deal with them in person and I haven't found much to link Daniel to them," Carter stated matter-of-factly.

"Carter, you're too much. Hey, I'm placing my bag in my office and then doing the most important task of the morning. Coming along for the ride?" Alex said mysteriously.

"Sure!" Carter smiled.

The firm's cafeteria was as elegant as the rest of the building. Breakfast was set-up buffet style in three separate areas. The warm buffet consisted of pancakes, scrambled eggs, bacon, and sausage. The cold buffet included different cereals, milk, yogurt, fruit salad, bread for toasting, and jam. The drinks section included a coffee bar, hot chocolate, tea, water, and various juices. Alex loved eating at the cafeteria. Nowhere else could she get a meal for such a cheap price. Alex filled her plate with pancakes, bacon, and a few packets of maple syrup. While wondering where the biscuits were, Carter walked up beside her with his yogurt and fruit salad.

"This really is wrong," Carter stated.

"What do you mean?" Alex said confused.

"This should be the other way around. Why do I have the weight problem, and you get to eat whatever you want every day?" Carter exclaimed.

"Hmm, I'll think of an answer while I'm trying to find the biscuits," Alex said smugly.

"I'm really jealous. Do you know how fattening that food is, and look at you," Carter stated while reviewing Alex's plate in the elevator.

"Look at it this way, Carter. Maybe I'll gain fifty pounds when I'm older and won't be able to see my legs past my hips," Alex commented staring at Carter.

Alex munched on her pancakes while flipping through the morning mail that Carter had already placed on her desk. She wondered how she would be able to get through a work day without him. She never had to worry about anything while he was around. The mail seemed to be normal: a letter from the national paralegal association, weekly memo from the paralegal manager, letter from the general manager announcing the Fourth of July firm picnic, and an envelope that didn't look familiar. Alex reached for a slice of bacon and then opened the envelope. It was a vacancy announcement for a paralegal position.

The firm had been retained to defend General Kimbala before the International War Crimes Tribunal located in The Hague, and they wanted to put a special team together consisting of employees from each of the firm's offices worldwide. Alex had heard about General Kimbala, but had no idea that the firm had been retained to defend him. Maybe she needed to attend Sunday dinners more often at her parent's house. Carter popped his head into the office.

"I take it that you've read the vacancy announcement?" Carter smiled mischievously.

"How did you know about the announcement?" Alex asked stunned.

"You have to ask?" Carter laughed.

"Actually no…" Alex paused looking at the announcement.

"So, when are you going to apply?" Carter asked.

"Who me? Are you serious?" Alex asked.

"Well, you're looking at it intently and we both know that you're looking for something new and challenging. I'm not a genius, but I think that this will fit the description," Carter said.

"You're right. It does sound interesting," Alex commented never taking her eyes off of the announcement. This could be the opportunity that she had been waiting for.

"Good because I've cleared your morning appointments already for you. You have until twelve noon and then your application is going into this self-addressed envelope," Carter said waving the envelope in the air.

"You're crazy, Carter. By the way, it looks like you're trying to get rid of me. I'm truly offended," Alex said laughing.

"Honey, they're going to need secretaries too. I'm hoping that you'll take me with you," Carter said while walking back to his desk.

CHAPTER 4

Rowland walked into the plush conference room and sat down at the head of the thirty chair dark wood mahogany conference room table. He liked this conference room the best. Oil paintings of the founding members hung on the right side wall in between two large windows, while two large frosted glass doors stood on the opposite wall. Rowland had the feeling that the founding members were staring down at him every time a decision was made in this room.

Rowland looked down the table and saw the faces of his best staff members looking back at him. He had spent the last five years making sure that Sanders Cayhill remained one of the best law firms in the country. The firm had not only expanded into other fields of law, but had also increased in staff numbers, and had become an international law firm. Now, the firm had obtained the retainer to represent General Kimbala. This was an important retainer and Rowland didn't want to screw it up.

"Now, as you all know, we have been retained to represent General Kimbala. Janice mailed a dossier concerning the case to each one of you. I trust that you've brought it along with you and that you've not only read the dossier, but have also learned it like the back of your hand. Henry is going to be the lead counsel on this case and is going to take over and give a presentation soon. I want everyone to treat this case as a priority. If we do well here, then the firm will be set for a very long time. Henry..." Rowland gestured for Henry Boome to begin.

Henry stood at his full height of six feet three inches and pulled on his shirt sleeves. He was an impressive handsome middle aged man and it was easy for him to captivate his audience. Everyone turned to him and forgot to watch time pass by on the wall clock. Henry opened up his silver pointer stick as he walked over to the podium at the front of the conference room.

"Good morning, everyone," Henry said in his deep melodic voice. "Just as James stated, we're here to talk about the General Kimbala case. Now, I see that everyone has their dossiers and hopefully, like James also stated, you have read through it thoroughly. This is going to be a high profile case and tough to beat. I just got off of the phone with our retainers and we have been given a go to place as many people on this case as we want and our budget has no boundaries. That is why we have called this meeting to talk with each of the firm's branch managers. We are looking to assemble a complete team that will focus completely on the Kimbala case," Boome stated as he pointed to the projector screen.

Henry continued, "The team will include me of course, three additional attorneys, one paralegal, two paralegal assistants, two investigators, five secretaries, and two interns. The team may expand as the case evolves, but we'll begin with a small team. I am looking for the best talent that we have in this firm. This morning, as you know, a vacancy announcement was sent to all possible candidates firm wide. There is one exception, the attorneys and paralegal assigned to this case will bring their own secretaries. Therefore, we will not be interviewing secretaries.

"We've given a deadline of one week and all resumes and cover letters are to be sent to their respective branch managers, in other words, you. I want you to sift carefully through the resumes, pick two people for each field, and remember that I'm a picky man. I don't have time for projects or emotional baggage cases. I want people who can do the job, have talent, take initiative, and need little supervision. The decision on who to put through for final interviews with me and James is on you. Your candidates will be a reflection on you and your branch. Today is Monday. The candidates have until Friday close of business to hand in their cover letters and resumes. You have until the following Monday at twelve noon to have your list attaching the qualified candidate's materials to Janice. You should have a good idea of what we're looking for by reading the dossier and from what I just told you. Don't disappoint us."

CHAPTER 5

Boome walked into the conference room holding a thick file under his left arm. It was Tuesday evening and Boome and Rowland had decided to stay late, discuss the resumes and eat take-out Chinese food. Janice, as the general manager's secretary, also had to change her plans and be on call for anything that Boome and Rowland needed for as long as they decided to stay. She hoped that this meeting wouldn't last past eight-o'clock. Sometimes she pondered early retirement more heavily than other times. This was one of them.

What did they really need her for? Was she supposed to sit and wait for the Chinese food delivery guy, then wait for coffee orders? Why hadn't she finished her paralegal degree fifteen years ago? Oh yeah, that's when Arnold left her with their one year old child for a better life. She couldn't finish school because she had a child to raise. And why take this crap from Rowland? Because she needed to fund Bethany's college tuition. Janice began reviewing and organizing the filing backlog. Well, she thought while placing the documents in alphabetical order ...at least I can get some of the filing done and have a more peaceful day tomorrow.

"Okay, so how about we go through the three attorneys first and then work our way down?" Rowland asked Boome.

"Sounds good to me, Jimmy," Henry stated. "The first one to impress me was Sam Richardson. He works in this office's general criminal law department, lectures two nights a week at American University teaching International Criminal Law, and is single. I've worked with him before. He takes direction well, is mature, and can also work well on his own. I think that he would be perfect on the team," Henry finished.

"I agree with you on Richardson. I not only think that he will be a great addition to the team, but someone who can second you too," James added. "Okay, onto the next candidate. I believe that Martie Candell should be added to the team," James stated.

"I've seen her resume, but you're going to have to win me over on this one because I don't know her or her work," Henry stated.

"Well, she works at our London branch in the fraud department. She's defended many corporations and executives against fraud and corruption allegations. Her specialty regions are Africa and Asia. I must say that she has a great track record and has won most of her cases. She's probably looking to broaden her experience on this case. I think that her experience and knowledge over Africa will be a strong advantage and help for you in this case. She's also pretty cute so you'll have something nice to look at while working," James stated with a smile.

"Jimmy, you're always working with both heads. I only need to deal with the one that I can see. Okay, she's in and now for the third candidate," Henry commented. "I think that Paul Jameson should be the third lawyer. He's Dutch-American and has lived in both countries, but is currently working at our Belgium office. He understands both common and civil law, and can help us to sway through the Dutch culture and laws," Henry commented holding Jameson's file in both hands.

"Are you sure you're not looking for someone who will only follow your directions? He's a junior attorney and you need people with strong backbones and experience behind you. I don't want you to carry people. This case is too important to the firm… we can't screw it up," James said sternly.

"Hmm, well it never did hurt to have someone who follows orders," Henry commented. "Come on, Jimmy," Henry laughed out loud. "Seriously, I do think that Jameson would be a good addition. He's young, intelligent, has only received excellent recommendations, and understands both countries. We should give him a chance," Henry stated.

James sat back in his plush leather chair and looked up at the ceiling.

The ceiling was the best feature of this conference room. James could stare at the off-white ceiling with its intricate impressions for hours. He's seen this type of work during his European travels. In the center of the ceiling hung a hundred grand chandelier.

The chandelier was purchased at a Sotheby's auction and was previously owned by Chief Justice Marshall. Special cleaners came in two times a month to clean the chandelier. It took six hours to clean each detailed piece. The chandelier fitted perfectly with the dark mahogany conference table and dark red and brown Victorian colored walls and oil paintings of the founding members. The only modern features, besides the service bar and vases and table decoration were the frosted sliding doors. This room held some history to it and James didn't want to be the one to change the course of history. Sanders Cayhill was the first American based law firm to ever be retained by a defendant accused of international war crimes. James wanted to make sure that the firm not only prospered, but that the Kimbala case set a precedent.

"Okay, Henry. I'll let you have this one, but only because I trust your judgment. But, understand that it's your problem if he screws up. We have too much on the line for this case to be screwed up by a twenty-five year old aspiring junior attorney," James sighed.

"We have our three attorneys then: Sam Richardson, Martie Candell, and Paul Jameson. Now, on to the paralegal and paralegal assistants. I don't think that we have much choice on the paralegal. We both know that there would be a fight from the top if we didn't take on Alexandra Cayhill. The good thing is that we know her and she performs well," Henry commented knowingly.

"Yeah, but she's only dealt with a few criminal law cases and on a limited basis. Her specialty is malpractice negligence cases. I know what certain members of this firm want, but do you think that she can cut it and come up to speed quickly?" James asked not sounding convinced.

Henry glanced over Alexandra Cayhill's file and thought about the times that she's completed projects for him. He looked up from her file and looked straight into James' eyes. "I've always been impressed with the research that she's completed for me, and you know my expectations, Jimmy. I believe that she can do it," Henry finished.

"Okay, then. So, the paralegal will be Alexandra Cayhill. I also think that we should assign Alex's personal paralegal assistants to the case in order to make the transition phase into the case easier. The good thing is that the paralegal assistants also applied. Their names are Cindy Hughes and Claire Matthews. Sound good to you?" James asked Henry.

"Definitely a good idea. This is going faster than I thought. Maybe I'll still make it to the Raven's game after party. Then everything won't be lost tonight." Henry looked at his watch.

"You and your football games. When are you going to enjoy a real sport, like golf or soccer? You're going to temporarily reside in Holland in the near future. You might want to look at converting to soccer, my friend!" James laughed.

"Hah, I've done my research already and they have the Amsterdam Admirals football team. I'll just hop over to Amsterdam for a few games. Feel free to stop by and catch a game with me. I'm just hoping that it's not too disappointing," Henry chuckled.

"I'll stick to golf, but maybe I'll take you to an Ajax Amsterdam or ADO Den Haag soccer game while I'm there checking up on you. See, I did my research too," James laughed. "Okay, now onto the investigator…" James yawned.

"It is getting a little late, but we're almost to the finish line. How about Max Kayhorn? He's a retired naval officer, has worked on three different United Nation's missions, and is now working for us in the fraud department. Two of his missions were on the African continent and he has provided information and statements on another case for the International War Crimes Tribunal. He will be able to provide some intelligence information along with background knowledge on Kilambèa and still has contacts at the International War Crimes Tribunal," Henry finished.

"I agree with you. Now, for the interns. We only need two for the time being and preferably mature third year law students or someone that's just graduated law school looking for a break. I've found one candidate that has already done some work for me. His name is Jack Sanders and he is attending the University of Baltimore Law School. He's in his third year and attends school at night. According to his application he's willing to work full-time during the day and can take his courses long distance when it's time to move to the Netherlands for the case. He's single and has no children so that shouldn't be a problem," James added putting Sander's file down gently on the table.

"I like Jack. He seems to have his head on his shoulders and is a hard worker. Okay, then for the second intern I suggest Carolyn Schmidt. She is an intern working at our Brussel's office, is of Dutch origin, and is attending Leiden University Law School as an external student. Her concentration is International Law," Henry stated.

"Great! It's nine-o'clock. You may just make that party after all. So, we have the attorneys, paralegal, paralegal assistants, investigator, and interns picked out. As for the secretaries, the attorneys and paralegal will bring their own to the team. That means that Edith Straw, Carter Rowens, Jennifer Van Landen, and Kirsten Lamberth will be added as the secretarial force. Edith, being your secretary and consequently that of Sam Richardson's, will be the lead secretary with the others reporting to her. Shouldn't be too hard seeing how she's the lead secretary for her floor. Carter Rowens is the secretary for Alexandra Cayhill. Jennifer Van Landen is the secretary for Paul Jameson, and Kirsten Lamberth is Martie Candell's secretary. This also means that we'll have four secretaries instead of five. I can't believe that we're finished here. I think that I'll surprise my wife and actually make it home before ten thirty tonight," James added pleased with himself.

"Look, I'll hand the approved list over to Janice, who must be thrilled by now to still be here, and instruct that the acceptance letters be sent out tomorrow. We can hold a meeting with everyone on Monday," Henry added.

"Good. I think that you have a good team here. I'm looking forward to seeing this case through," James stated as he stood up, gathered his files and walked to the door. "Get a good night's sleep because now the game really begins." James smiled, opened the frosted sliding door and walked out.

---------------------- CHAPTER 6 ----------------------

Martie Candell had just gotten off of her direct flight from England. She always enjoyed flying with British Airways, but this time was the best. She was feeling wonderful after receiving the faxed acceptance letter the previous Wednesday. Even though she only had three days to hand over her current cases, she made time to not only book her flight with the firm's travel agent, but to tell them that she would pay the extra amount for first class. She was going to enjoy this flight.

Martie had started working ten years ago for Sanders Cayhill when they first opened the London branch.

Many of her colleagues thought that she was crazy to leave her cozy one hundred thousand pound job to begin working with a start-up American based law firm. She had her own secretary, a wonderful view of the Westminster Abbey and Parliament, a private car and chauffeur, stock options provided for by the firm, and she had just made partnership one year before. Why would she change to a small firm that held no reputable standing in the British legal community? Moreover, her salary took a dive, but Martie had known better.

She had researched the firm, the annual reports, and its attorneys and had known that she was joining a gold mine. Martie knew that she was going to gain everything back in the long run and she was right. She came in as one of the first attorneys and was now a corporate partner in the firm. She not only gained the salary and benefits that she had ten years ago, but also many more including respect from her colleagues. Martie Candell was now seen as one of the best attorneys in Britain.

She walked towards a cab sitting outside of BWI Airport. The cab driver stared at Martie as she approached and couldn't believe his eyes. Martie had just flown eight hours, but looked as if she hadn't just stepped out of a plane. She was five feet nine inches, wore a sleek black pantsuit with a beautiful matching silver and diamond necklace and bracelet set. Her watch was just as stunning and her dark hair flowed down to her shoulders and café latte skin. The cab driver looked down to find three inch heels, but the most stunning factor was her green eyes. He looked up to find her smiling at him.

"Let me take your baggage, Miss. You can go ahead and get in the backseat," the cab driver hesitated.

"Thank you. I will keep this one bag with me, but the suitcase can be placed in the trunk of the cab," Martie stated pointing to her brown leather briefcase. She then proceeded to step inside the cab. Martie thought back to the plane ride. The food was delicious. She had always wondered how it would be to fly first class abroad. Sure, she had flown first class in Europe, but only for short trips and the only pleasure she had received was having a seat that she could move in.

This trip was different. She had received a glass of champagne as soon as she had sat down and the food had been delicious. She had expected pork tenderloin or Filet Mignon, but not the choice of lobster, crab, or shrimp. Breakfast had also been wonderful. She was used to a cold breakfast of fruit salad and a cold croissant, but this time she had had a choice of pancakes, sausage, various omelets, and scones. And she couldn't forget the fresh juice besides the coffee and tea. But, the best part of the trip was the ability to turn her seat into a bed and have the use of high quality wool blankets. Martie had never slept better during a flight before.

Now, she was off to meet people that she would be working with for the next two to three years. Martie had to admit to herself that she was a bit nervous. She shouldn't be because she had earned this opportunity, but she couldn't help the feeling of butterflies in her stomach. She knew only one person: James Rowland. The rest of the people she only knew from the internet research she had been able to complete in the British Airway's lounge before heading to the departure gate.

The cab driver got into the front seat of the cab. "Where to, Miss?" the cab driver asked.

"The Sheraton Hotel on Charles Street please," Martie responded.

"Sure, we'll be there in about fifteen minutes as long as there's no traffic or accidents," the cab driver stated while looking at Martie in the rear-view mirror.

"Sounds good," Martie responded looking at the cab driver briefly before looking outside the window. Baltimore hadn't changed much since her last visit.

The last visit had occurred when she came to interview for the attorney position ten years before. She remembered walking into the lobby of Sanders Cayhill and having the immediate feeling that she had made the right decision. If the firm's lobby exuded such power and influence, then she couldn't wait to see what the rest of the firm was like. That had been her first meeting with James Rowland. Ever since then she had kept herself busy with the London branch, never making it to firm wide capital partner meetings held at the Baltimore branch. Now, she was returning to where it had all begun.

Martie thought back to her research results at Heathrow Airport. From what she could tell and the picture that she was able to find, Mr. Henry Boome was a very talented attorney, not to mention very handsome. She knew that his name was respected throughout the entire firm and that everyone wanted a chance to work and learn from him. He had graduated cum laude from Howard University, was in his mid-fifties, and had won most of his cases. He had come into the firm as a junior attorney and become a capital partner within five years. He was also on a few of the most important boards in the firm and lectured once a week at the University of Maryland Law School. No wonder the man had never been married, Martie thought to herself while watching the towering glass buildings pass her by. Martie wondered if they were close to the hotel.

Martie decided to turn her thoughts to Sam Richardson. She had seen him once at the London Branch. He had come over for some business meeting that lasted for an afternoon. Then he had gone. She had been introduced to him briefly in the hallway before he entered the conference room for the meeting. He had been professional yet very down to earth. She had liked his navy blue suit and pink and white striped shirt. She had also noticed the polished black shoes and that he didn't have a tie on. The two top buttons had been open. Martie had been able to tell that he took care in grooming himself. He had been clean shaven, every piece of black hair had been smoothed down and stayed in place and his fingernails were manicured. He had definitely been a dish, but had he been available? She had known that he worked a lot with Boome, and wondered if that had helped his chances with getting a spot on the Kimbala case.

As for Paul Jameson, he was a junior attorney that Martie had never met or heard about. She had been able to find his bio on the firm's website. All of a sudden the cab drove past a Starbucks and Martie had a strong urge to ask the cab driver to pull over. She could taste the Toffee Nut Latte on her tongue. No, I need to get to the hotel and get some rest, Martie thought.

She had remembered seeing a young kid staring back at her on the firm's website. He had dirty blond hair spiked with the help of some gel, blue eyes. Typical Dutch, Martie thought. She wondered if the kid was more Dutch or American or if his parents were able to balance it out. She wasn't quite sure why Jameson had been added to the team. He worked in the Belgium office's banking department. He didn't seem to have a background in criminal law, but he had a hidden talent that only they knew about. She only hoped that the hidden talent would be an advantage for the team. Martie knew that she wanted to work on the Kimbala case, but she wondered how it was going to be working with these people for the next two or three years.

"Miss, we're here. You can go ahead and walk inside. I'll be right behind you with the luggage," the cab driver said.

"Thank you," Martie said, happy to be one step closer to the peace and quiet of her hotel room. She wanted to be fresh and clear-minded for the eight-o'clock meeting the following morning.

------------------ CHAPTER 7 ------------------

Janice had come in at seven to prepare the conference room. She was expecting a heavy day. This was going to be the true start for the team of the Kimbala case for the firm, and she wanted to have at least an hour of preparation time. Janice was expecting eight people for this meeting. She was going to be on hand for the team during the morning hours that week and Edith, Henry Boome's secretary, was going to take over for the afternoon sessions. That way Janice could get her work done for Rowland in the afternoons and Edith could get Boome's work done in the morning. They figured that it was the best way, and both Rowland and Boome were fine with it. She hoped that they had made the right decision.

Janice picked up the eight portfolios, walked into the conference room and turned on the light to show a naked room. The chandelier had a dimmer, but it didn't matter how high Janice turned the light up if it was dark outside. She started placing the portfolios around the conference table. Boome would be sitting at the head of the table, and Janice planned on going to his office at seven thirty to pick up the materials that he was going to use during the meeting, but first she wanted to organize the room. She ordered breakfast to be delivered at seven forty-five, which included muffins, bagels with cream cheese, various pastries, coffee, juice, water, and tea. The kitchen service was also supposed to bring cutlery, cloth napkins, mugs, and tea cups. She hoped that they wouldn't forget anything. They were to be in and out before seven fifty so that there wouldn't be a traffic jam between the team members and the kitchen staff.

Janice placed the last portfolio on the table and then picked up the remote control for the projector screen. She pushed the button in order to bring the projector screen down and then proceeded to turn the computer on and turn the microphones off at each seat. They wouldn't need them since it was only going to be eight people. The last thing that Janice did before leaving the conference room was to open the heavy curtains, only to see the sun rising outside.

Sam walked into the conference room. He was forty years old and cared about his appearance. He not only wanted to make a good first impression for his new teammates, but also give the illusion that he was self-confident and knew what he was doing. He was wearing a nine hundred dollar navy blue pinstripe suite with a contrasting white shirt. He wasn't wearing a tie and had left the first two buttons open. He also wanted to give the team the idea that he could be laid back and fun. Sam had had a meeting the night before with Henry and knew that he was going to be the second in command. The rest of the team was going to be informed at the meeting today.

Sam was happy to be working on the Kimbala case. Henry had become Sam's mentor when Sam had begun working at Sanders Cayhill fifteen years ago. Many of Sam's colleagues could recall horror stories of their beginnings at Sanders Cayhill. Their mentors either used them as paper filers and memo writers or they treated them as if they were lower than ants. But, Henry had taken Sam under his wing, coached him, challenged him, and finally helped Sam become a partner in the firm. He had liked working with Henry and always learned something new. Henry had become more than a mentor and colleague. He was like a father to Sam.

Sam walked around the table shaking hands and introducing himself to the other team members before finally taking a seat towards the head of the table. The only person missing was Henry. Sam knew that Henry would show up exactly at eight-o'clock. They had one more minute to wait.

Finally, Henry walked into the conference room, smiled at everyone, and then proceeded to walk around the table for individual introductions. He began with Martie Candell and ended with Max Kayhorn. Henry then took up his position at the head of the table.

"Thank you for coming this morning. I understand that a couple of you had to travel overseas to get here and I hope that your trips were pleasant. I also understand that all of you had to quickly finish any loose ends on the cases that you were working on and hand them over to other attorneys. I appreciate your cooperation thus far, and we have a reason for the haste. The Kimbala case may seem like a simple case to some. One defendant shouldn't take up too much time or need too many resources, but the one defendant in this case was in charge of a country and has now been indicted in front of the International War Crimes Tribunal located in The Hague. This case is more complex then you may think. It will take each and every one of us to complete this case. We may even find that we need more resources down the road. There will be many stressful moments and our energy will be absorbed during the trial. I don't want you to have any delusions as to the work that will have to be put into this case..." Henry walked toward the table. "All of the material that we will go through today has been added to the portfolios that have been placed before you."

Henry paused looking at each team member. He then picked up the remote control and said, "Let's begin." Henry pushed a button and the lights dimmed.

Janice, who was standing in the corner between the projector screen and window, began closing the curtains. She walked out once the last curtain had been drawn. Henry knew that he could summon her with one click of a button on the remote control. Henry turned the little lamp on and then proceeded to turn the projector on. An introduction slide appeared on the screen entitled, 'The Defense of General Joseph Kimbala.'

Henry drank a sip of water before beginning. "The Kilambèan government gained independence from the British government in 1959 on the condition that the British government would cede power slowly over a period of five years. The presidency was handed over immediately to a popular Kilambèan rebel, along with the cabinet. The British government installed a small office of British nationals to act as consultants to the new Kilambèan president and cabinet. The British government made it publicly known that the Kilambèan government would have the freedom to navigate the course of the land, and that the British government would only be there to advise and consult with the new government. It was found out later that the truth was exceptionally different. The British government played a key role behind closed doors and the new president did not act without receiving orders first from the British government. It was also later learned that opposition was quickly disposed of.

"Everything was going well for the new president, his cabinet, and anyone that the president hired. Unfortunately, the economy was disintegrating, and at the same time the unemployment rate soared along with the crime rate, and the people were becoming restless. Enter Karim Kimbala. Karim Kimbala was a rebel and national hero by early 1963. He was known by all for his patriotic speeches and call for reform. He even had a prison record because of his work as an opposition leader, but for some reason he never mysteriously disappeared.

"In September 1963, Karim Kimbala attempted a coup and was successful. The Kilambèans believed that Karim Kimbala was their saving grace. He would make everything alright. Karim Kimbala began his tenure as a democratic president, and made many promises to the citizens of Kilambèa. He made the usual promises that all politicians make around election time, and desperate people grasp at every chance even if that chance is slim. But, by 1973 the country looked the same and the problems remained. The promises of Karim Kimbala had not come through.

"One thing that Karim did not foresee was his brother, Joseph, entering into the story as a threat to his presidency. Joseph Kimbala came in the picture by giving a speech accusing the current government of killing its citizens at a rally on July 7, 1973; ten years after Karim took power. Joseph promised to take action where Karim only provided words. He promised to improve the economy and eliminate poverty. He also promised to come down hard on corrupt government politicians, improve the job market, and make it easier for the common person to approach government officials. Word reached Karim quickly and the family feud had begun. The brothers never spoke again and Joseph continued to speak against the government for the following seven years. During this time, Joseph formed the Kilambèan People's Reformation Army (KPRA), and Joseph's popularity rose while that of Karim's dropped. On 5 April 1980, Joseph, along with members of his party attempted an assassination hit on his brother, but ended up killing Karim's wife and two children instead. Karim escaped narrowly and fled into hiding. With Karim in hiding it was easy for Joseph and the KPRA to round up Karim's cabinet members and anyone else that would oppose him and take over the government. Joseph Kimbala became president of Kilambèa and remained so until his capture on 3 May 2006.

"Joseph Kimbala was meeting with Lewell when a guard burst into the room and passed on information that international troops were driving towards the palace. This guard also told Kimbala that the troop's purpose was to take Kimbala into custody. We know that the peacekeeper's special ops force searched the presidential palace including his residence without finding General Kimbala. It took them four days before finding the general on the outskirts of the capital. The rumor is that the general was waiting until it was safe for him to leave the country and seek refuge in Tanzania. General Kimbala was found in his mistress's vacation home, supposedly still warm in bed lying next to the mistress.

"Joseph Kimbala was then escorted under guard by the peace keeper force to The Hague, Netherlands, where he now sits in a cell at the detention center in The Hague waiting for his trial to commence at the International War Crimes Tribunal.

"I've just given you a summary of the political situation in Kilambèa. Now, if you open up the portfolios sitting in front of you, then you will see that the first ten pages give you a complete description of the historical political situation of the country along with the names of the most important figures in the Kilambèan government. I want all of you to read this section because it's a good introduction to understanding this case. The next eighteen pages consist of the indictment against General Joseph Kimbala. The following page, page twenty-nine, is a contact list with all of our names and telephone numbers.

"Page thirty contains a schedule with projects, tasks, and deadlines. You will also note that there is an additional column identifying who will be working on each task or project. I expect each and every one of you to meet your deadlines. If you can't meet a deadline, then I expect you to inform me immediately. Let's take an hour and a half break so that everyone can read the portfolio. It's eight forty-five right now. We will reconvene at ten fifteen sharp."

Henry stood up, reached over for a bagel and then walked out of the room. He had a few telephone calls to return before the meeting resumed.

"Welcome back, everyone." Henry smiled, sitting down in the plush black leather chair. "I hope that you were able to read all of the materials in the portfolio. We've gone through a summary of the historical background of the country. Now, I want to take the rest of this time to open up the floor for questions. Feel free to ask questions about the government, the indictment, or the tasks and projects listed on page thirty in the portfolio," Henry stated.

"Are there other people who have been indicted besides General Kimbala, such as people from Kimbala's cabinet or from the military?" Alex asked.

"Yes, the Tribunal has moved to indict fifteen other people besides General Kimbala. Ten of the people indicted have either been caught or surrendered voluntarily. The remaining five people are still at large. This is a good question because we're going to have to follow the other cases. I'm sure that General Kimbala's name will be surfacing in each case and it will not be positive. Other defense teams are going to put all of the blame on our client and bring witnesses in to confirm their position. Watching these cases for any possible exculpatory or inculpatory evidence will be one of your jobs, Alex. We will need to know what will hurt us and what will give us some hope," Henry finished.

Alex finished writing on her legal pad and looked up and said, "Okay, I'll take care of that."

"I'm sure that the portfolio will give us a beginning to understanding the history of the Kilambèan government along with pertinent information on General Kimbala, but can you tell us if you have any favorite websites that provide helpful or pretty accurate reports on the situation in Kilambèa?" Jack asked.

"Well…"Henry paused to think before answering. "BBC has a good website along with the Tribunal's own website. The Economist country files are also a good source, but remember that the media cannot be trusted one hundred percent. You'll have to take what you read with a grain of salt. The best information that we can receive is by researching the original documents from the government's archives, local newspaper archives, and conducting witness interviews." Henry began to walk around the room. "By doing this we will be able to reconstruct an actual story that can be told throughout the trial."

Max Kayhorn looked around the room before speaking. "Seeing how we have an international team here, will everyone be working in the same office building or will people work from their main offices?" Max questioned, wondering if some people would have to relocate to the Baltimore branch.

"Everyone will work from this location and offices have been made available for them. They'll receive a tour this afternoon. Those in question will be able to go home every once in awhile for vacation or to do some other work in their main office locations," Henry answered calmly.

"Will we be conducting any field visits in the next couple of months to visit the region and get a feel for the country's culture and people?" Martie looked at Henry.

"Yes, the team is scheduled for a field visit in two weeks. You will be receiving more information and plane tickets by the end of this week. By the way, while we're on the subject everyone in this room will be receiving a firm credit card, if you don't have one already. The credit card should be used to pay for any expenses incurred while working on this case. This will include any business trips that you may take, and outsourcing of work. You will need to itemize each bill on the firm's expense report, and hand the completed form with the receipts attached to your secretary. Please make sure that you make this a ritual at the end of each month," Henry stated sternly. On the one hand, Henry was eager to answer their questions, but on the other hand he wanted to begin work and make more telephone calls in his office. Hopefully they didn't have too many more questions to ask.

Martie looked up from her portfolio anxious to see her new office and begin work. "Has the discovery process begun? Have we received documents yet from the prosecutor?" Martie asked.

"Yes, we've received three thousand documents so far and the prosecutor told me that we will be receiving more documents by the end of this month. All of the documents are being processed now by the document archives unit. They are almost finished and we will be receiving comprehensive spreadsheets with document descriptions, bates numbers, hyperlinks to the electronic version of the documents, and any problems that they've found with the documents by the end of this week," Henry stated.

"Can we see the documents?" Martie inquired.

"Sure, you can visit the archives unit now. Maybe Alex can volunteer to take you and also give a short tour of the office?" Henry stated looking at Alex relieved that the meeting could end any moment.

"Well then, let's get started," Martie said smiling. She was ready to see what the documents looked like. Alex could see no way out and decided to see this as a way to get to know Martie Candell a little better.

Alex and Martie walked down the hallway. Martie was watching Alex as Alex gestured towards the offices and explained the office set-up. The Baltimore location was set-up differently than her office in London and it was much bigger holding ten floors of lawyers, paralegals, specialists, interns, secretaries, and other support staff. Alex pressed the elevator button before turning back to Martie.

"How about we begin downstairs?"

Martie agreed with a small laugh. "I'll follow you. I've only been to this office once and that was for my initial interview. The only room I remember seeing is a conference room. So, I'm eager to see the rest of the building even if I won't remember everything."

Alex stepped into the elevator with Martie following. "I can guarantee that you'll be lost your first week here, but it'll get better after that." The two ladies walked out onto the basement level. Alex gestured around the room as she spoke, "This is a common area for everyone in the firm. We have vending machines to the left and as we walk around the corner here you'll see the cafeteria on the right. They serve breakfast, lunch, and a light dinner service during work days. Breakfast begins at seven thirty and dinner service ends by six thirty. You can always take your food back up to your office, but they do ask that you return your dishes and tray to the cafeteria. If we walk over to the left, then you can see the lounge area. Here is where people come to get away from their desks and talk with each other. A flat screen television is located on that wall while a magazine rack and book stand are here around this corner. Most of the magazines and books are donated by the employees. The firm pays for two magazine and newspaper subscriptions." Alex and Martie walked back to the elevator.

"Now, on the first floor we have the mail and fax room. You'll also find all types of supplies on this floor, but I'm sure that your secretary will take care of your supplies for you along with mail and faxes."

They walked through before going back to the elevator. Martie felt comfortable and remained silent. She wanted to listen carefully and try to remember what Alex was telling her.

"On the second floor we have training rooms, the computer help desk, and the archive unit's main office. The archive unit also has another office on the third floor. All computer and educational training takes place on this floor. I don't know how it is at the London branch, but there are a few mandatory courses, especially educational courses, but your secretary will keep you informed about those courses. The rest of the floors are divided into disciplines and each floor contains one or two conference rooms depending on the conference room size. We're the exception, seeing how our case doesn't fit the norm. We're spread throughout the building unfortunately," Alex said as she and Martie were standing in front of an office.

"This is your office."

Martie looked shocked and walked inside the office. She looked outside and was quite pleased with the view. They were on the eighth floor, but a skyscraper didn't ruin her view of the harbor. Martie turned around at the sound of Alex's voice.

"How about I pick you up for lunch at twelve? We can eat at a nice restaurant down the street before being pulled back in by Henry for more meetings?"

Martie was grateful for Alex's offer. "That sounds nice. Should we meet here? I have a feeling that I'll get lost if I try to find your office."

"Sure. I'll pick you up here. Oh, and the lunch is on the office. See you at twelve." Alex walked out of Martie's office and made her way back to her own office. She also wanted to check her email and voicemail before they left for lunch.

CHAPTER 8

Alex raced through BWI airport to catch her plane. She had just barely checked in and was told that the plane was going to depart in twenty minutes. The attendant hastily handed Alex her boarding pass while gesturing the way to security, the terminal and finally her gate. This walk would normally, with a stop off at Starbucks, take thirty minutes, but Alex had to do it in less than twenty minutes if she wanted to fly with her colleagues. She thought about the past two weeks and had to admit that it wasn't the smoothest two weeks of her life.

Alex brushed past a tour group and barely ran into a family of five when her mind turned to the secretaries in the newly formed group. There was a tumultuous clash amongst the secretaries when they were told that Edith would be the lead secretary and counted as their supervisor. Alex understood their position and quickly remembered the nights that she had to listen to Carter complain about his new found situation. She was happy with the firm's resolution. It had been decided that all of the secretaries would answer to their respective attorneys or paralegal in terms of workload, but that the secretary manager would continue to deal with their administrative issues and any work related frustrations and complaints. Edith, it was decided would help to organize the secretaries during vacation and leave periods, but had no power over the secretaries workload. Alex had to admit that she was also worried about Carter's workload if Edith became a mediator, instead of

Alex being able to talk directly with Carter. They had a good relationship and she didn't want unnecessary changes affecting that.

Alex slowed down as she approached the Starbucks. She had missed breakfast and thought quickly about whether she could still make it before deciding against and picking up speed again. She adjusted the shoulder strap of her briefcase and pulled her black leather suitcase along behind her. She loved the fact, especially now, that she could attach her briefcase and laptop to her suitcase. She was hoping that this fieldtrip would help bring the team together as one unit. They hardly knew each other, which was felt over the past two weeks. They were not only dealing with different nationalities, cultures, and specializations in law. They were also dealing with large egos, misunderstandings, and learning curves with a new working structure. Sure, everyone worked for the same law firm, but it was quickly ascertained that all of the law firm's offices only used a skeleton feature of the firm's mission statement and policies. Every location molded the policies to fit their country's standards.

Alex rounded the corner and bumped into a young man causing both of their suitcases to fall unceremoniously to the ground. Alex apologized, picked up her bags and left the man in mid-sentence not realizing that the man didn't care about his suitcase. He was too busy asking for her name hoping that the conversation would lead to a phone number. Instead, the man watched Alex's backside as she ran down the terminal with a dash of hope as the gate came into view. Alex could see that the last two people in line were passing the flight attendant after handing their boarding passes over.

Alex reached the attendant and finally slowed down to take a breath. She boarded the plane and waved to Martie and Sam before placing her suitcase in the overhead and sitting down. Alex laid her head against the head rest and felt a great sense of relief as the airplane door closed. Alex repeated to herself that this was going to be a good trip. She opened her laptop and pushed the power button as soon as the seatbelt sign light was turned off. Alex knew that the flight was only going to last forty minutes, but she had to use every minute of the working day if she wanted to keep up with the pace of the case. She accepted a glass of water from the airline hostess and tapped away while keeping one eye on the clock.

The plane landed in Philadelphia and the team raced to their commuting plane. Alex walked in a pack with the attorneys and investigator. The first commute was relaxing, but the next flight would be a working flight. The team had first class seats and was flying to Vienna. They were due to stay overnight in Vienna before departing for Kilambèa. The team's field visit was scheduled for one week. Henry wanted this to be a firsthand crash course for them on Kilambèa. He wanted his team to have a feel for Kilambèa's people, society, culture and history. The week was completely booked with little room to maneuver or have free time. Henry even had Edith order a minibus so that everyone would stay together.

The team was set to visit the location sites mentioned in the indictment, meet with a few of the inside witnesses, take a small tour of the capital and outskirts, and then visit the government archive's building. Alex was looking forward to this field visit even though it would only produce more work for her and the team. The team would first have to struggle with the delicious food and wonderful atmosphere of Vienna before moving onto the long continuous work days.

CHAPTER 9

Edwards was sitting in the waiting room located directly outside the boardroom. They would be calling him inside any minute now and Edwards tried to remain cool. Anyone passing Edwards while walking through the hallway would immediately think that Edwards was lounging and waiting for his lunch date to arrive. He was dressed in a casual dark suit and was tie-less. He was sitting back with his legs crossed.

Edwards had just returned from a trip to the Chad Republic. He was exhausted and wanted only to rest, but had received an urgent phone call to report to the main office at two-o'clock sharp. He had driven straight from the airport. He wondered what the urgency was. Why couldn't he at least get a few hours sleep before coming to the office? The boardroom doors opened and Edwards was summoned in. Edwards walked in the boardroom only to see three people sitting at the boardroom table staring back at him. Why was the director sitting here? What was going on and how did it involve him? Edwards asked himself.

"You're probably wondering why you've been summoned to meet with us?" Director Henley inquired. The Director continued without waiting for an answer. "The Kilambèan president, Kimbala, was arrested last night at eleven-o'clock and immediately transferred to The Hague. I understand that this is your case, and seeing our agency's involvement over the past few years, I wanted a debriefing personally from you," Henley stated.

"Kimbala was arrested last night?" Edwards looked at Henley and the other two in astonishment.

"Yes, he was arrested at his home while entertaining guests. He was celebrating his recent win during the presidential election even though we know that it was a one-sided race anyway." Henley continued, "I heard that you visited General Kimbala six months ago. What I would like to know is what happened during that visit?" Henley waited for Edwards to begin.

"Pardon? I included everything in my report once I returned," Edwards replied confused.

"I read the report and now I want to hear it from your lips," Henley stated leaning forward onto the table staring at Edwards.

Edwards looked at the three faces staring back at him. He recognized the woman sitting next to Henley as the assistant director of the agency and his boss was sitting next to the assistant director. Edwards was beginning to feel a little nervous and drops of sweat started to drip down the sleeves of his arms.

"I met with General Kimbala at his house. We ate breakfast together and we talked about the situation in Kilambèa. I reminded General Kimbala of our country's relationship and informed him that the British government was disturbed about what was happening in Kilambèa. I also made it blatantly clear that General Kimbala had to reverse the situation and that my government would be watching." Edwards stopped not knowing whether or not to proceed.

"And now he is enjoying the inside of a cell at the detention center in The Hague. Is there anything that can put our government into a negative spotlight?" Henley inquired.

"Not that I'm aware of, Sir. We dealt with General Kimbala legally. Any documents passed between the two governments are clean," Edwards stated.

"Good. Go home and get some sleep. I want you back here tomorrow morning at eight thirty sharp. You will be working with us until further notice on the Kimbala situation," Henley confirmed.

"But, Sir, I was supposed to travel to Ghana in three days," Edwards blurted out.

"That trip is cancelled, Mr. Edwards. You will be spending some quality time with us. Go and get some rest," Henley stated briskly and then turned immediately to talk with his assistant director.

Edwards knew that he had been dismissed, stood up, and walked out of the door. He couldn't understand why they needed him to stay at the agency for this. All Edwards knew was that he couldn't think clearly and needed some sleep. He stepped into the elevator and looked into the mirror to see red puffy eyes staring back. He was beyond exhausted after the meeting and couldn't wait to see his car.

The parking lot was almost full, but Edwards was able to find a parking spot close by the elevator. He turned the alarm off of his Audi and stepped in. Fifteen more minutes and he would be home.

-------------------- CHAPTER 10 --------------------

Sam had just cancelled his date and started to make himself a drink. He had met her two months ago and they had already been on five uninterrupted dates. This was the first time that he had cancelled a date, but that was about to change seeing how he was now on the Kimbala case. He didn't have much success in long term relationships and wondered how long this one would hold out. Sam picked up his rum and coke and sat down in the study. He was a creature of habit during the week. He was used to rising at six-o'clock, driving into the parking garage by six fifty-five, and sitting in his black leather chair by seven-o'clock. He worked the entire day including business lunches, and then retired home to his apartment's living room to work for an additional two hours. He usually ate dinner while reading over a pleading or correspondence from clients.

Tonight, Sam planned on reading through the indictment against Kimbala. He was in charge of making sure that the defense could counter any evidence that the prosecution had and to make sure that the defense could spot the prosecution's weaknesses. He knew that he could only do this if he studied the indictment and knew it like the back of his hand. Sam also wanted to do a good job. Henry was not going to be disappointed with making Sam second chair on this case.

Sam looked at the document piles on his desk, picked up the indictment, sat back in the chair, and began to read. He knew that this was going to be a long night.

General Kimbala was accused of many things according to the indictment including crimes against humanity. The indictment stated that the General was directly and indirectly involved in murder, torture, enforced disappearance of persons, political persecution, and sexual slavery. In other words, General Kimbala was being indicted under Articles six and seven of the Court's Statute for Crimes against Humanity and War Crimes. Henry had told him earlier today that they would be receiving an initial witness list of two hundred people, but there were only five names mentioned under murder, and fifteen people under torture. Maybe these were the people that the prosecution has the strongest evidence on? Sam wondered what evidence they had on these twenty people. Could they weaken the prosecution's case?

Sam read further. General Kimbala was accused of ordering the attempted assassination of his brother, Karim. The assassination attempt had been a disaster. A bomb had been placed under the president's car the night before. Two hit men had waited outside of the gates in a parked car for the president's car to drive out of the gated entrance. It had been a known fact that the president liked to leave his residence every morning at nine-o'clock for work. The car had driven through the gated entrance at the same time and the assassin sitting in the passenger seat had pushed the button on the receiver. Their orders had been to push the button, confirm that the car had exploded, and then leave. Hence, they hadn't waited to see President Karim running out of the house towards the car screaming his wife and children's names.

The next few minutes had seemed like eternity to Karim and anyone around him recounted for days the first minutes of the beginning of President Karim's demise. The yellow red hot blazing flames and small explosions from the car had been abandoned while everyone focused on their president brought to his knees sobbing uncontrollably. He, who was their invincible president, was on his knees crying for his wife and children in one breath and promising revenge to the killers in the next. No one had dared to move near him, nor console him.

President Karim had then received a visit from his brother three days after the assassination attempt. Joseph had arrived at the meeting with three of his colonels. Joseph had told his brother, at that meeting that Karim had two days to pack his suitcase and leave the presidential palace. Karim had thought that his brother was joking until Joseph had told him that he had planned the assassination against his brother.

Sam remembered hearing about the assassination attempt on the news. It was also reported that Karim had fled to the neighboring country, Chad, and become the head of the resistance movement against his brother three years later.

General Joseph Kimbala was also being accused of enslaving the wives of anyone who opposed him. The rumor was that the wives were transported to various sex clubs near the military camps. They were forced to perform sexual acts and provide companionship for the officers. Some of the husbands were forced to watch as their wives were raped and molested by the officers, while others were killed immediately. Sam could see that the prosecution placed three pseudonyms down for the enforced sexual slavery. Sam wrote a note that they would have to figure out the real names behind the pseudonyms.

Sam thought back to last year this time. The stories of the sex clubs were well known. Sam remembered watching a documentary about it on *60 Minutes*, but the story was everywhere, including all of the leading newspapers. He even remembered being shocked at seeing a *Good Morning America* commercial with the sex clubs as a headliner. Sam only knew one thing for sure: this wasn't going to look good for the defense. They were going to have to figure out how to handle this aspect of the case because the prosecution was going to embrace this and maybe even exploit the facts for their benefit.

It was also well known that some of the men escaped and were living in other countries. A few of the later taped documentaries even located men, shown in previous documentaries, still living in Kilambèa who were supposedly known opposition members. They found out during the later documentaries that the stories were false and created to magnify the negative rumors surrounding Kimbala's government. Sam made a further note that those men needed to be found and interviewed.

CHAPTER 11

It was six-o'clock and Alex was half asleep drinking her coffee. She would have preferred sleeping another hour, but wanted to get a head start on the day. The team had received three thousand documents the previous month, and a new disclosure shipment had arrived the day before consisting of two thousand more documents, two hundred videos, and one hundred photos. Alex had yet to organize the three thousand and now she had to worry about a large amount of additional material. She had set a meeting for that morning at nine-o'clock with her two paralegal assistants, but wanted to organize herself before meeting with them.

The team had a special war room where all of their disclosure materials were going to be kept. All future meetings were also going to be held there. One of Alex's tasks was to organize the war room and make it functional, a working library. Alex didn't want to disappoint the team and wanted to keep everyone as content as possible.

She walked into her office and placed her half-full Starbuck's coffee cup on her desk. The other offices were dark and Carter's desk was empty. Good, she thought to herself, I can actually get some work done without people interrupting me. The laptop began to hum as she tapped in her user name and password. Alex opened the case calendar to see what motions were due, if any, today.

"Okay..." she said out loud. "We have two motions due today and

Martie is the drafter. Crap, we also have a team meeting later on this morning. This is going to be a busy day." Alex sighed.

She drafted an email to Martie inquiring about the drafting process and then turned her mind over to disclosure.

With one tap of her keyboard, Alex opened the War Room Directory Archive, or in other words the WRDA. She loved that program. It was a 3-D layout of the team's war room, making it capable for Alex to design the layout of the war room. Her paralegal assistants would be organizing the war room that and the following days according to her design. Each section of the war room had a different color. Alex looked at the entrance of the war room and moved her mouse to the left. She had written history and general research on the first section, which had a burgundy color. All of the open source materials, including books on Kilambèa, articles, and press clippings, would be included in this section. She moved her mouse a little to the right and looked at the section.

The master registry filings, including all pleadings and filed correspondence, would be placed in this yellow section. Alex took a sip of her coffee and looked at the clock. It was almost seven twenty. The kitchen would be setting the breakfast out at seven thirty and Alex planned on being their first guest. She moved the mouse a little further to the right and saw the brown section where all of the master correspondence binders, including party and third party correspondence would be shelved and maintained. She shifted a little to the right and saw the computer area.

Each team member had their own laptop in their offices, but these computers would make it easier for members to conduct research without having to move continuously from the office to the war room. There were a total of three computers at the stations and each computer was set to have the reference library installed in two days. The reference library would include a summary of every item located in the war room along with an index so that the item can easily be found.

Alex moved the mouse further to the right and ended up at the far back end of the other side of the war room, and landed on the green section. The disclosure materials that they received from the prosecution would be shelved there. She added another section for this purpose. All of the materials that they receive from the prosecution were being archived in the system electronically by the archive unit. After archival, the unit was to send an email to Alex with a detailed spreadsheet of the contents and drop the electronic items into Alex's special folder for this purpose. They were also going to deliver one hard copy set of the materials to her office. So far the Archival Unit had never let Alex down.

She moved the mouse a little farther to the right and saw the light blue section. That section would hold all of the materials that the defense team was going to gather from their investigative work, from the government of Kilambèa, and interviews with witnesses. Alex was expecting the first batch of materials, around fifteen hundred documents, to arrive sometime the following week. Alex looked at the clock and it was seven thirty on the dot. Time for some breakfast, she thought.

Alex returned to her office with a tray full of food, juice and coffee. It was seven forty-five. She took one more look at the WRDA design, felt satisfied and began to eat her waffle. She had a pile of mail to go through before the day started. She opened the interoffice envelope resting on top of the pile. Carter organized her mail by placing the most important mail towards the top. She opened the envelope to find an interoffice memorandum from the paralegal manager. She was expected to make a presentation of the case to all of the paralegals at the next paralegal meeting. The presentation should be no longer than ten minutes, but give everyone an idea of what the case was about and who the players were, including the team members on the defense team. The memo also stated that all of the legal secretaries and paralegal assistants would be allowed to attend.

Great... Alex thought. I have two days to supervise the building of the war room, do my daily work, and somewhere in between prepare a presentation for over fifty people... "Wonderful!" Alex stated aloud.

"What's wonderful?" Carter stuck his head around the door and asked.

"I just read this memo from Cleo saying that I have to give a presentation on the case in two days. I have too much work to do to have to worry about a presentation," Alex said throwing the paper down on the desk.

"Phew, good morning to you too," Carter retorted. "Look, you'll be fine. I'm here to assist you and make sure that you get everything done. That's why I'm here, right?" Carter looked at Alex. "Take a deep breath and focus on the meeting that you have in one hour. We can worry about the presentation after that. How does that sound?"

"You're right. I still need to make some notes for the meeting, and it's not worth getting anxious about right now," Alex said.

"Good. I'm going downstairs to get some breakfast. You want some more coffee?" Carter asked.

"No, but I wouldn't mind some lemon tea," Alex commented.

"How could I forget? It's not Starbucks, so you won't want it." Carter laughed.

"You're making me out to be a snob. Now, don't forget to add a piece of lemon and some honey."

"No, you're not a snob. If you weren't by boss, then I would accurately call you a princess." Carter walked hastily away before Alex had a chance to respond.

Alex turned to her computer and printed out three copies of the WRDA for her meeting with Cindy and Claire. She always felt that visuals were important whenever she needed to explain the organization of a project. Alex had just finished jotting down her last agenda item for the meeting when Carter walked in with her cup of tea. Just in time, Alex thought. She gathered her printouts and memo pad before picking up her cup of tea and walked towards the war room. She didn't want to be late and keep the ladies waiting.

Cindy and Claire were waiting for Alex in the war room. It was eight fifty-nine and they knew that Alex would be walking in any moment with the instructions. They also knew that Alex liked to be prompt, and neither of them wanted to hear her speech about being late. Just then, Alex walked in smiling, holding two small binders and her memo pad in one hand and a cup of tea in the other.

"Good morning ladies, let's begin," she said taking a seat at the head of the table.

CHAPTER 12

Edwards stepped in the back seat of the British Embassy's car at Schipol Airport in Amsterdam. It had been a while since his last visit to the Netherlands, but from the looks of it, nothing had changed. The chauffeur turned onto the A44 towards The Hague and Edwards tried to recount his last meeting with the assistant director. His instructions were to find out more about General Kimbala's case firsthand, and to see if the Government had anything to worry about. All of his inquiries were to be discreet. This was a one day trip and Edwards was disappointed that he wouldn't be able to sightsee around Amsterdam this time around.

The driver pulled into a driveway and Edwards looked at the nice red bricked attached house. He walked up the path to find Sir Richard Hanley staring back at him.

"Henley told me that you were coming. This is extremely inappropriate," Sir Richard said angrily towards Edwards.

"Forgive me Sir Hanley, but I am only following orders. May I come in?" Edwards replied.

"Do I have a choice?" Sir Hanley replied with only a stare as Edwards's response. "Come further and tell me what the bloody hell you want to know," Sir Hanley retorted with a flicker of the arm.

Edwards followed Sir Hanley into the library. Each wall was covered with legal and academic books. A small section was reserved for hobby books. There was a fireplace located in the center wall with a desk located ten feet away. Edwards decided to sit on the couch while Sir Hanley sat in the large ottoman chair next to the fire place. The housekeeper came in to see if they wanted anything to drink. Edwards decided to be polite and asked for tea.

"Why are you here?" Sir Hanley asked.

"Sir Hanley, we understand that General Kimbala is being detained at the detention center in Scheveningen and that he has been indicted by the International Tribunal. We would like to know how the General is doing, and what sort of information the Tribunal has against him," Edwards finished, taking a sip of his tea. Sir Hanley looked at Edwards in disbelief.

"Do you understand that I'm the president of the court?" Sir Hanley replied aghast.

"Yes. That is precisely why I'm here," Edwards replied.

Sir Hanley stared back at Edwards in disbelief. "Get out of my house right now," Sir Hanley stammered. He was furious, staring back at Edwards while gripping the sides of his armchair.

Edwards rose and remained cool. "Sir Hanley, I didn't come here to make your life difficult. I will leave now, but I may return." Edwards left Sir Hanley sitting in his armchair, still in disbelief.

CHAPTER 13

"Good morning, everyone. As you know, this meeting was organized so that I can give you some information on the prosecution," Max began. "Alright, I researched the prosecution team and this is what I've come up with. Look at the screen. The lead attorney is Jan Paul De Loon. He's a Belgian attorney, Flemish side. He's an international boy. Studied at Oxford and then attended law school here at Boston College. He's learned in both civil and common law. Worked in Belgium and England and has now been with the court for ten years. This is his second case as lead attorney there. The other three attorneys on the team are American, British, and French. Let's continue with the French attorney: Henri Dupree. Now, Henri stepped over the border for the first time in his life one year ago, and that was to come and work for the Tribunal. His background is in civil law, and his experience, before the tribunal, centered on little chump cases like traffic offences and small demeanors. No one knows why he got a job with the prosecution, but the rumor is that his cousin, the deputy prosecutor, handed it to him. For the past year he's worked on a small case and now his cousin thinks that he's ready to play with the big wigs.

"The British attorney is Meredith Smith. Smith is the third in line of superiority while Dupree is on the bottom of the pool. Smith attended Oxford law school, is a barrister, and has ten years of legal experience, five of which were gained at the Tribunal. This is her second big case at the

Tribunal, and I heard that you don't want to cross her. Supposedly, she has a reputation for climbing over people to get to the top. She's left a few skeletons behind her. According to what I've heard, she's more arrogant than the Frenchman."

"The last of the attorneys is Gabriel Hart, an American. Hart grew up here in Baltimore, attended College Park and then moved onto Stanford Law School. He practiced criminal law here in the States for ten years and has been working at the Tribunal for the past five years. He's on route to becoming a senior trial attorney, is charismatic and the number two on the team."

"I've saved the best for last." Max turned around and winked at Alex. "The prosecution's paralegal is Analise Morgan. Most of the paralegals that they hire don't have any legal training, but Morgan does. She's a British paralegal who has worked in one of London's largest firms and was brought in exclusively for this case. Alex, you have some competition here. She has a team of three people working for her. They also have analysts, an investigation team with five investigators, three investigator assistants, and a team of language assistants. Each of the attorneys that I mentioned shares a pool of junior attorneys and interns."

"I know Meredith. We went to Oxford together. She was a nerd and hardly talked to anyone at all, and now you're telling us that she's arrogant and a nightmare?" Martie asked Max.

Max looked at Martie and sighed. "Yep. I think that she's been making up for her childhood. She's also known for taking on a male intern each term and personally mentoring them. I've heard that her mentorship has nothing to do with international law and she's quick to find a new puppy once they screw up. In two words: she's ruthless."

"Okay, so what do we really know about these people besides the fact that they all went to good universities and can be heartless?" Sam asked.

Alex leaned forward and began to talk. "We completed a search on each lawyer's legal background to see what type of cases, if any, they have worked on. We also tried to find out, with Max's help of course, how successful they were in private practice, what cases they worked on in the past at the Tribunal, and what roles they have played on their teams at the Tribunal. We've also been able to locate past trial footage for the lawyers that have actually stepped foot into the courtroom. Each of you will be receiving CDs with both examination and cross-examination samples for every case where the lawyer may have taken a witness. The footage is already on the network and you can view it anytime.

"Now, if we turn back to Jan Paul De Loon. Can you please put De Loon's picture back up on the screen?" Alex asked. De Loon's picture appeared on the screen and everyone stared at a well groomed handsome man with dark hair and blue eyes. He was wearing a Bulova watch and an Armani navy blue suit. Besides the watch he wore his father's ring. This was the only jewelry that Jan Paul wore.

"Like Max said, he's worked in both Belgium and England. Jan Paul began his career in England with the help of the French government. He worked on white collar crime cases at a prominent London firm, and helped out on pro bono civil litigation cases when he could. He moved to France after six years and began working with the prosecutor's office specializing in terrorism. According to the press his experience on white collar crime helped the prosecutor's office. The French government then pushed his name forward as a candidate ten years ago once a position for a lead counsel opened up at the Tribunal. He was hired quickly without a formal interview process seeing how there were no other French lead counsel and the Security Council wanted to keep the nationalities balanced.

"His first case involved atrocities that had occurred in both Ecuador and Colombia. You probably remember reading about this. Ecuador believed that there were a few Columbian high government officials involved with cartels smuggling drugs into Ecuador. As you may know, Columbian drug traffickers have used Ecuador as a transit country for cocaine intended for sale in the United States. This involvement caused a leak of a number of undercover agent's names, which resulted in their deaths. Relations between the two countries broke down. This was the last straw for the Ecuadorian government.

"Ecuador gathered troops and stormed into Columbia in search of anyone that had been involved. It didn't matter if they were government officials or members of a drug cartel. The Ecuadorians were out for revenge. It had been reported that the Ecuadorians killed approximately three hundred people before the international community gained control. But, the Columbians weren't happy and entered Ecuador one week later. It had been reported that they killed around five hundred people. Jan Paul was in charge of prosecuting the Columbians. The case lasted for almost two years ending in mistrial. During those two years the prosecution lost most of its insider witnesses, three members of the prosecution team were threatened with one resulting in death. The prosecution decided to keep the threats from the public and was later torn apart by the public and press once the death occurred. It turned out that the female attorney that was killed left a husband and three children behind.

"The husband gave interviews afterwards to anyone that would listen telling them how the Tribunal wanted to keep things quiet and his wife was dead because of their negligent actions. With the loss of the insiders and the turmoil on the team it's no wonder that the prosecution was bound to lose on all fronts. Ecuador demanded a turnover and resignations, including that of Jan Paul, in the prosecution's office. They further demanded that the trial be commenced again. Colombia demanded that its citizens be returned to Colombia. To appease both countries, a new trial commenced, lasted about one year, and the defendants were then set free because of a lack of hard core evidence. All of this happened two years ago. He needs to rectify his reputation with the Kimbala case," Alex finished.

"I talked with a friend of mine from the prosecution's office and it looks like we have a wounded man here. He lost face at work and in France by not being able to keep things together. His personality has hardened since the Colombia fiasco and he'll do anything to save face with the Kimbala case. He's stressed out, works long hours, and expects his team to do the same. It's also been rumored that his wife is about to leave him if things don't change," Max added.

"Thanks Max. Let's move onto Gabriel Hart. As Max mentioned, Hart worked as a senior partner at Brooke & Watts, LLP. He worked on white collar crime cases and also advised on cases for the mergers and acquisitions group. During this time, he helped senior prominent businessmen win cases and stay out of jail. He finally received a conscience and decided that he needed to use his knowledge and help the less fortunate. One call to a friend and he landed a job at the Tribunal. The rest is history. He's very charismatic and a skilled trial attorney. He's been able to stay in good graces with the right people and sailed up the chain. It's believed that he will receive his own case once Kimbala is finished.

"Now, on to Meredith Smith. She was a research assistant to Sir

Richard Hanley at Oxford. Sir Hanley is, by the way, the president of the court now. Smith then worked for two years as a junior attorney for the national prison board in England. She became bored and then took her knowledge to the European Committee for Prevention Against Torture. She worked as a senior researcher with the Committee for five years. She then began working for the prosecution in The Hague as a legal officer and was just promoted, with Sir Hanley's help, as a trial attorney. She has very limited experience in the courtroom even though this is her second trial. She's trying to turn from researcher to skilled advocate," Alex took a breath to review her notes.

"That's like a veterinarian trying to perform heart surgery," Sam smirked. Alex looked up from her notes. Her glasses had moved down the bridge of her nose. She moved them up and looked around the table, glancing slightly in the mirror. Good, her ponytail was still intact.

"I'm guessing that Smith is trying hard to compensate for what she doesn't have, but that's for you to figure out."

CHAPTER 14

Gabriel was sitting in his favorite Thai restaurant situated in the center of The Hague. He had ridden his bike straight from work and arrived a few minutes before the others. He was actually glad to be alone for a little bit and hoped to let go of the day's stress through a glass of Belgium beer. He was sitting on the right hand side of the restaurant watching the filled trams and walkers pass by. It was a warm sunny day and Gabriel was happy that the lights were still off in the restaurant. He wondered how the Dutch could live without air conditioning especially with windows that didn't open.

Gabriel looked around and took in the décor. The dark colors and Asian interior would have transplanted him to Thailand if it weren't for the sight of the tram outside. The walls were covered in a special dark red carpet with an intricate gold colored design. The ceiling was covered with drawings of different cities in Thailand, and the dark wood tables were covered with beige tablecloths. Each table was surrounded by equally dark chairs and a single long white candle adorned each table. The lights were dimmed at night to fit the atmosphere. He especially liked the draw cords hanging down from the ceiling at each table's end. He always wondered what would happen if he pulled on a draw cord. Did they really work? Would someone come if he pulled the cord?

"Hi sweetie." Gabriel looked to his left and saw Suzanne bending down to give him a kiss. His office mate and friend, Gert, was standing on the other side of the table with his wife, Marieke.

"Hey, guys," Gabriel got up to shake hands with Gert and walked around to perform the three kisses on the cheek ritual with Marieke.

"I see that you started without us," Gert said smiling and pointing to Gabriel's beer glass.

"Ah, you know what type of a day I had. You should be surprised to hear that this is my first glass!" Gabriel sat down again and waved to the waiter.

Marieke and Suzanne looked at each other. They knew what would happen if they didn't intervene immediately. The night would end up with conversations about work, exactly what they didn't want for tonight.

"Mannen, tonight we are going to talk about everything except work," Marieke began.

"Yes, but because we love you the two of you have five minutes to talk about work and then we don't want to hear anything else about it. Agree?" Suzanne added.

Gabriel and Gert looked at each other. They knew that they would have to concede if they wanted a pleasant evening. "You're right. We shouldn't fill up the evening about our work day," Gert said knowing that it would please Marieke. Maybe it would please her enough and he could release some tension tonight before going to sleep. They hadn't had sex for two months now and Gert felt that it was long overdue.

"Hey, Jan Paul came by the office after you left. He mentioned that you have a meeting tomorrow morning at ten-o'clock and that it's important for you to be there," Gert told Gabriel.

"Another meeting? I was just in a three hour useless meeting with the man today. Did he mention what this meeting was going to be about and if I have any chance to get some work done tomorrow?" Gabriel asked.

"Nope. Just that you had a ten-o'clock meeting tomorrow." Gert looked back down at his menu.

"This man is going to drive me crazy. It is Thursday evening. I have had nine freakin' hours of meetings already this week and he can't give me a free no meeting day tomorrow! What's wrong with this man? What have I done to deserve him as…"

"Right, time is up." Suzanne looked at her watch.

"What are we having for starters? I'm fancying the mini loempia myself," Marieke added smiling at Suzanne.

Gabriel took a large gulp of his beer, sat back, and proceeded to calm down. The lead counsel wasn't going to ruin his night. "Make that two loempias. Tomorrow's going to be another awful day, but I'll be damned if the bastard's going to screw my evening up too," Gabriel said leaning forward to look at his menu.

CHAPTER 15

Analise was being escorted into the paralegal manager's office by Carolyne, the paralegal manager's secretary. She had just arrived and took a taxi directly to the Tribunal for her early evening meeting with Claire Brown, the paralegal manager. Analise carried a visitor's badge knowing that she would officially begin tomorrow morning starting with receiving her personal badge from administration. She looked around and was immediately impressed with the circular lobby. She felt a sense of importance, but also had a feeling that something bigger than her own existence was happening at the same time. The walls and ceiling were made of white marble with grey abstract markings running across the walls and ceiling.

Lush, dark burgundy carpeting adorned every inch of the floor while four white marble pillars stood at each corner of the lobby. A large beautiful chandelier hung from the center of the ceiling while pictures telling the court's history hung from the walls. Leather benches formed an inner circle of the lobby, but what impressed Analise the most was the bronze statue of the lady of justice that was positioned by the guard's austere large white marble desk. Analise showed her visitor's pass to the security officer and walked through with Carolyne. She had gone through the scanner already before entering the main lobby. They had a separate trailer on the outside with a scanning machine. Analise was glad that they hadn't spoiled this beautiful lobby by adding scanning equipment to the décor.

"Claire, this is Analise," Carolyne introduced Analise and showed her to one of the chairs positioned in front of Claire's desk.

"Hi, Analise. I'm Claire Brown, the prosecution's Paralegal Manager. Please sit down." Claire motioned to the empty seat while taking her own seat. Analise placed her luggage next to the chair and sat down.

"Welcome to the International War Crimes Tribunal. How was your flight?" Claire looked at Analise.

"The flight was superb. I flew from one of our American offices so I'm a little tired, but at the same time I'm anxious to see what awaits me here. I've heard so much about this Tribunal and am privileged to have the opportunity to work here." Analise smiled at Claire.

Claire felt as if she had just heard a commercial. "Wonderful. And we're happy to have you here too. You have high recommendations from your former employer and I think that you'll be happy here. How about we start with going through the ropes and then I'll show you to your office." Claire touched the pile of paper and documents on her desk. Analise nodded in agreement. "First of all, we have your contract, which states that you are temporarily working for the Tribunal. This means that you are employed at the Tribunal for as long as the Kimbala case is active up to the judgment. Your salary is also mentioned on your contract. Here is a copy of the original for your records. Next, I have a general new staff packet for you. Included are documents explaining the health insurance, tax system, pension fund, staff counseling services, staff union, and general items such as a diagram of the Tribunal. This envelope here includes your personal code for the long distance telephone calls, the fax machine, and copiers. You'll need this code at all times when using these services. The badge that you receive tomorrow will need to be worn at all times while you're on the premises. Every department and courtroom is closed off and you can only access the departments that are applicable to you.

"Each department adheres to strict rules. The outside world looks up to us to hold the rules that we try to enforce. Therefore, there is no fraternizing with the other departments. Now, this doesn't mean that you can't have a cup of coffee with someone from another department, but what it does mean is that you are not allowed to date people from other departments or have unexplainable relationships that might call for a conflict of interest. I'll take you around first thing tomorrow morning on a tour of the building. We'll take a copy of the diagram to help orient you with the building.

"Here is a booklet giving a short explanation of the prosecution. It includes a who's who from the prosecutor down to the copy clerks. You'll also find summaries of present cases along with snip-its of past cases. Here is a booklet concerning the paralegal division of the prosecution's office. You'll find various standard operating procedures of the division, such as disclosure policies, exhibit lists, and regulations on cite-checking and proofreading. Basically we have formats for everything and everyone sticks to the specified formatting style. This way the case can go on if someone resigns.

"You will also find information on the computer programs and databases that we use. You will feel more confident if you read through this booklet. The last booklet that I have here pertains to the Kimbala case. Inside is the indictment against Kimbala, a list of your team members along with extensions and room numbers, a case history brief, and the Tribunal's Rules of Procedures. Last, but not least, here is a time table for your first week here at the Tribunal. Every new staff member begins with an induction week. During this week you will complete specific computer training courses. You will also have an introduction meeting tomorrow morning with the other new prosecution staff members, and short lectures from each department explaining their functions here at the Tribunal.

"The introduction meeting begins at nine thirty tomorrow morning and lasts until ten-o'clock. I'll pick you up and then we'll make the rounds so that you can meet your team members. After that, you will go to your first training at eleven-o'clock, which lasts one hour and then you get to have lunch and a break from twelve noon to one-o'clock. Then you'll have a short introduction from the chief of prosecution followed by more training. And it will go on like this until your induction is over.

"You will be communicating directly with your attorneys and other members of your team. You can come to me if any problems arise. The attorneys and staff understand that you are the first point of contact and only come to me if there are problems, administrative or otherwise, that need to be sorted out. If a problem arises, then we will solve it together. I prefer to have it this way to eliminate any confusion on who is doing what and who the contact person is for the team. Also, if you need advice, then understand that my door is always open. Now, how about we take a walk to your office, and you can ask me any questions on the way?" Claire asked.

The two ladies walked out of Claire's office and headed past the other offices, including the secretary's desks towards the hallway door. The interior was basic, but professional. All of the office doors were made of dark red wood. A green plant adorned each corner wall. Maybe that was a way of cheering up the windowless cubicles covering the middle of the room that the secretaries sat in. She had to admit that the cubicles were pretty nice and modern considering the fact that it looked like two secretaries shared a cubicle. Each desk was separated by a divider and the inhabitants could only see their cubicle mate's face when standing.

Claire and Analise made it to the elevator. "Now, we're going to leave the second floor and take the elevator to the fifth floor. This half of the building belongs to the prosecution. Only people from the prosecution are allowed to walk freely throughout our side of the building. If you need to bring someone in from the outside, then you will need to notify your lead counsel and myself for security purposes. Each floor in this building has its own purpose. The second floor is home to many of the managers' offices in the prosecution department, such as finance, Chief Lead Counsel, Deputy Prosecutor, HR manager, and myself. The lead counsels, the prosecutor, and the prosecutor's assistants are on the third floor.

"The rest of the floors are divided into regions. The fourth floor deals with any cases coming from Asia. The Fifth floor, your floor, deals with west and mid-west Africa. The sixth floor deals with the rest of Africa. The seventh floor deals with Latin America and the eighth floor deals with the Middle Eastern Countries. One day we're hoping to have a section for the Western countries. Each country floor holds the trial attorneys, paralegals, paralegal assistants, investigators, analysts, assistants, secretaries, and interpreters. We looked at our predecessors, past interim international courts, and believe that region concentration would work better if we wanted to have teams that understood their cases.

"Some people worry that they will be seen by outsiders as 'specialists,' but this type of layout is working better." Claire stepped out of the elevator. Claire used her badge to open the door to the offices on the fifth floor. They entered and turned to the right. The fifth floor had the same lay out as the second. Cubicles were in the middle and offices along the corridors. They walked to the end of the corridor, turned left and stopped at the third door. Analise read the name tag on the right side of the wall next to the door. The name tag read Greta Van Huizen. Claire opened the door and walked in with Analise following. "This is your office and here's your desk. Your roommate is Greta. There is one thing that I failed to mention. Each new staff member is paired with a senior staff member for a period of three months. This is to help new staff integrate into the system more easily. Greta is not only your roommate, but the person that I'm pairing you with for the next three months. She's not here to supervise or change your work. She's only there as your senior for guidance. Greta's been working in this department for six years and knows her job. She'll be a wonderful guide for you. It looks like she's left already for the day so you'll meet her tomorrow. Your computer and telephone will be delivered this week, but it won't matter seeing how you will be busy with the various training courses," Claire stated.

Analise glanced around to the left of the room. An empty beige top desk with dark mahogany wooden legs and bare walls signaled a new start. She couldn't even find a topless pen or leftover post it notes on the desk, wall or window seal. She noticed that an equally vacant filing cabinet stood behind the desk. Analise looked to the right to find an inhabited existence. The computer screen was on, but in stand-by mode. A cartoon monkey was dancing over the screen. Analise would have to figure out where Greta got the screen saver from. The desk was covered with paper work and the monitor was framed with different colored post-it notes.

Analise looked at the background wall to find an Anton Heyboer poster. To the right of the poster was an extremely organized filing cabinet. The top of the filing cabinet was covered with various mementoes. It looked like she collected a souvenir from every country that she'd visited. It looked like Greta was going to be an interesting roommate. Claire and Analise walked out of the room and continued to walk around the outer parameter of the cubicles.

"I'll introduce you to everyone tomorrow. One of the analysts had their last day today and will be moving back to their native homeland, Gambia. He is having his farewell party tonight. That's why no one is here at this hour. Each floor has the same lay out as you've been able to see. This way you will be able to find your way with no problem. All of the trial attorneys sit with two to a room and their offices are grouped together.

"Right now, your division has three paralegals with you being the third paralegal. Your other colleague is sitting in the office next door. As soon as a fourth case appears, then we'll hire a fourth paralegal. There is a pool of paralegal assistants that sit on the other side of your office. Currently, you have three assistants that will begin working with you on the Kimbala case. Seeing how this is a big case, just let me know if you need more assistance. I want you to be able to work smoothly and efficiently. The investigators sit two to a room down the corridor and the analysts sit near the investigators.

"The interpreters, translators and interpreters, sit on the other side of the investigators. What you see here in the middle of the floor on the left side of the corridor are the cubicles for the secretaries. On the right side are filing cabinets for the secretaries and trial attorneys. Last, but not least, at the opposite end of the corridor is the war room. The war room holds general information regarding your region, and more specific information regarding all of the cases pertaining to your region, past and present. Do you have any questions or do you want to wait, read through the materials, and soak in what's just happened first?" Claire smiled at Analise.

Analise looked at Claire and smiled back.

"I think I'll go with the latter. This is a lot to take take in. I'm sure that I'll have questions after reading and meeting every one, so I'll wait with the questions if you don't mind." Analise finished.

"Fair enough. There is one person that I would like you to meet this evening and that's your lead counsel, Jan Paul. He's waiting downstairs for us." Claire began to lead the way to the elevator.

"I would have thought that he was at the farewell with the others," Analise commented.

"He is going, but wanted to meet you first," Claire retorted.

"Oh, that's flattering," Analise stated.

Jan Paul hung the telephone up. He was in the middle of telling his wife, Lizette, that he would be home late when Lizette ended the conversation. Jan Paul found himself talking to silence. He was working a lot of hours at the office and Lizette was feeling lonely and overwhelmed with the three children that they shared. Lizette adored their lifestyle. They lived in a posh area with a park down the street. The house was lovely with two levels and the rooms were bigger than the European norm. Their three children, all under the age of ten, were healthy and loving life. Lizette only missed the comfort of her husband's attention. Besides that his personality was changing. When he was home, which wasn't often, he talked about the case, and complained about his staff. He didn't know what was going on with the children half of the time or her. It was as if he had become obsessed with this case. But, Lizette didn't know what to do or how to make things better. She only knew that it simply had to get better.

Jan Paul was massaging his temple when Claire knocked on his door. He took a deep breath, placed his glasses on, and asked for them to enter. He first saw Claire and then Analise. He saw a tall beautiful woman with flowing long dark hair and green eyes. She was wearing a black suit with a green blouse underneath, which really brought out her eyes.

Claire began, "Jan Paul, this is Analise Morgan, the new paralegal."

Jan Paul stood up and shook Analise's hand. "Hello, Analise. How was your trip here?"

"It was a very long trip, but nice. Thank you for asking," Analise replied.

"Has Claire already shown you the offices and set you up?" Jan Paul continued.

"Yes, I've seen the fifth floor and Claire has provided me with all of the introduction materials," Analise replied.

"Wonderful. I'm sure that Claire has already mentioned this, but the work is very rewarding and the people are not only nice, but helpful. I think that you will enjoy your time with us."

"I think that I will," Analise replied with a smile.

"Good. Well, you must be tired, but if you want the team is down the street for a farewell party. Would you like to come along? I'm going to leave and join them for a drink." Jan Paul waited for her answer.

"That's a lovely offer, but I think that I need to find my housing, and get a good night's sleep for my first day tomorrow," Analise replied.

"Okay, then have a good night and I'll see you tomorrow." Jan Paul shook Analise's hand again and watched the two depart his office. He answered a few emails before logging off to join the team.

------------------ CHAPTER 16 ------------------

Adam stepped into the white UN truck after stepping out of the airplane at Kilambèa's only working airport. His interpreter, Sabrina, was sitting in the back seat. It was going to be a long day for them. They were heading to the refugee camp located twenty miles from Kilambèa's center, St. Germaine. He had to conduct five interviews today and wanted to get into the mind-set. He looked outside and was happy that the tires of the jeep were creating a thick brown layer of dust around the car from the dry dirt road. Then he wouldn't have to see the lost faces as they drove by. The worst was looking into their eyes to see sadness, anger, and frustration staring back. No, the worst was not having the answer or means to give them their lives and family back. Adam looked in the mirror at Sabrina. She was a native who began working as a translator for the first UN troops after the war.

He remembered the day that Sabrina finally opened up to him about her past. They had worked closely with each other for a year, but had never past the superficial relationship until the day that Sabrina was sitting in his office after hours sipping on a drink. Adam remembered the room filling with silence until Sabrina's voice had pierced the air. She had taken Adam into her confidence for which Adam was forever grateful. She had described the events that took place around her in her small village. Adam had heard a flowing story about how the war was still affecting Sabrina's life years after its dissolve. Adam had thought it amazing that Sabrina first earned money for her and her family by working as an interpreter for the peace keeping force before seeking asylum as a refugee in Holland.

She had confessed that it was hard leaving her family behind, but had known that moving outside of Kilambèa was the only way that she could support her family and save her own young life. Sabrina had lived in an asylum center after she had been taken into custody by immigration officials at Schipol Airport in Amsterdam. During her stay, she had endured the interviews, fought depression and dreamed of the day that she could earn money again.

The day that Sabrina had received her asylum decision was beautiful, warm and sunny, but Sabrina had fought mixed emotions inside. She had been entering a new phase in life in her new country and leaving the country she had known her entire life behind.

Adam looked in the mirror again knowing that he would have to watch her carefully on this trip. The anniversary date of the beginning of the war was approaching, and Adam knew that this time of year was especially difficult for Sabrina.

Sabrina was looking straight ahead not daring to look to the left or right. She hated coming back to Kilambèa, but knew that this was the only way to see justice served. This war had taken six years of her life away. Because of these power hungry psychopaths, Sabrina had lost the only home she had ever known, her parents had lost their jobs because they didn't support their 'brothers.' Her twin brother had been killed in cross fire. Now her parents were reduced to waiting for rations from the UN, monetary help from Sabrina, and stability in the government and their future. Sabrina knew that they shouldn't hold their breath, but didn't want to discourage them. Their children's lives were torn apart with one in the grave and the other living in The Hague. She just had to hold on for the next four days and then she would return to a sense of normalcy in The Hague, a safe feeling that she feverishly gripped onto every moment in The Hague.

The jeep entered the refugee camp and continued to drive straight through. The left of the camp looked the same as the right side. Multiple white tents covered the grounds like clouds with a few white trailers intricately located inside the parameter of the camp. Adam knew what the trailers were used for. There was always a trailer for registration, two more for cooking volumes of food, two trailers for medical help, three trailers containing the showers, and two trailers for administration and shelter for the aides. The jeep was headed for the administration trailer. They knew that Adam was coming and he was hoping that a spare room had been set up for his use. He needed privacy if the victims were going to not only talk, but hopefully talk freely.

Cathy, the lead coordinator of the camp, was standing in the door way. Adam got out of the car.

"Good morning, Cathy. I'm shocked to see you standing here." Adam walked over to give Cathy a hug. "How are you?" he asked.

"I couldn't miss seeing you. I'm about to walk over to registration, but wanted to personally show you to your office. How are you doing?" Cathy looked inquisitively at Adam. Cathy was Adam's mother's best friend and she wanted to make sure that Adam was as comfortable as could be in this type of situation.

"I'm doing fine, Cat. I always feel a sense of humility when I come here or travel to any worn torn country, but I'm good. How are things going here?" Adam inquired.

"Oh, we'd have to take longer than the walk to your office for me to answer that question. How about you get settled here and we meet for dinner tonight? The British base is nearby and we could go and have some dinner there tonight. Get you away from this mess for a little bit," Cathy said.

"Cat, I'm sure you know the answer to that," Adam replied.

"Great. Here's your office and I'll pick you up at the end of the day." Cathy gestured towards the trailer before walking away to begin her long day.

Adam walked inside to find a sparsely decorated office that contained a portable collapsible desk, four chairs, a telephone, water bottles, an ash tray, and an electrical outlet. He began organizing his materials and setting up his computer. Sabrina walked in and began to do the same. He would remember later to invite her to dinner with Cat. He was sure that she would also want a break from the refugee camp and hopefully the memories.

There was a knock on the trailer door and a small old woman walked in and sat down. She was very grandmotherly, but at the same time you could see that she had had a harsh life. The wrinkles in her ash brown skin told many stories of a harsh life. Her eyes were dull as if life had already escaped her body. Adam wondered if she even remembered how to smile. According to the summary provided to Adam, she was seventy-six years old and had lost every single family member in the war.

She was alone, but contrary to her outer look, it was said that she was very helpful in the camp with her fellow residents. Maybe, Alex thought, helping the others is how she was able to get up on a daily basis and carry on. It also stated that she had no home to return to. They wondered, with her age and all, if she would even survive to testify at trial, whenever that would occur. At least she could testify today in the form of a statement, Adam thought.

"Good morning, Ms. Ntanga. My name is Adam Ferguson and this is Ms. Sabrina Ndabala. Thank you for coming to talk with us this morning. I am an investigator at the prosecutor's office at the International War Crimes Tribunal and Ms. Sabrina is an interpreter for the same office. As you've been told, we've come today to talk to you about your experiences during the war. I'll ask you specific questions that I will record here on my laptop and Ms. Sabrina is going to translate our entire conversation. Now, I do need to let you know that your answers may help the prosecution build a case against Mr. Kimbala. You may even be called to testify during the trial. You don't have to make a decision now on whether you would like to testify. I'm just letting you know that the option exists."

Ms. Ntanga interrupted Adam, "I have no problem with telling my story at a trial."

"I see. Thank you for letting me know. I will note it in your statement, but you will still have time to think about it. Also, within two to three days a copy of your statement will be available in your own language. I would appreciate it if you could come back here to read it and then sign verifying that the statement is accurate. Shall we begin, Ms. Ntanga?" Adam inquired.

"Yes, Mr. Ferguson. I'm ready," Ms. Ntanga replied as she sat back, crossed her hands on her lap, and waited for the first question.

"Ms. Ntanga, you lived in a small village called Jonestown located about fifty miles from the capital of Kilambèa. Can you please tell us how life was in your village before the war started? And please take your time."

"You want to know how life was in my village?" she asked. Adam nodded. Ms. Ntanga looked away from Adam to the outside and began.

"My village was small with twenty families. We were common farmers living off the land. We would make trips to the city for any materials that we couldn't make or grow ourselves, such as the newspaper. We kept ourselves in tune with the country through our televisions or radio and ventures into the city. We had a good life, but began to slowly see our country and lifestyle deteriorate as the years went by. We sold vegetables to the government for income. But, the money that we received over time started to decrease. They told us that inflation was the problem. We had to grow and sell more in order to make the same amount of money.

We also started to notice that the materials we bought in the city were becoming more and more expensive. Unfortunately, our government officials didn't look like they were hurting from the same inflation that we were told about. Then the Kimbalas started to make speeches. They were our saviors." Ms. Ntanga looked at Adam with a hint of light coming into her eyes. "Karim Kimbala began the revolution and, we thought, gave us our lives back. We thought that life would begin again. Then, after a few years, our hope dissolved." Ms. Ntanga looked back outside and continued, "Karim made many promises to the people, but didn't deliver. Instead he became corrupted. Life became worse than what we knew before the Kimbalas and then we had a second hope, Karim's brother, Joseph Kimbala.

"He seized power from his brother and we couldn't do anything but regain hope. We had to. Then the district chiefs came in. Joseph Kimbala appointed a person from each village to be that village's district chief. He also sent in assistant district chiefs. These people were not from nor did they ever live in the villages they were assigned to. We were told that assigning assistant district chiefs would make sure that all decisions made were fair and impartial. You see, you had to take any problems you had with neighbors, your farmland, or government to your district chief. He was seen as the extension of our national government. We saw it as Joseph Kimbala's way of bettering our people and providing some type of security and organization. We wouldn't have to worry about high prices too much longer, or high unemployment, or tribal wars to gain food. Joseph Kimbala was our true savior."

Adam didn't see the addition of district chiefs as a plus for the Kilambèan people, but he wasn't there to argue with Ms. Ntanga. "Ms. Ntanga, I'm sorry to interrupt, but can you please tell us where you were when the outbreak of the war started?" Adam asked.

Ms. Ntanga hesitated and Adam thought that he would have to give her a short break, but then she began. "I was sitting in front of the house cleaning the breakfast dishes. I had just said goodbye to my husband. He was going to the city to pick up the necessary items. He did this once every two weeks so it was nothing new. After cleaning the dishes, I picked up my needle and an old pair of my husband's pants and sat back outside. They needed some mending. I also liked to talk to my neighbors and watch the children play.

"Then I saw a truck come into the town. A green army truck, the kind with no hood and there were soldiers standing inside. They went directly to the district chief's office where the man sitting in the passenger's seat in the cabin of the truck got out and walked in with some documents. Everyone continued looking at the district chief's office. The district chief himself came outside with the man from the truck and walked to the center of our village."

"Ms. Ntanga, may I ask what their names were? Who was the district chief and the man that delivered the documents? And were the assistant deputy chiefs there at that moment?" Adam asked.

"The district chief's name was Sam Muntanga. The man that he was talking to was Captain Delucroix. The assistants weren't there at that moment. I don't know where they were. Sam walked to the center of the village, opened a document, and began to call names. He told us to come towards him if our name was called. He called seven people to the center. They were taken into Sam's office..."

"Do you need a break or would you like some water?" Adam began pouring water into a glass for her.

"Water is good. Thank you. The next few hours changed my country forever. We didn't know why those seven people were taken into Sam's office, but the sounds that came out of his office that afternoon were terrible. I never heard such screams in my life. No one dared to ask what was going on in fear of having to join their seven neighbors. It lasted for most of the day. Most of us sought shelter in our homes hoping to muffle the high pitch screams and avoid the sight of the soldiers guarding the office. It was as if we could deny what was going on if we didn't have the imagery.

"I remember the sun setting and wondering where my husband, Tim, was. He was late and I was worried what would happen if he returned to the sight of soldiers in our village. Sam finally appeared outside with the captain and soldiers dragging our seven neighbors behind him. The soldiers screamed at our seven neighbors while they forced each one to stand in a straight line. Once our neighbors were standing in a straight line, their shoulders barely touching, Sam shouted orders for the soldiers to kill our neighbors. It was over in seconds. The soldiers then quickly made a pile of our neighbor's lifeless bodies. We were told to come outside. The captain walked over to Soliel, one of our younger men, and told us that this was the result of disloyalty. He wanted us to take a good luck at our neighbor's faces and bodies, and reminded us that anyone of us could have been lying on the ground too. The arms and legs of our neighbors were strewn in the most unnatural way. I will never forget their lifeless eyes as if they were staring at me, accusing me of not helping them. Then the captain took his revolver out and shot Soliel in the head. We didn't know why Sam and the captain were doing these things. The captain reminded us that General Joseph Kimbala was our leader, that he worked hard and fought for us, that we should be loyal to him for all that he has provided. The captain told us that Sam would be watching over us and that he would be back if there was a hint of disloyalty. We watched the back of the truck leave along with any hope that was left. I also never saw my husband again," Ms. Ntanga finished.

"Ms. Ntanga, would you be willing to give the names of the seven people to us?" Adam asked.

"Yes, son, I will." Ms. Ntanga replied.

Adam knew why the soldiers had entered her village that day. Karim Kimbala had just failed at a coup attack to take the country back. Soliel provided Karim with inside information he received from Sam, and therefore needed to be eliminated. The other seven people were innocents, but Joseph Kimbala wanted to make a strong point of who was in charge.

"Thank you again, Ms. Ntanga for coming to speak with us," Adam said. Adam watched Ms. Ntanga leave the office before letting out a sigh of relief.

"Are you okay?" Sabrina looked earnestly at Adam.

Adam looked down at his trembling hands. He needed some fresh air. "I'll be back in a couple of minutes."

Adam was standing on the office's porch for a short break. There was a sea of color moving like a slow tide among the white tents in front of him.

He could also see Cat walking around. She was a plain woman in contrast to the colorful dress of the refugee women in the camp. Cat had been doing the job for years, but he didn't know where she got her countless energy and enthusiasm from. He was just glad that they had someone like her there. He walked back in to prepare for the next witness interview.

Cathy picked Adam and Sabrina up and drove them to the British base for dinner. Tonight was Mexican fiesta night and Cathy thought that it would be good to bring some normalcy back for her visitors. She also needed a break from the camp life herself. They would have a window of three hours for dinner with curfew starting at ten-o'clock. Cathy would have to drive them back to their motel and get back to the camp before lockdown. She was looking forward to seeing Adam and catching up on what he'd been up to. Sabrina sat in the front seat with Adam getting in the back.

"Okay Cat, where are we going to tonight?" Adam asked excited to exit his motel room for he hoped at least two hours.

"Well, darlings, we are off to the British base for Mexican fiesta night. I thought that the two of you wouldn't mind mixing with the Brits tonight. I haven't seen the two of you for a long time, and want to hear what you've been up to in The Hague. Love, I want to hear from you first." Cat looked over at Sabrina.

"Well, I'm ready for the change of scenery and it's good to see you again too, Cathy," Sabrina smiled at her.

CHAPTER 17

The team had arrived in The Hague the day before and were having breakfast downstairs in the hotel's restaurant. It was Alex's first time in The Hague and she hoped that she would get to see some of the city before leaving. Amsterdam would have to wait until she had more time. She had woken up with a slight headache and was still jet lagged, but was also too excited and pumped with adrenaline to notice.

"No matter how often I visit Europe, I'll never get used to the breakfast. Give me scrambled eggs, sausage, and toast anytime," Henry said looking down at his croissant and eggs.

At least he got his eggs even though they were poached. Alex was happy to find yoghurt and some toast, but she was pretty sure that she would need more than this to sustain her once the jet lag was over.

"Let's get over to the office. I want to make sure that everyone gets settled in and then Sam and I are going to head over to the detention center for a meeting with the General," Henry said.

Everyone stood up and moved to the taxi. They were staying at a secluded hotel off of Noordeinde, right behind one of the Dutch Queen's palaces. Alex watched the houses and little shops as they passed by and fantasized about what she would find inside. She was also amazed to see so many people riding bicycles. They seemed to be everywhere, even grannies were cycling. She nudged Martie and pointed to granny. Martie smiled enjoying Alex's fresh look at a country she had visited many times during university. She had spent most of her time in Amsterdam's pubs and house parties, but she had visited The Hague a couple of times, and from the looks of things the city hadn't changed that much.

The taxi stopped in front of an office building, and the team stepped out. The office space was bare. Alex didn't expect the first supply shipment to arrive until the following day. Today, they were going to claim their office space and set up a temporary working space until the supplies arrived. At least they had their laptops and had carried any important documents and supplies with them on the plane ride. Martie and Alex were going to stay behind at the office and work on a few motions that needed to be filed with the court the following day. Henry and Sam, after setting up their work stations, departed for their meeting.

Alex walked into Martie's office holding a stack of files in her left arm. She looked around the room and took in the starkness of the décor. The off-white walls contrasted with the dark grey rug.

Alex sighed and looked at Martie. "We'll definitely have to buy some plants for the offices," she said.

"We'll need more then plants if we want to improve the décor. A couple of nice paintings or at least posters will help a lot." Martie searched for a pen in her bag.

Alex sat down in the only available seat and placed her stack of files on the desk. "What's the game plan for today?"

Martie used her teeth to take the cap of the pen and shuffled through the pile of documents on her desk before picking up her note pad. "We need to complete our response to the protective measures motion today. Henry also wanted us to complete the draft motion on witness summaries. Once these two filings are finished, then we can turn to the agreed facts. Have you completed reviewing your set of the witness summaries? I'm finished reviewing my set."

Alex grabbed one of the files and pulled a pile of paper out. She also pulled out an excel spreadsheet and handed it to Martie. "Yes, I finished my review and created an excel spreadsheet with all of the necessary information. I included each witnesses name, the contents of their witness summary, any inconsistencies that I found in the witness summary, and I also made a note about what I believed was missing from the summary."

71

"Yes, I noticed that the prosecution provided one paragraph witness summaries for a few of the witnesses. I can't even tell why those witnesses are relevant to the case. Okay, can you please draft a short motion requesting more information in the witness summaries and add my notes concerning the witness summaries that I reviewed to your excel spreadsheet? Then we can meet this afternoon to review your draft and make any changes. We'll add the excel spreadsheet as an annex to the motion so please make sure that it is formatted correctly for filing." Martie handed her notes to Alex.

Alex placed the notes in the folder. "Sure, I can do that. Are you going to work on the protective measures motion? Do you need any help?" Alex asked.

"Yes, I already have the draft response ready. I just want to review what I've written and read through their motion again. I want our facts to be completely correct. I can understand why the prosecution is seeking protective measures for some of its witnesses. I don't understand though why they're requesting protective measures for the international witnesses. Those witnesses aren't living in Kilambéa and have no one to fear. Why would they want or need protective measures?"

"I don't know. Maybe they are afraid of providing sensitive or confidential information to the public?"

"But, then I still don't get it. The judges can order that the information not be provided to the public. They can order that the witness testify in closed session when providing sensitive information. They don't need protective measures," Martie stated perplexed.

"Seriously, I have no idea. Hopefully, we will find out once our response is filed."

"Yes, I hope so. Okay, let's get to work. Let me know if you need anything while drafting the motion. Otherwise, let's have a follow-up meeting at two-o'clock this afternoon. Sound good?" Martie tapped her pen on the pile of documents.

"Sounds good to me." Alex stood up, picked up her stack of files, and walked out of Martie's office.

CHAPTER 18

Henry and Sam entered the detention center, emptied their pockets into the box and walked through the scanners. "Gentlemen, can I please see a photo ID?" the security officer asked. The English accent was unmistakably Dutch. Henry and Sam both handed over their passports. "Thank you. I understand that you are here to see inmate Kimbala. We'll hold onto your passports and in exchange give you these visitor badges. Please wear them on your outer front jacket at all times. You will need to sign the visitor's list every time you come here for a visit. Officer Jonas will take you to the interview room and explain the rules on the way. Officer Jonas, they're ready." The security officer looked in Jonas' direction and motioned for him to lead the gentlemen away.

"Gentlemen, please place your cell phones and personal property in one of the lockers to your left, and then follow me. We're going to walk through the door straight ahead and immediately turn to the right where the interview rooms are contained." Officer Jonas swiped his key card and the door unlocked. "Inmate Kimbala will be escorted to the interview room once you are inside. There is video monitoring in both the interview room and all hallways."

The men entered the interview room and the door closed behind them. "The door locks automatically. If you need to exit, then push this button. The bathroom is located down the hall. If you need to go, then push the button, and someone will come. Oh, and your visits can last up to two hours. Do you have any questions?" Officer Jonas asked.

"I think it's pretty clear," Henry replied.

"Good, then I'll have inmate Kimbala brought over."

General Kimbala was escorted into the interview room ten minutes later by two officers. He was dressed in plain clothes. The only reminder that he was a detainee was the handcuffs contrasting with his black shirt. Otherwise, he looked like everyone's average grandfather. The General was clutching a manila envelope under his right arm. Henry and Sam rose to their feet to greet the General and shake hands. The officers left the room.

"Good afternoon, General Kimbala." Henry and Sam talked in unison.

"Good afternoon, gentlemen. How was your flight?" General Kimbala inquired.

"The flight was fine, but we're happy to finally be here. We wanted to meet with you and give an update on what we've been working on and what you can expect to happen over the next couple of days. Now, you know that we have a status conference coming up in two days and it's obligatory that you attend. I understand if you would rather not, but this will be a good time to let the judge know if you're experiencing any problems here in the detention center. Are you experiencing any problems here?" Henry asked.

"No, they are treating me very well here at the center. Please go on," the General requested.

"Well, seeing how we'll be going to trial pretty soon, the judge will want to discuss a few issues, such as disclosure, agreed facts, witnesses, exhibits, and protective measures. Therefore, we have a long status conference that may last four hours. Now, we received the prosecution's pre-trial brief, witness list and summaries, and list of exhibits. Our response is due next week, but we've already been able to spot some mistakes in their brief. We'll also be contending some of the witness summaries that we obtained due to the fact that they are vague. Lastly, we have some problems with some protective measures that they've requested for some of the witnesses and after double checking we were able to verify that we haven't received some of the materials listed on their exhibit list through disclosure. General Kimbala, were you able to read the prosecution's pre-trial brief?" Henry

Boome asked. He was curious to know what his client thought. More importantly, Henry wanted to know if the General had found the same mistakes or even more gaps that his team missed. He would take anything that would help them with this case.

"I have read the brief in its entirety and made notes. The prosecution has made many mistakes and I wanted to hand my notes over to you. It actually amazes me what they got wrong, and this is supposed to be the almighty prosecution," the General laughed and handed over his notes.

"Thank you, General. It amazed us too. We'll compare your notes with ours and see what we've possibly missed. We're going to counter any gaps or mistakes in our response next week. What we're going to do this week is talk to the prosecution and the judge about the missing exhibits. I don't feel comfortable filing our response until we've been able to see those exhibits. So, I want to see if we can get those exhibits by the end of this week if not before.

"You probably looked at the witness list too. Can you please tell me if any of the crime based or local witnesses' names look familiar to you?" Henry placed a copy of the witness list in front of the General.

"Yes, I looked at the list already and there were only three names that looked familiar," he replied.

"Okay, and out of the international and sensitive witnesses are there any names that we should be particularly careful with?" Henry asked.

"I spoke personally to three of these internationals during my presidency, and of course I know the sensitive witnesses," the General replied.

"Would you be able to give us specific details about your meetings with the internationals and any information that you can give on the sensitive witnesses? I mean their relationship to you, what their functions were, did they have any personal access to you and the decision making, are there any skeletons in their closet, were they hard to handle? Any type of information that you are aware of no matter how minute. We need to figure out why their names have made it onto the prosecution's witness list," Henry finished.

"When do you need this to be completed by?" the General asked.

Henry smiled and replied, "Within the next two weeks would be ideal. What we need to know urgently is whether or not you have any objections to the various protective measures that they have requested for some of the witnesses."

"That's an easy answer. I object to all of their requests. If these people want to testify against me, then they should do so in the open. I have nothing to hide, and if they're telling the truth, then they should be willing to speak openly and without regret," the General replied indignantly.

"Okay. That's one of the responses that Martie and Alex are working on now back at the office. We'll let them know your wishes," Henry stated. "Besides protective measures, Martie and Alex are working on two other small motions. One motion requests that the prosecution provides more detail in some of the witness summaries. The information that they provided us doesn't help us to prepare our case at all, and we'll need more information about who these people are and what they plan on testifying about. We're trying to minimize any blindsiding from the prosecution. And talking about blindsiding the agreed facts..."

The General interrupted Henry again laughing. "Sorry, Henry, but that was funny. I didn't like most of the statements that they made about me or what happened in my country. Do they expect us to agree to these statements?"

"No, General this is a tactic used to shorten the trial and to make sure that we're only arguing what both sides disagree on. For instance, we can agree with the prosecution that you took office in April 1980, but we do not agree that you attempted to assassinate your brother in 1980. Sam and I will be working on a response to the agreed facts proposed and will come back tomorrow so that you can have a look and advise," Henry stated.

Alex and Martie were hunched over their desk with each completely focused at the task at hand when Henry and Sam walked in. Alex was proofreading the motion requesting more detail for various witness summaries while Martie was placing the finishing touches on the protective measures motion. Martie looked up first.

"How is our client holding up?" Martie asked.

"He looks good and has been doing his own homework. He gave us his notes on the prosecution's pre-trial brief, and he'll be working tomorrow on the draft agreed facts response that we want to file," Henry exclaimed.

"Wow, a working client. This is good." Alex smiled.

"It's our first night here. I suggest that we go back to the hotel, get something to eat, and then everyone can work in their hotel room. We can re-group at nine-o'clock in my suite, review the motions, and discuss what we've come up with on agreed facts," Henry said.

"That sounds good to me," Sam said.

"I don't think that you have to ask us twice," Martie said.

The ladies began to pack.

CHAPTER 19

Calvin appeared suddenly in the girl's doorway. "How about we go out after work for some drinks?" he asked. The girls laughed.

"What's the special occasion?" Greta asked. It was four thirty and the ladies had just had a busy day. They were waiting for the clock to strike five thirty and then they could make good on their pact: they were both leaving at five thirty today and not one minute later.

"What's the special occasion, you ask? How can you not know? Analise has been here for three months as of today and has yet to talk about resigning! I call that a call for celebration!" Calvin exclaimed.

"Cal, I've been here for six years. I call that a cause for celebration; not three months!" Greta growled back laughing.

"Okay, okay call it whatever you want, but we should go out for drinks tonight. First round is on me. Are the two of you in?" Calvin asked.

"Cal, you just want to go out. Okay, I'm in." Greta laughed.

Analise joined in. "Count me in too. I need some strong liquor. We have been preparing for this status conference for a week now and I'm exhausted." Analise sighed.

"Are you prepared?" Calvin asked.

"Of course she's prepared. Look who she had to help her." Greta smirked at Calvin with a hurt look.

"How modest you are. You know that the puppy dog look doesn't work on me. What time are we heading out of here tonight?" Calvin asked.

Both girls answered in unison, "Five thirty and not one minute later!" Both Analise and Greta filled the room with laughter while Calvin stared in amazement, turned around, and left the room.

----------------- CHAPTER 20 -----------------

It was eight-o'clock and the defense team's taxi had just pulled up in front of the Tribunal's front gate. Alex was sitting in the back seat on the right side of the car. She looked out of the window at the massive building and was immediately impressed. A wide half moon sidewalk and tall spear headed grey iron gate separated the stone street from the Tribunal's housing. The large gate opened in the middle for cars with two welcoming doors.

A smaller opening for pedestrians was also visible. It was already open that morning, but there were two moveable metal poles protruding from the ground eliminating the possibility for just any car to enter. A security officer stood in a single booth just beyond the gate's entrance. The defense team stepped out of the cab and walked towards the security officer. Alex looked around as they walked up the path to the booth. The Tribunal building looked small from the outside and she wondered how they could fit all of the offices and work space into this tiny building. Her last internet search estimate was that the Tribunal contained fifteen hundred employees.

Even though the building looked small from the outside, Alex was impressed. The building's character was from the fifteenth century and looked like a renovated castle. The walls were made of brick with a tower accentuating each angle of the Tribunal's walls. The windows were decorated with stain glass adding an additional enchantment. Alex thought that a mistake had been made until she saw the Tribunal's flag waving above.

Henry spoke to the security officer who in turn checked his list. They were then escorted to the security office in the main lobby where they received their badges. Afterwards the team was escorted to one of the vacant defense conference rooms where Hanna Van Hout was waiting.

"Good morning, everyone. My name is Hanna and I'm your contact person from the Office of Defense Counsel or ODC for short." Hanna shook everyone's hand. "I understand that you have a status conference tomorrow and probably want to start working as soon as possible, but I would like to point out a few things about the Tribunal and take you on a tour of the building. This will take two hours of your time this morning, but I assure you that these two hours are important in regards to your working and stay here at the Tribunal. If you take a seat at the table, then we can begin." Hanna gestured towards the table.

---------------- CHAPTER 21 ----------------

"All rise, the court is now in session," the court deputy recited. The pre-trial chamber of judges filed into the courtroom, stepped up onto the bench, and sat down.

The presiding judge began to speak. "Good morning to everyone present. This is the first status conference for the Prosecution v. Joseph Kimbala, case number nine hundred and seventy-one. My name is Judge Theonus Atkinson, to my left is Judge Adrienne Reinhold, and to my right is Judge Jeremy Robinson. Can we have the appearance of the parties please?" Judge Atkinson looked straight ahead at the parties.

The court usher, legal officers for the court, and stenographer sat at a long oak table directly in front of the bench. The prosecution was sitting on the opposite side of the oak table to Judge Atkinson's left while the defense and the accused sat to his right. An off-white wall, decorated with pictures of the Tribunal, acted as the back wall behind the prosecution and defense tables. The witness booth sat in between the bench and prosecution on the left side, while the public gallery was located on the right side of the bench. A bullet proof glass pane separated the public gallery from the courtroom. The interpreter booths and video production unit were positioned directly behind the witness booth, separated from the witness by another thick paned glass wall.

Jan Paul stood and spoke. "Good morning your honors. Paul Jan De

Loon for the prosecution. Here with me today are Gabriel Hart and the paralegal, Analise Morgan." Jan Paul returned to his seat.

"Thank you, Sir. The defense, please?" Judge Atkinson asked.

"Henry Boome for the defense your honors. With me today are Sam Richardson, Martie Candell, and our paralegal, Alexandra Cayhill," Henry stated returning to his seat.

"Will the accused please stand?" Judge Atkinson turned to face the accused. General Kimbala stood between two security officers. "Good morning, Mr. Kimbala. Is there anything that you would like to share in regards to your stay at the detention center or your health?"

"No, your honors. Thank you for asking," General Kimbala replied.

"Then you may sit down," Judge Atkinson said looking down at his paperwork. "I trust that you received the agenda for today from my legal officer. We have a lot of issues to get through so let's begin." Judge Atkinson looked up from his paperwork and readjusted his eyeglasses.

"The first item of business is the prosecution's pre-trial brief. The defense has filed a few motions including a request concerning witness summaries provided for by the prosecution, and a response regarding protective measures sought by some of the prosecution's witnesses. I'm going to start with the defense. Would you like to provide any further information at this time, Mr. Boome?" Judge Atkinson looked over at Henry.

Henry stood up and turned the microphone on before answering. "Your Honor, we believe that our position is clearly stated in each motion. We have read the prosecution's brief, the summaries, and reviewed the exhibit list. The witness summaries are inexplicably vague and the defense is unable to work with the limited information provided to us. We also would like to note that the prosecution has requested protective measures and the defense is in no position to provide a response with the vague summaries that have been provided. Furthermore, we noticed that we are missing a few of the exhibits and would like to have copies furnished to us by the end of this Friday seeing how our response is due next week." Henry remained standing and waited for Judge Atkinson.

"I see." Judge Atkinson looked up from his paperwork. He looked above the rim of his reading glasses. "And would your position to the protective measures be any different if you already had the information you deem to be evident?" Judge Atkinson smiled at Henry.

Henry smiled back. "No, your Honor, our position would be the same," Henry replied.

"That's more honest. Mr. De Loon, I'm sure that you've read these motions. What is your position?" Judge Atkinson requested. Henry sat down while Jan Paul rose to his feet.

"Your Honor, I believe that the witness summaries are sufficient and shouldn't hinder the defense. We also only request protective measures in urgent situations when the witness' life could be in danger. We have done so in this case. As for the exhibits, we disclosed copies of all of the exhibits, but if the defense can provide a list, then we will be happy to provide the information again," Jan Paul strongly stated.

Henry waved a piece of paper in the air. "I have the list of missing exhibits here for the prosecution." Henry stated rising to his feet.

"Very efficient, Mr. Boome. Will the court officer please accept the piece of paper and hand it over to the prosecution? Now, we read the summaries too and they are inadequate. I suggest that the defense provide the prosecution with a list of names where they want more substantial information. You will then have, Mr. De Loon, five days to provide sufficient summaries to the defense. You also have until the end of the week to provide copies of the missing exhibits. Now, onto agreed facts. Have you been able to agree on any facts?" Judge Atkinson requested looking at the prosecution.

"We provided the defense with a list of facts one month ago. We have yet to hear a response," Jan Paul stated.

"Mr. Boome, what do you have to add to this productive conversation?" Judge Atkinson asked.

"Your Honor, we did receive their agreed facts and have been working on our response. Up to today, I can say that we will object to most of the facts proposed by the prosecution," Henry stated.

Judge Atkinson looked at his two colleagues and mumbled, "This is going to be a long trial." He resumed. "Okay then, it is important that you both sit down and come to a decision on agreed facts. We don't want to waste the court's time and resources debating facts that both parties can agree on. Do you understand?" Judge Atkinson asked. Everyone knew that this was a rhetorical question. "How are we dealing with disclosure? Are there any matters to be raised besides the exhibit's issue?" Judge Atkinson asked.

"We are still reviewing the materials that have been disclosed by the prosecution. Therefore, we're unable to give a cohesive answer at this time," Henry replied.

"Does the prosecution want to add anything to this?" Judge Atkinson turned to Jan Paul.

"No, your honor," Jan Paul stated.

"Well, then we have a court date set for three months from now. We will have another status conference in six weeks. I expect to hear that you've been very productive at the next conference. Does anyone wish to raise any other issues?" Judge Atkinson looked around the room before adjourning the Status Conference.

The three judges rose with everyone else in tempo, turned to the left, and walked out of the courtroom. Henry walked over to speak quickly with Jan Paul while Sam and Martie walked over to the General. Alex closed down her laptop and put the paperwork back into her roller briefcase before leaving the courtroom.

CHAPTER 22

Jan Paul was bending forward and staring intensely at the white board. Silence filled the room while everyone waited for him to speak. Three large white boards hung from the walls. The white board on the left contained a hierarchy chart of Kimbala's government and military officials while the middle white board contained a timeline of important events that occurred in Kilambèa. The third white board contained all of the information from the first two white boards in 3D by linking the officials to the events that occurred. Gabriel figured out that the Dutch loved their white boards, and he could understand why looking at the mass of information before him in a single glance.

They wanted to prove that General Kimbala had been either directly or indirectly involved in murder, torture, enforced disappearance of persons, political persecution, and sexual slavery while most attorneys have enough problems trying to deal with one charge let alone multiple counts.

Jan Paul looked at the second board. Kilambèa gained independence in 1959 and Karim Kimbala led a successful coup in September 1963. Ten years later his brother, Joseph, who fought by his brother's side, gives a speech on July 7, 1973, condemning his brother's government. Seven years later, Joseph leads an attempted assassination against his brother killing his brother's wife and children, his brother flees, and Joseph takes control of Kilambèa. Joseph Kimbala is arrested in 2006 and now, in 2007, they are going to trial in three months. Jan Paul looked at the third board and Gabriel saw a flicker of anxiety in Jan Paul's eyes. There were a few important missing links on the third board and the tension was rising as every day passed to connect the dots and eliminate the gaps.

Jan Paul spoke finally, "Adam, what did you find on the mission last week?"

Adam sat up in his chair and began talking, "I took five interviews of crime based victims and collected some promising documents from the archive's unit. The interviews were very productive and we've been able to eliminate some of the questions that we had and link a few more of the perpetrators to the crimes themselves.

"For instance, one victim, Ms. Ntanga provides a link to Delucroix and we all know that Delucroix answered to Lewell, Kimbala's number two man. Fortunately, we do have documentary and visual evidence already adding weight to Ms. Ntanga's story. I did run into a problem though with the archive's unit. I still couldn't gain access to one of the vaults. The archive unit's director told me that he tried, but couldn't get permission from the Justice Department. I called the Justice Department and was told that they had given permission already. I couldn't get the two departments to talk to each other over the phone and left with the same run around," Adam stated.

"At least they had a new story this time," Gabriel chuckled.

"I'll talk to the prosecutor and see if a formal telephone call can be made. Maybe the office can remind the government of what could happen if they don't cooperate," Jan Paul said looking back at the white boards.

"How are the witnesses coming along? Is the witness unit able to secure our first fifteen witness' travel arrangements?" Jan Paul looked at Mandy, one of the investigators.

Mandy cleared her throat. "Ten of the witnesses have their passports and visas already. Two of the witnesses told us yesterday that they haven't received their passports yet so we're working on chasing them up. Three witnesses are having second doubts and are afraid to testify, one being a key insider witness. Riek Van Helden and I are working on clearing these things up." Mandy looked at Jan Paul and felt the tension rise in the room.

"I want the passport issue handled by tomorrow and a briefing this afternoon about the three scared witnesses, especially the insider." Jan

Paul stated while turning to Analise. "Analise, how are we doing with disclosure?"

"Everything seems to be moving right along. We disclosed another thousand items last week to the defense and now we're looking at disclosing the materials that Adam brought back from last week's mission. We've already requested translations for the relevant documents from his mission," Analise finished.

"Good work. Let me know if any problems arise with disclosure. How are the exhibits coming along?" Jan Paul asked.

"All of our exhibits have been uploaded and of course the defense has access. The videos are an exception. Cohen and Derek are reviewing the tapes to see which remaining portions should be translated and synchronized in the database. Once we have that information from them and Gabriel gives the okay, then the videos will be uploaded into the database and notification will be sent to the defense," Analise said.

"Great. At least something is running smoothly. People, we have less than three months now to prepare for trial. The defense is stalling with the agreed facts. It seems as if they don't want to agree to anything. We have witnesses without passports and three witnesses that don't want to testify. We're also having trouble with filling in the gaps. Now, I know that we're going to have to try to fill some gaps during the trial, but we need to fill the important gaps now. I don't want to hear any excuses. I only want results." Jan Paul looked at everyone, stood up, and walked out.

CHAPTER 23

Jan Paul placed his hands on the stand and rose to his feet. His presentation lay neatly on the stand. The room was bathed in silence. He looked at the judges, the defense counsel, and then the journalists and public audience sitting in the gallery. The accused, Joseph Kimbala, sat alone in his box. Kimbala was wearing a dark suit and head phones. He ignored the flashing lights from the journalists' cameras in the gallery and stared indignantly at Jan Paul. This was a mock trial that wasted everyone's time. He knew that he had done the right thing for his people, for Kilambèa. Who was this prosecutor to say differently? What did this prosecutor know of his homeland, his people or their sufferings all of these years. Who was he or any foreigner to judge his actions?

Jan Paul ignored Kimbala's cold stare and began after clearing his throat. "Good morning, your Honors and learned colleagues. Today is an important day for Kilambèa. Today is the beginning for the search for truth and justice for the Kilambèan people. Today, the prosecution can show the international community why the Kilambèan people are better off without the accused, Joseph Kimbala. Today, the international community can say enough is enough. We will not condone the inhumanity and crimes committed by the accused, Joseph Kimbala in Kilambèa.

"The Kilambèans were given false hope in 1959 when they gained their independence from the United Kingdom, but their dreams were given new life in 1963 when Karim Kimbala, Joseph Kimbala's brother, staged a successful coupe and filled the Kilambèan people's minds with new and reanimated dreams for the future. On 7 July 1973, the accused sitting before us spoke to the Kilambèan people and told them many things that they had already heard multiple times before. On 5 April 1980, the world saw a rebirth of the Kilambèan government. A sigh of relief rushed across the world when the accused took control of the government from his brother. We all believed that his 1973 speech would become reality. Kilambèa was finally going to progress, the economy was going to improve, and the people would receive much needed food, housing, employment, and other necessary benefits in order to have decent lives. Kilambèa was finally going to be free.

"Unfortunately, this dream of progress and decency didn't last for long. A truth did appear, but it was not the truth that we wanted to see. We were given a firsthand account of the real General Joseph Kimbala who was in reality a man filled with hate, corruption, greed, and void of compassion and good will. The people that the accused fought to lead became the sufferers, the victims.

"The accused has, rightfully so, been charged directly and indirectly with murder, torture, enforced disappearance of persons, political persecution, and sexual slavery. Between 1980 and 2006, the Kilambèans lived under a reign of terror. District chiefs were established in every community, and had the help of assistants. The district chiefs reported to regional chiefs, who then reported to the National Intelligence Service. The National Intelligence Service, or NIS for short, reported to one of Kimbala's lieutenant generals and advisory board who in turn reported to Joseph Kimbala. As you will see, the NIS was a subsection of the army. It not only created orders and decisions, but also supervised the national prison system. The NIS breathed fear into the average citizen's life.

"It is important to note that the NIS received its orders and decisions directly from Joseph Kimbala. Furthermore, the NIS leadership received direction at their weekly meetings with Joseph Kimbala. This was a large intelligence agency with many legs, but Joseph Kimbala kept a pulse on the organization. But, this was not enough. Joseph Kimbala also imposed his rule in the media by enforcing state sponsored television, newspaper, and radio programming. Kilambèa was completely under the control of the accused.

"As I mentioned a little earlier, the accused is charged with murder, torture, enforced disappearance of persons, political persecution, and sexual slavery. These are grave charges and therefore I want to take you through them one by one. We will begin with the murder charge. For the most part, the accused was able to keep his hands clean. He delegated his killing orders to the NIS, but the prosecution will not only prove that the accused provided killing orders to the NIS. We will also prove that the accused took part directly in three killings."

Jan Paul turned, looked at the accused, took a deep breath and then began again. "The accused took power on 5 April 1980 after his attempted assassination of his brother failed. To cement his leadership beginning his reign of terror, the accused single-handedly shot and killed three members of his brother's advisory group in cold blood. Furthermore, he gave orders for other key governmental officials to be assassinated. The accused wanted word to spread quickly that he was to be obeyed. He knew that in order to keep control he would need a central organization that would have eyes and ears in every village across the land. The former intelligence agency, formed by the British government, was disbanded and the NIS was born. The accused placed some of his most trusted friends from the army in key NIS positions. These trusted friends also sat on his advisory panel. Throughout the prosecution's investigation, we found more than fifty killing orders, all coming directly from the office of the accused.

"Later on, during the prosecution's case, you are going to meet an eyewitness to an event stemming from one of these killing orders. She will describe how seven people were taken to the district chief's office for interrogation. She will also tell us how she couldn't avoid hearing excruciating screams vibrating through the village while her neighbors were tortured for countless hours. This witness will further tell us how these same seven neighbors were dragged outside covered in blood. She and her neighbors were told to come outside and were given a speech that disloyalty to the accused would come with a price. The seven neighbors were shot to death while the remaining villagers were forced to watch. The men that visited this witness' village worked for the NIS, and the prosecution will prove that their killing orders came directly from the accused.

"I mentioned a few minutes ago that the accused has also been charged with torture. The prosecution is going to produce a witness that will recall a chilling event from her childhood. This witness's father was a member of Karim Kimbala's presidential advisory group and the Minister of Finance for the Kilambèan government during Karim Kimbala's presidency. This witness's father was one of the men killed in cold blood by the accused. The witness will recall the day that the accused arrived at her home unannounced. The family, including the witness's father, was sitting at the dining room table. It was the witness's birthday and her father was about to cut the birthday cake when the accused and two armed men walked into the dining room. The witness will tell you that the accused immediately began threatening her father, accusing him of treachery to the nation. Furthermore, the witness will tell how the accused made her father rise from his chair and kneel in front of him. The accused threatened to kill the witness's mother if he didn't recant his past dealings with Karim Kimbala and promise loyalty to the accused and new government. Through this witness's testimony, you will learn that her father pleaded for his family's life to no avail. The accused looked down at the former Minister of Finance, the father of the witness, spat in his face, and then shot him once in the head. The witness will also tell of how the accused then picked up the knife that would cut the birthday cake and offered pieces to the two other men stating that good cake should not be wasted. The witness and her mother were then escorted to one of the many military camp brothels. The witness was thirteen years old when she became what is famously known in China as a 'comfort woman.'

"This witness's story is chilling to the bone, but unfortunately it's not the only story that the prosecution will be able to share with you. There are many excruciating stories of former governmental officials and party sympathizers whose right to chose their own political affiliation was snatched away in Kimbala's thirst to control the country, his country. You will hear how the NIS gathered all known governmental officials from Karim Kimbala's regime and held them in the now infamous prison camp for its ironic name, 'Free Town Hotel.' Free Town was synonymous with torture and killing. Kilambèans tell nowadays that many people who checked into the hotel never checked out. The precious few that did check out lived through unheard of torture, an intensive brain washing program, and in the end devoted their loyalties to the accused and new regime. One former inmate of Free Town will share his story with us. He escaped and fled to Nigeria where he's been living ever since, too afraid to return even now to his home country.

"The stories that I just shared with you cover the range of crimes that the accused has been indicted on: murder, torture, enforced disappearance of persons, political persecution, and sexual slavery. Over the next few months you will hear from experts that study the Kilambèan government. They will give a summary of the government's history. You will also hear from international witnesses who worked in Kilambèa after the accused was arrested. Insider witnesses will tell the truth of what happened in Kilambèa and authenticate many of the documents in the prosecution's possession. Finally, you will hear from the victims. These are the people that have the most to say. They are Kilambèa. The prosecution, through every single witness, will paint a grave picture and show the world how the accused selfishly led his people to despair. The prosecution will show how the Kilambèans no longer whisper the words of hope and prosperity, but firmly speak of improved lives in the absence of their fearful leader, Joseph Kimbala. The prosecution thanks you for your time and patience." Jan Paul sat down. He could feel the perspiration dripping down his arms, chest, and groin.

"Thank you, Mr. De Loon. Would the defense like to begin?" Judge Atkinson turned to the defense table.

Henry looked at the clock and stood up. "Your Honors, I believe that we are reaching the time for a break. May I suggest that we break now and then I can start once we return? This is a grave matter and it is important that the defense's statement is not interrupted." Henry looked towards the chamber for an answer.

"You are absolutely correct, Mr. Boome. We will break now for thirty minutes and resume at twelve thirty. How long do you expect to be?" Judge Atkinson asked.

"Actually, your Honor I believe that I will not take more than forty-five minutes of your time," Henry replied.

Judge Atkinson smiled. "That sounds good. Let's break."

"All rise, the court is now in recess," the court usher's voice echoed in the courtroom.

The defense team was sitting in the defense room discussing the prosecution's opening statements. Sam and Martie were both eating a sandwich while

Henry sipped his coffee and gathered his thoughts. Alex had decided to coordinate with the audiovisual booth, interpreters, and stenographers. She wanted to make sure that they were ready. Alex had a copy of Henry's opening statement so that the interpreters and stenographer could follow Henry more easily. She also had a special copy for the audio visual department which incorporated the video segments that Henry wanted to show during his presentation. Alex wanted their first day to be as organized as possible. She also hoped to minimize any problems that could arise. Alex was a little nervous, but staying busy helped to calm the nerves.

"So, what did you think about their opening statement?" Martie asked.

Sam was swallowing a piece of his sandwich. A ham cheese croissant sandwich in Baltimore definitely tasted different than what he was eating here. He would never be able to eat another croissant back home. He made a mental note that a trip to France was a must.

"I thought it was very emotional and didn't give too much guidance as to what they want to prove. I'm not quite sure if they know what they want to prove. We can do better. What were all of the notes that the General kept passing over to you, Henry?" Sam looked over at Henry with an inquisitive look.

Henry snapped out of his trance and looked over the table at Sam. "They were notes concerning the prosecution's opening. He was letting me know where the holes were," Henry finished.

"Was it good advice? Does it look like he'll be helpful or will we get a lot of rubbish during the trial?" Martie asked.

"Most of the notes were actually pretty good and there were a couple of things that I hadn't picked up on," Henry stated.

Alex walked in. "It's show time. Are you ready, Henry?" Alex looked at him in anticipation.

"As I'll ever be. Come on everybody, let's get this party started," Henry said as he rose from his chair and gathered his notes.

CHAPTER 24

The defense team returned to the office to find pizza boxes awaiting them in the kitchen. Carter knew that they would be famished and wasn't sure if it was going to be a long night, but he did want to make sure that everyone had something to eat. It also gave him an excuse to use the firm's credit card. There was nothing better than using someone else's money he thought, especially your boss's money. Alex picked up two slices of pizza and a coke before racing to the war room and turning on CNN. She had seen their reporting van stationed out front of the Tribunal that morning and knew that they would show coverage of the process. Others filed in after Alex and took a seat covering the table with filled dinner plates and pizza boxes.

The news reporter replaced the Black Berry commercial and began talking about the process. Alex thought that she would have to wait patiently while wading through three or four other reports, but it was her luck that they were starting off directly with the Kimbala trial. The reporter began by giving a brief history of Kilambèa while showing a picture of Joseph Kimbala dressed in a military uniform in the background. They then moved to a picture of the Tribunal in The Hague before showing footage of the courtroom including images of Henry, Jan Paul, the judges and Joseph Kimbala surrounded by three security officers. Alex reached for a third slice of pizza while Sam took a gulp of his beer. The news anchor turned and began talking to the correspondent in the field whose picture replaced the courtroom footage.

"Jane, you have been talking to many people in Kilambèa over the past few days. What can you tell us about the atmosphere in Kilambèa? Are the people happy or confused and upset at the fact that their former president was arrested for grave international war crimes and is now standing trial in The Hague?"

The correspondent shook her head while listening to the feed through her ear piece. Jane was standing on a hotel balcony with the dark sky and bright city with twinkling lights as her scenic background. She spoke once the final word disappeared through the earpiece.

"Carly, yes I have been walking through the streets of Kilambèa over the last five days to gain a feeling of how the Kilambèans are reacting to this piece of their history. So far, we have heard mixed feelings. At one moment we're talking to loyal Kimbala supporters while at the next moment we're confronted with angry stories stereotypical of a past dictatorship."

"Were the people watching the beginning of the court process today, especially the opening statements or was this just another typical day in Kilambèa?"

Jane broke the silence once the last word disappeared. "It seemed as if everyone was watching today. Every store and restaurant seemed to have the television turned onto the trial. The people here are very interested in the court process and how the Tribunal is dealing with their former leader. They feel a part of this process because it's focused on their lives, past and present. Of course they want to know what's going on because it concerns them."

"And what did they think about the prosecution's opening statement?"

"Once again," Jane began, "we received mixed feelings. Some people believe that the prosecution presented a weak opening statement while others either thought that it was sufficient or had no comment."

"And what did they think about the defense's opening statement?"

Jane listened before answering. "The overall consensus was confusion. They couldn't believe that the defense delivered an opening statement for only twenty minutes. Many people didn't know if the defense had already given up or thought that the prosecution's case was weak and therefore did not need a proper response."

Carly shuffled the paperwork placed before her before responding. "That's very interesting Jane. I understand that you're coming back tomorrow. Have a safe trip, okay?"

Jane responded after a pause with a smile. "Thanks, Carly. Have a good night."

Joseph Kimbala's picture replaced Jane's picture and Carly began to speak again. "The trial process against former president Joseph Kimbala is set to continue for the coming months. CNN will be following the process in detail and you can too by tuning in and visiting our special website dedicated exclusively to updates on the Kimbala Trial. The following story takes us to…" Alex turned the volume down on the television and reached for a brownie.

Henry took a bite of his salad and contemplated the news coverage. He didn't put too much into the news seeing how it was circumstantial anyway.

Sam pointed to the television with his beer glass. "Well, it sounds like no one knows what our strategy is. It's good to keep everyone guessing, at least for television ratings."

Henry stood up and pushed his chair under the table. "Well, at least they didn't say anything new or shocking. Everyone, I'm going to get some work done before heading back to the apartment for some sleep. I suggest that you all do the same." Henry exited the war room and everyone else followed agreeing that Henry was correct.

CHAPTER 25

Alex was working in the office. It was an early Saturday morning, but she needed to prepare for the next witness. Alex knew that the rest of the team would be in later on in the day, and she loved the peace and quiet during the morning hours. If Alex was lucky, then she could finish her work and get out of the office in time to do some shopping and enjoy some of the day.

The prosecution's case was about to end after a parade of experts, internationals, military personnel, and local witnesses. Alex had known that this was going to be a difficult case, but she had no idea that it was going to be this bad. She not only had to adapt to a new working environment, but was also working extremely long hours with little breaks in between. She was also experiencing a foreign culture, food and language. Alex missed her daily Starbuck's coffee, salad bars amongst other things, but she was also grateful for having the opportunity to live temporarily in Europe. And after three months, Alex felt comfortable taking the tram and bus through The Hague. She had even tried a few of the common foods even though she would be okay if she didn't ever eat the Dutch kroket again in her life. She could also find her way around town. Alex stood and looked outside the front window while sipping on her second cup of coffee. Early risers were cycling past probably on the way to the city for early morning shopping. A mother cycled past with a funny looking wooden box attached to the front of the bicycle. Two laughing children sat inside the box. Alex was still getting used to the large volume of bicycle riders; actually bicycle riding as a means of public transport for a large percentage of the population.

Alex finished reading her emails from the office and decided to turn to preparing for next week. She had received the exhibit list for the next witness the previous night and wanted to print out the documents and make binders for the attorneys. They already had binders for each of the prosecution witnesses including the witness summary provided by the prosecution, an evaluation summary sheet with information concerning any witness statements that the witness had given, previous testimony given, documents authored by the witness, any research that was conducted on the witness, and any documents that could be used during the witnesses testimony on this case. Alex liked to match the prosecution's exhibit list with what was contained in the binder and then add any additional items from the prosecution's list that they may have missed. She wished that she could organize the binders more ahead of time, but the prosecution released their individual witness exhibit list only the night before the witness testified. Alex turned around at the sound of the door opening and the floor creaking under heavy footsteps.

Henry and Sam walked in. "We have a problem. Martie's on her way in," Henry stated.

Alex put her coffee cup down and sighed. Her afternoon shopping would have to wait. "What's going on?" she asked.

"Call Max and tell him to get over here. I don't care what he does, but he needs to be here by tomorrow afternoon. We found out that the British government has been contacting our witnesses. We're losing them and need to get our people to Kilambèa as soon as possible. They also visited our client yesterday afternoon. They're not being very subtle about this," Henry replied.

"But, what do they want with our witnesses?" Alex asked while picking the phone receiver up. She began dialing the country code and telephone number for Max's cell phone.

"It looks like there's more behind the British government's support of Kilambèa over the past few years. This is the last thing we need with this next witness coming up," Sam said.

"Sam, I want you to coordinate with Max and find out what's going on. We can't lose our witnesses," Henry stated.

"Max is on the line," Alex said.

"Put him on speaker, please," Henry replied. "Max, we have a problem with our witnesses," Henry began.

"I know. One of them called me yesterday. He was approached by a British agent..." Max started.

"How long have you known this? And you didn't call us immediately?" Henry interrupted Max.

"Wait a second, Henry. Calm down, okay. It's three-o'clock here for freakin' sakes and I was called late last night. I was going to call you this morning first thing," Max replied angrily.

"Okay, I'm sorry Max, but we can't lose our witnesses. We're doing well here and I don't want to lose any angles. Who contacted you and do you have any idea why the British government is contacting our witnesses?" Henry waited for Max to reply.

"James Rhodan gave me a call last night around ten-o'clock in a frantic state. Some British agent showed up at his front door showing a badge and asking questions about Kilambèa and James' testimony for us. James wanted to know how this guy got his name and contact information especially seeing how he's a protected witness. I was able to calm him down, but I don't know how long he'll stay that way. He may pull out of testifying for us," Max finished. A short pause filled the room with silence.

Sam and Henry looked at each other and then Henry began. "Rhodan is one of our top witnesses. We know that he won't testify without a guarantee of anonymity. We know that the British government kept a close eye on Kilambèa and our client after independence. What happened during this time that is scaring the British government? They're afraid that we're going to uncover something that should remain hidden. Max, I need you over here by tomorrow afternoon and bring two of your best people. Sam, start looking at Rhodan's file to see if you can find anything that might help us to solve this mystery. Alex, I want you to gather any information that we have on the relationship between Kilambèa and the British Government. Max, one thing that I want you to start doing once you're here is to contact our witnesses. I don't want to cause alarm. It's just a follow-up call to see how they're doing. If they mention being approached, then we ask more questions. Do you hear me, Max?" Henry asked.

"Loud and clear. I'll organize some things here and be there tomorrow first thing," Max replied. Silence filled the room again. Max was gone.

Martie walked into the office in her exercise clothes. "What's going on?" she asked.

Henry, Sam, and Alex stared back through the thickened silence.

-------------------- CHAPTER 26 --------------------

Max was sitting across from Carter Thompson, a prime witness for the defense, in the bar lounge of the Savoy hotel in Kilambèa. Although the lounge, except for two other tables, was empty Max and Carter spoke quietly aware that someone may be monitoring their every move. The lounge was spacious with dark wood and leather furniture and dim lighting. One bartender served the bar and waited on the tables. Max was sipping on his rum and coke while Carter drank a Cola light.

"Who contacted you, Carter?" Max inquired softly.

"A man with a British accent. He gave me a name, but I believe that it was false. So, it doesn't matter," Carter replied brusquely.

"I know that this has frightened you, but I need to get as much detail as possible from you so that we can figure out who this person is and what they're up to. Do you remember what he looked like and did he show some type of identification or say which organization or agency he worked with?" Max asked waiting to write down any useful information he could gather from Carter's account.

"He was a tall thin man, dark short hair, green eyes, and wore casual clothing. He stated that he worked for the secret service for the British Government and wanted to know if he could enter my residence. Of course, I let him in. Once inside, he began to tell me how he found me; that I was a witness in General Kimbala's trial. He wanted to know what I was going to testify about and if I had received any coaching or materials from the defense for my testimony. I asked him why did he need this information, but he didn't give me a clear answer. I told him that I was feeling uncomfortable with the visit. He told me that he or one of his colleagues would return if I didn't provide him with the answers to his questions. I could tell that it was a threat and decided to cooperate," Carter finished.

"I want you to write down an account of what questions this man asked along with the name that he gave you. Has he or anyone else suspicious contacted you since then?" Max asked.

"No, Max no one has contacted me." Carter took the pencil and paper from Max and began writing.

"Okay, I'm going to get the menus so that we can order some lunch. We'll talk more once you've finished writing your summary. I also have some information concerning your proofing and testimony dates." Max rose from the table and walked over to get two menus from the bar.

Max grabbed the two menus and heard two gunshots as he was turning around to walk back to the table. He ducked under a table and waited until the screams from the nearby table stopped. Max rose hesitantly from under the table only to find Carter lying on the floor with one bullet in the head and another in the chest. Whomever it was wanted to make sure that Carter didn't walk out of the lounge. Max didn't know what was going on, but he was going to find out. He walked over to the table and found it empty. The killer had taken the paper that Carter was writing on. Carter was still clutching onto the pencil. His dead eyes were wide open filled with shock and fright.

Max entered his hotel room exhausted. He had waited at the bar for the police to arrive and then had given a statement of what occurred. Now, three hours later, he was happy to see his hotel room and hopefully a bit of privacy. He took ten minutes of peace and silence before picking the phone up to call Henry.

The telephone rang. "Boome," Henry stated briskly.

"Henry, it's Max here," Max began in a somber voice. "Thompson is dead, Henry. We were sitting downstairs in the bar. I walked away for a few seconds to pick up some menus and someone shot him dead." Max fell silent looking at the white wall while waiting for Henry to speak.

"One of our prime witnesses is dead?" Henry asked in a whisper.

"I'm sorry, Henry. He was also writing down an account of his meeting with the British agent when I left to pick the menus up," Max stated.

Henry interrupted him. "Did he write much? Do you have what he wrote?"

"No, Henry. I'm really sorry," Max replied.

"Okay, do you need to take some time off? Maybe go home and rest?" Henry inquired further.

"No, I want to stay here and finish the job. I'll see the other witnesses and give you an update once I'm done. I'm not going to let the team down, Henry, but seeing how things are taking a turn I want Scott to come out here and help. Then I don't have to worry about turning my head to pick up some menus. Can you have that arranged?" Max asked.

"That won't be a problem. I'll have Alex call him and he'll be on the plane first thing tomorrow morning. Take care of yourself and pull out immediately at the first sign of danger," Henry stated.

Max hung the phone on the receiver.

CHAPTER 27

"Good evening, Sir Hanley," Edwards sat down in the dark burgundy leather chair opposite Sir Hanley. Sir Hanley looked up from his newspaper. He was holding a glass of brandy in his other hand and a pipe was sitting on the side table waiting to be lit.

"What are you doing here? This is a private club," Sir Hanley asked after looking around to see if anyone was listening.

They were sitting in the only British cigar club in The Hague. Edwards could see Sir Hanley's mood change immediately. He knew that this was Sir Hanley's private time. He came here three days out of the week to smoke one pipe, savor two glasses of brandy, and read the newspaper in peace away from the public, the cameras, and his wife. Edwards also knew that Sir Hanley had never missed an evening at the club since his move to The Hague.

"I know the manager, Sir Hanley. You don't have to worry. I will not make this regular although they always have wonderful brandy and cigars here. I could also deal with a little bit of relaxation. These trips are becoming cumbersome and creating tension in my lower back. Should I make an appointment with the house masseuse?" Edwards looked at Sir Hanley while pointing to his lower back.

He decided to continue the conversation seeing how Sir Hanley didn't respond. "Well, I guess you're not in the mood to give advice. You have to do that all day. What am I doing… you don't want to have to deal with my ailments. You're here to relax." Edwards sat back and ushered the waiter over for a drink. "I'll have a Martini. My friend will have another brandy." Edwards smiled at the waiter.

"Why do you insist on harassing me? This is highly inappropriate and I suggest that you leave this instant! I will contact your superior if you don't leave at once." Sir Hanley motioned for the manager to come over.

"Well, Sir Hanley, I didn't mean to be unfriendly. I also wouldn't say anything to the manager if I was you. If you do, then I can also talk about your friend, Ben. I believe he's your newest conquest. The problem, I believe, is his age. I don't think that the court or your wife would be happy to hear that you're fondling a fifteen year old boy nevertheless conducting online sex chats with strange men. Is the sex life with the missus that bad, your Honor?" Edwards paused to take a sip of his Martini. "Ah, yes this is a delicious drink," Edwards commented. Sir Hanley stared at Edwards in shock.

The manager was standing at Sir Hanley's chair. "How may I assist you this evening, your Honor?" The manager bowed towards Sir Hanley.

"Uhm, I'm sorry George. I thought that I had misplaced my pipe, but I see that it's right here," Sir Hanley replied sheepishly.

"That's okay, your Honor. Feel free to signal me if you need anything else. We're here to make your visit satisfactory," the manager stated before walking away.

"Why are you doing this? Making these accusations. What do you want from me?" Sir Hanley asked.

Edwards could see a slight tremble of the newspaper that Sir Hanley was holding. "Your Honor, you're usually such an intelligent man. I'm sure that you can figure it out." Edwards finished his Martini and stood up. "I'll let you finish reading your newspaper. Expect a telephone call from me soon," Edwards said before walking out of the room.

CHAPTER 28

"Good morning, Ms. Ntanga. As you already know, my name is Jan Paul De Loon and I will be asking you a few questions about Kilambèa and your village. We'll have short breaks once an hour, but please let us know if you need to take a break at any other time during your testimony. We want to make this situation as comfortable as possible for you. Do you understand what I'm saying? Good and one last thing before we begin. It's very important that you speak slowly and begin your answer only after I have finished speaking. This way, we will make the interpreters and stenographer's jobs easier. Can you please state your full name for the record?"

Witness: Susan Ntanga.

Prosecutor: Thank you. Can you please confirm that you were born in 1920 in the village of Jameson?

Witness: Yes.

Prosecutor: Thank you. Now, you've come here to testify in the trial of Joseph Kimbala, but I want to first talk to you about your village. Can you tell us how your village was before Joseph Kimbala took over as president of Kilambèa? Was it a small village? How many people lived there? What type of lives did you lead?

Witness: Before the Kimbalas? Our lives were hopeless. We had a small village back then, which is even smaller now. Everyone knew and helped each other in my village. We grew most of our food and sold what we could of it back then to the government for income, but the incomes became worse over the years. It didn't matter if we took the same amount or more, the money that we received got worse. The government told us that it was inflation.

Prosecutor: I'm sorry to interrupt, Ms. Ntanga, but can you please tell us how the rise in inflation affected you?

Witness: Our lives changed dramatically. We had to grow and sell more. We couldn't afford to drive the car more than twice a week. We used to travel to the city two to three times a week and had to cut it down to once a week if that. We couldn't afford the hospitals and doctors. The good thing is that we all pulled together. If one person got sick, then the rest of us came together to help out with food and nurturing. One of the ladies was also good at delivering babies. I don't know where we would have been without her.

Prosecutor: Thank you, Ms. Ntanga. What happened when the Kimbala's took over the power of the government?

Witness: We regained hope. We thought that things would only get better because they had too. We waited and hope slowly drifted away as the years passed. Our suffering did not increase too much, but it also didn't improve.

Prosecutor: What do you mean by that, that your suffering did not improve?

Witness: What do I mean, Mr. De Loon? I mean that we continued to be hungry. I mean that the government continued to cheat us out of our hard earned money. Karim Kimbala promised us a better life, but all we saw were empty promises and smoke screened speeches to the outside world. But, at least he treated us better than his brother.

Prosecutor: And what happened under the rule of his brother, Joseph Kimbala?

Witness: Then our lives became worthless. Joseph Kimbala had forsaken his people for money, affluence, and the love of outsiders. We, his people, became the dirt that he couldn't wash off of the shoes sole. District chiefs were installed in every village along with spies. We also had the NIS. Everyone feared them.

Prosecutor: May I stop you here, please. Who were these district chiefs and what was their importance?

Witness: The district chiefs were placed in our villages shortly after

Joseph Kimbala took over as president. We were told that they were there to help things run more smoothly. If we had a problem with our neighbors or the government for some reason, then we were to go to our local district chief and report the problem. The district chief acted as a go-between person. We thought that it would be easier to have a district chief to complain to instead of writing or visiting the nearest city's civil affairs office, which was twenty kilometers away. Instead, they didn't help us at all with our problems. They turned out to be snitches. We learned that any complaints we had about the government were passed onto the NIS.

Prosecutor: Did any of the villages, to your knowledge, have a police department?

Witness: No. We only had the district chiefs and their assistants.

Prosecutor: And who were these assistants?

Witness: Whoever the district chief trusted, but they were all approved by the NIS.

Prosecutor: Ms. Ntanga, I need to take you back to the start of the war when the brother of the accused attempted a coup to take the country back. You talked to one of our investigators and gave him a statement concerning the afternoon that a green army truck entered your village. Do you remember that interview and the statement that you signed?

Witness: Yes.

Prosecutor: And do you remember the events that took place that afternoon and night after the green army truck entered your village?

Witness: How could I ever forget that day? It was the first time that I had seen someone shot to death and lost my husband. How can I ever forget that?

Prosecutor: I'm sorry, Ms. Ntanga. I'm going to be asking a few questions that may not make sense, but the judges sitting here in the courtroom and people sitting in the gallery are unaware of what happened. You and I only know what happened and I'm trying to make things very clear for the judges.

Witness: Ask your questions then.

Prosecutor: Thank you. This will not take long. Now, you stated that a green army truck entered your village. Can you please tell us what happened on that day?

Witness: A green army truck entered our village and drove straight to the district chief's office. A soldier got out of the truck with documents in his hands and walked into the district chief's office.

Prosecutor: And who was your district chief?

Witness: Sam Muntanga.

Prosecutor: And the soldier that stepped out of the truck. What was his name?

Witness: Captain Delucroix.

Prosecutor: And what happened while Captain Delucroix was there in your village? And was it only Captain Delucroix in the truck?

Witness: No, there was a driver and soldiers standing and sitting in the back of the truck. Captain Delucroix went into the office while the soldiers from the back of the truck got out and took up positions in front of the district chief's office and around the village. Captain Delucroix and Sam then appeared in the center of our village and Sam began calling names out from a piece of paper that he was holding. He called out seven names, seven of my neighbors.

Prosecutor: And then what happened?

Witness: They took all seven neighbors into Sam's office. We didn't know what was going on or why these particular people were taken into Sam's office, but we began to hear screams coming from his office and we knew that they were being tortured. We couldn't take it after a while so everyone went inside their houses. We thought that we could run away from the tortured screams if we did that, but the screams followed us through the walls. We couldn't escape.

Prosecutor: What did you do in your house while the seven people were being tortured in this man's, Sam's office?

Witness: I sat in my chair at the kitchen table rocking myself back and forth and humming an old song that I know. I kept humming louder and louder hoping that the screaming would stop. I wanted it to be a nightmare that I would wake up from, but the screaming wouldn't stop and I didn't wake up so I kept on humming.

Prosecutor: Was anyone else with you? Were you allowed to go and stay with other neighbors at their own houses?

Witness: No. We were told to go to our individual houses. The soldiers were stationed all around our village and we were told that there would be consequences if we congregated together.

Prosecutor: And what consequences would there be? Did these soldiers tell you?

Witness: Only that there were grave consequences. One of the soldiers pointed to his gun and stated that he still needed to do his target training for the day. That was enough for us to obey them.

Prosecutor: I understand. Did the screaming stop at any point?

Witness: Yes, after a few hours.

Prosecutor: And what happened after the screaming stopped?

Witness: Our district chief came outside, along with Captain Delucroix. Soldiers were dragging our neighbors outside to the center of our village. We were told to come outside.

Prosecutor: And then what happened?

Witness: They killed them. They killed them right in front of our eyes and they told us that this is what happens when you're disloyal to Joseph Kimbala.

Prosecutor: Who told you this?

Witness: Captain Delucriox. He said that Sam would be watching us and he would be back if any of us were disloyal.

Prosecutor: And who was killed? What are their names?

Witness: Patrick was killed first and then the rest followed one by one, James, Laney, Raymond, Brenda, Richard, and Rebecca was the last one, the youngest of them all. Then Sam killed another neighbor, Soleil.

Prosecutor: And do you know why these people, these eight neighbors were killed? Why no one else in your village was hurt physically or killed that day?

Witness: We were told that Soleil was killed because he gave important information to Joseph Kimbala's brother, Karim. Karim had failed a few days before in an attempted coup to regain governmental control. The others were killed to make a point: disloyalty deserves death.

Prosecutor: Ms. Ntanga, we're almost finished. Can you please tell me if you know where Captain Delucriox worked? Had you ever seen him before that day?

Witness: Yes, of course. He worked for the NIS. Everyone knows that.

Prosecutor: Thank you, Ms. Ntanga. Your testimony has been very helpful. I have no further questions.

Henry stood up and took a moment to reorganize his notes and pen on the portable mahogany podium. Ms. Ntanga reminded him of his grandmother. She exuded the same strength and wisdom. Henry was not going to enjoy this cross-examination as he usually does. He just wanted to get this over with. He wiped his brow with his hand in an attempt to quickly massage his brow and unconsciously let out a sigh. He would keep this one short and try to make the judges understand that memories were all relative, the only thing that mattered was who was re-telling the memory.

Defense: Good afternoon, Ms. Ntanga. I also want to share my gratitude for your willingness to come here today and share your story. My name is Henry Boome and I am representing General Kimbala. You have answered many questions today and I don't want to keep you here any longer than what is absolutely necessary. Now, Ms. Ntanga, I'm not going to jog your memory or question that your neighbors are dead. What I would like to focus on are the orders that were supposedly given to the men that entered your village that day. You stated that your neighbors were killed as a warning for all of you. How do you know that?

Witness: It was told to us by Delucroix when he killed them. That is how I know. Are you trying to say that I'm lying?

Defense: No, Madam, I am not, but how do you know that this order to torture and kill really came directly from General Kimbala? Did you see a written order?

Witness: No, I did not see a written order.

Defense: Then there is no way to verify that this order came from General Kimbala, am I correct? For all we know this Delucroix could have been acting on his own behalf.

Witness: We didn't need a written order to know that the message came from Mr. Kimbala.

Defense: Thank you, Ms. Ntanga. I beg to differ with you.

Henry sat back down and felt a stabbing pain in his stomach. He was confident that Ms. Ntanga was telling the truth, but he had a job to do. Henry needed to defend his client completely even if his client wasn't exactly an angel. He hoped that Ms. Ntanga would forgive him. Sam looked over at Henry and knew that Henry had gone easy on this witness. Ms. Ntanga was very motherly in appearance. He would have had the same problem, but hoped that their softness to Ms. Ntanga didn't hurt their case in the long run.

CHAPTER 29

Gabriel was sitting in the middle of the office floor at one of the office's share tables in between the secretary's desks. He was playing poker with two of the investigators and one of the secretaries. They wanted to play strip poker, but decided that too many eyebrows would be raised with the security officers patrolling the hallways twice an hour. They settled for pizza, beer and wine. The other team members were scattered around the office with the majority of the food displayed in the war room.

Gabriel always liked the office parties. They were always international in flavor with the team being so diverse. He actually had the feeling that he was eating traditional native food instead of what was served in the restaurants. He could hear the music coming from the war room. It was Sabrina's turn to pick the music and she fittingly chose music from her homeland. This was the team's celebration of the end of the prosecution case.

Everyone was exhausted, but they were excited to finally see the end of the long haul; to have a breather. The defense was given two months to prepare its case. Gabriel was looking forward to a week in France. He had already booked most of the days with visiting vineyards and wine tasting. He was even debating whether or not to leave his cell phone in The Hague. What he really wanted to do was sleep, but he knew that Suzanne would be disappointed if they didn't spend time together and take in the sights. She had missed him those past few months.

Jan Paul retired to his office with a glass of red wine. The others were drinking heavier liquor, but Jan Paul wanted to savor that moment. He sat back in his leather chair and looked up at the ceiling. He could feel the release of tension slowly fading from his body. He continued to look up at the white ceiling while his door opened and gently closed. Analise came over to his desk with a glass of white wine in her left hand. She was dressed especially for that day in a dark grey blazer, matching knee high skirt, and off white tank top.

She sat on his desk, and kicked off her three inch high black patent pumps before she lifted her left leg and rested her foot on the right arm of his chair. She then placed her right foot on the other arm of the chair, set her wine glass aside, and laid down on the table. Jan Paul moved closer and Analise cupped his face tenderly in her hands urging him to move even closer. He grasped her right leg with his left arm and began to kiss her ever so gently on the inside of her right wrist while he reached under her skirt with his right hand to find that she wasn't wearing any underpants. He began to gently massage her between the legs before entering with his fingers. She slowly began to move her hips, held onto his arms and gently pulled him closer. Analise arched her butt forward and pressed her feet down hard on the arm rests. She closed her eyes and mentally followed every move of Jan Paul's fingers until she couldn't take it anymore. Analise felt her body relax as she reached the height of an orgasm. She hoped that this was the first of many orgasms for that evening.

She sat up and looked at Jan Paul. "I thought I'd come down here and personally congratulate you on a job well done," Analise commented with a smile.

"Hmm, thanks but it's not over yet. We still have a defense case to get through and our case wasn't the greatest," Jan Paul replied.

"Look, let's not spoil tonight. All of us have worked long and hard to get to tonight, darling. Let's just enjoy it while we can and look what needs to be done next week," Analise said.

"I don't think that you would say that if the Prosecutor was on your back," Jan Paul retorted.

Analise cupped Jan Paul's face in her hands and moved them slowly down his chest to his groin. "Look, I'm giving a small intimate celebratory party at my place. Can you make it?" Analise asked.

"Let me just get my coat."

Analise stood up and kissed Jan Paul on the neck just under his right ear. "I'll meet you downstairs."

Jan Paul and Analise walked towards Analise's apartment, two blocks away from the Tribunal. They entered her apartment and Jan Paul took her into his arms. They began to kiss and undress each other. Analise unzipped Jan Paul's pants and pulled them down while Jan Paul unbuttoned Analise's skirt. He then pulled her tank top over her head and raised her onto the hall table and pushed himself inside of her. Jan Paul could feel the stress and tension falling away in waves until his body shuddered and the last of the tension melted away. He dropped his head onto Analise's chest causing her to sink back onto the wall.

Lizette climbed into bed. She knew that this was the last day of the prosecution's case and that her husband, Jan Paul, was attending the team's celebratory party. He had already told her that she shouldn't wait up for him. Knowing him he would celebrate with the team and then go back to work, she thought. Lizette also thought that it would have been nice to celebrate with him at home, but that it was important to him that he celebrated with his team members. Jan Paul knew how hard they had worked these past few months and wanted to show his gratitude. Lizette knew that they had made the halfway point in the case. She would have her husband back again soon. Lizette turned the bedside lamp off and fell asleep.

Jan Paul woke up in the middle of the night and sat on the corner of the bed. What was he doing? He had never stayed this late at Analise's before. He looked over at her sleeping body in the moonlight. Why couldn't he say no to her? He looked down at his hands. He knew that he was putting his life and job in jeopardy. If anyone found out about this affair, then he would lose everything.

Analise woke up and found him sitting on the corner of the bed. She was hoping that he would stay the entire night this time. She longed to have his warm body sleeping next to hers while the sun came up. Analise moved the bed sheet down to uncover her breasts. Her nipples were hard.

"Jan Paul, I'm cold. Can you come and warm me up?" Analise looked at him.

Jan Paul turned towards her looking at her hard nipples in the moon light. He started moving on all fours towards Analise and she could tell that he was already hard. She threw the sheet away and opened her legs to welcome him. Jan Paul slid between her legs and began kissing her nipples. Just one more night he thought. Just one more night and then he'll figure out how to end it.

CHAPTER 30

Alex was cycling to the office. It had taken her two months to get into the habit of using a bicycle as a mode of transportation, but now she cycled every day with ease to the office without breaking a sweat. For the past two weeks she had been preparing the proofing binder for their first witness who was arriving that afternoon, and wanted to get to the office early to make sure that everything went as planned. It had been difficult managing the Dutch and Baltimore offices simultaneously along with the staff and documents, but she was getting a handle on it now. Both offices mirrored each other. She made sure that any document they received in the Dutch office made it over to the Baltimore office within one day. She had to admit that Carter was a big help in administering the offices.

Alex had prepared twelve proofing binders for this witness beginning with his statements; background information on the witness; public information found in newspapers, books, and the internet concerning the witness; and any possible already tendered exhibits and new documents that they could use. She had also included a diagram consisting of already tendered exhibits in relation to the testimony heard so far in the case and what effect the exhibits could have on the witness's testimony. Alex walked into the office to find Carter making coffee. He had become an addict while living in The Hague. I guess it's true what they say about our coffee, Alex thought.

"I'll take a cup too when it's finished," Alex said to Carter.

"Well, good morning to you too, sunshine!" Carter retorted.

"Sorry, Carter. Good morning, how are you? Oh, and by the way, I'll take a cup too when it's finished." Alex smiled patting Carter on the butt while walking past.

"Anything for you, sweetie. Did you get breakfast on the way in? I went to a new club last night in Amsterdam, have had three hours of sleep and am famished! Tell me that you picked up some croissants, Danishes, or that suikerbrood that we tried the other day. I could use some refueling," Carter said.

"I did one even better than that," Alex screamed from her office. She walked back into the kitchen carrying a bag. She had also become proficient in carrying bags while cycling through the busy city streets.

"I picked up two omelets, croissants and jam from our favorite place. We have a busy day today. Which club did you go to and why didn't you take me?" Alex looked upset.

"Child, I asked you last night and all I heard in return was a grunt. You didn't even look up from your binder," Carter replied.

"Oh, yeah. I'm sorry about that. It's just that this is a crucial witness and I don't want to mess up." Alex began unwrapping their breakfast.

"I understand that, but you can't continue working these long hours without any rest. The stress alone will make you sick." Carter looked concerned at Alex.

"I know and I promise to slow down a little after this witness. Come on, let's eat before it gets cold. Hey, did you reach the travel and victim's department this morning? Is everything going as planned this afternoon?" Alex asked inquisitively.

"Of course I did and yes. The car should be pulling up around three-o'clock this afternoon and dinner arrangements have been made for this evening at six-o'clock. It gives just enough time for him to see his hotel room, freshen up, and meet you and the gang for dinner on time," Carter said.

"Thanks, Carter. I promise, after this witness is finished I'll go out with you. Just choose the club and I'm there," Alex said.

"I'll believe it when I see it," Carter replied with a sigh.

"I have to watch out for Daniel's best interest," Alex added while walking back to her office holding a plate full of food.

CHAPTER 31

Thirty-six hours before the defense's first witness

It was nine-o'clock at night and Alex decided that she should get some rest. Tomorrow was a big day and she needed all the energy she could gather to make it through. Instead of taking the short cut, Alex cycled through the city to see The Hague Jazz. She had heard that this was a yearly event that occurred every summer and expected to hear live music and see people sitting out in cafes drinking wine, laughing, and having a good time. She made a promise to herself to come back to The Hague next summer to fully enjoy this event.

Maybe she could even bring Carter with her. She was sure that he wouldn't hesitate to come back. Alex turned into the Denneweg and began to hear pop music filtering out of a stereo. People were dressed in posh outfits and sitting outdoors drinking red and white wine. They were there to be seen. Alex cycled a little further and came across a more relaxed crowed of people. There was samba music and the people were dancing in the street holding their partner's hands with one hand while balancing a beer in the other and juggling cigarettes at the same time.

Alex turned into a side street and saw restaurants full of patrons happily eating their dinner. She made a right turn onto a larger street and stopped for a few minutes to listen to the band playing reggae on the stage. She was impressed with the variety of music that was being played and began to relax. She began cycling again and turned down yet another side street. This street wasn't populated so well and only a few tables were occupied at each of the restaurants. She liked the cozy effect of the street though. If people wanted a quiet or private dinner that night, then it is the perfect street to be on. Alex began to slow down. She saw their witness, Karim Kimbala, sitting inside one of the restaurants.

A glass window separated her from Mr. Kimbala who was happily eating a steak dinner. Alex thought about going inside to greet Mr. Kimbala and moved a little closer only to realize that he was not alone. Another man, a man that she had never seen before, was sitting opposite Karim and also enjoying a steak dinner. Alex knew that Karim Kimbala was charismatic and had probably run into a lonely tourist. She decided to cycle onwards. She also needed to eat some dinner before retiring for the night. A quick cycle through the streets would have to suffice. The Hague Jazz would have to wait another year.

Five hours before the defense's first witness

Alex walked into the office to find Sam sitting at his desk typing away. "Hey, good morning," Alex stood in Sam's doorway.

"Good morning, Alex. How's it going," Sam looked up from his laptop to greet Alex.

"Do you want some coffee? I'm about to set a pot on. Hey, who's this?" Alex inquired looking at a sketch of a man lying on Sam's desk.

"Oh, that's a sketch of the man that's been talking to our witnesses. Max and Scott had one of the insider witnesses describe the man while a sketch artist drew it, and then they emailed it this morning. The witness did a good job, huh?" Sam pushed the save button. He didn't want to lose this document.

"Sam, I've seen this person before," Alex began to worry because she knew exactly where she had seen this man.

"What are you talking about? Did you visit Africa last night instead of going back to your place?" Sam liked Alex and had even thought about asking her out on a date once, but he didn't know if she liked him and also worried about the consequences of dating someone at the work place. He was very strict when it came to dating women from the same firm – he just didn't do it. It was too complicated, especially if one of them got bored and wanted to move on.

Alex looked up from the sketch. Her look scared Sam and made him sit straight up in his chair.

"This isn't funny, Sam. I know where I've seen him before," Alex said.

Four hours before the defense's first witness

Henry and Martie had entered the room and all three attorneys were sitting around Alex in a semi-circle.

"Okay, Alex. We know how we obtained this sketch, but I want to know why you believe that you've seen this man in person before. Who do you think this man is and where do you think you've seen him before?" Henry asked. He was leaning forward facing Alex with his arms draping his knees.

Three hours and forty-five minutes before the defense's first witness

Henry picked up the sketch, looked at it, and then turned the sketch so that Alex could see it. "And this is the man that you saw with Karim?" Henry asked.

Alex looked at Henry and the others. "Yes, it is," Alex said.

"Are you one hundred percent sure that this is the man that you saw sitting with Karim?" Henry asked.

"Henry, you can doubt me all you want, but I know what I saw," Alex stared back at Henry.

Henry sighed and put his head in between his hands. "I'm sorry, Alex. It's just that this isn't good. This really is not good," Henry exclaimed.

"What are we going to do?" Sam asked.

Defense's First Witness

The gallery was full of photographers, journalists, and curious bystanders after weeks of hardly a soul visiting the court proceedings. The prosecution paraded fifty witnesses throughout its case, while the defense was rumored to have stated that they would call only ten witnesses to testify in the case. Everyone knew that the defense thought one of two things: either the prosecution had failed to prove its case or the defense felt that the evidence was too damning to fight and that ten witnesses was its way of waving the white flag. No one was sure which way to sway, but one thing was sure: everyone had their opinion. Alex knew this from Carter. Carter had attended a party that was attended by staff members from the registry, prosecution, and chambers.

Some of the people didn't know that Carter worked for the defense team and he was able to hear many of the rumors floating around about the case. The only problem was that the rumors contradicted each other. Everyone would just have to wait for the end before learning the truth.

"All rise, the court is now in session," the court deputy recited.

The judges filed into the courtroom, stepped up onto the bench, and sat down. Judge Atkinson began to speak. "Good afternoon, ladies and gentlemen. May the witness be escorted into the courtroom? You may begin, Mr. Boome."

Karim Kimbala walked into the courtroom escorted by the usher. Sounds of astonishment and surprise could be heard from the gallery and the journalists moved forward in their seats. The journalists had been given a copy of the defense's witness list a week ago and had seen Karim's name at the top of the list, but couldn't believe that Karim would come and testify for his brother, the person that not only attempted to kill him, but killed his wife and children. Karim sat down and adjusted his suit jacket. He was looking good for someone living in exile for the past twenty-seven years. He was thinner, but looked well fed and groomed. Someone had been taking good care of him.

Henry stood up and smiled towards Judge Atkinson. "Thank you, your honor. Good morning, Mr. Kimbala…"

CHAPTER 32

Sir Hanley opened the door and welcomed the Prosecutor inside. "Good evening, Laney. Come on inside. You know where to leave your things. I'm off to the kitchen. I think that our dinner is burning. Feel free to make yourself a drink and I'll join you in a second."

Elizabeth hung her jacket on the coat rack and walked into the library. It had been a long day with non-stop telephone calls to New York and she fancied a nice gin and tonic. Sir Hanley walked into the library to find Elizabeth sitting in the lazy boy with her feet up and cocktail in hand.

"Rough day, Laney?" Sir Hanley prepared a glass of red wine and sat down.

"It's been a hell of a day, Richard. Where is Sandra? Is she joining us for dinner?" Elizabeth looked around wondering if Richard's wife Sandra was going to walk around the corner.

"She's lecturing at Oxford and will not return until Monday. I'm sorry to say, but you have to deal with me alone this time." Sir Hanley smiled over his wine glass at Elizabeth.

"Don't worry, Richard. I think that I can handle whatever you throw my way. We've known each other a long time, correct?" Elizabeth looked over at Richard.

"Yes, about fifteen years now. Why do you ask?" Sir Hanley inquired.

"Then it's understandable if I know that something is bothering you. I was just here for dinner with both you and Sandra not too long ago. Why am I sitting here, Richard?" Elizabeth looked sternly in Richard's direction.

"Laney, can't I have you over for dinner just because you're a good friend, actually one of my best friends?" Sir Hanley put his wine glass down on the side table and wondered why he had invited her over knowing that she would be suspicious of his reasoning.

"If you don't tell me what's going on right now, then you can stop calling me Laney and one of your best friends. Only people that tell me the truth can do that. You know that I don't talk around a subject, Richard. So, come on out with it," Elizabeth was tired from the long day and minced words even less when she was tired. She was a tough prosecutor and no one questioned her ability to do a thorough job.

Sir Hanley shuffled from the left side of the chair to the right with his hips and crossed his left leg over his right. He began massaging his left calf with his left hand while rubbing the right arm chair with his other hand. He began after a long sigh.

"Laney, we have known each other for a long time and I should be straight with you. It's just that this is a delicate situation," Sir Hanley took a deep breath.

"Spit it out, Richard. If you keep up like this, then we'll never get to dinner." Elizabeth took a sip of her gin and tonic realizing that this was going to be an even longer evening.

Sir Hanley knew that he couldn't jeopardize his relationship with Laney. He was also aware that Laney had strong values and principles. Even if he asked her about the prosecution's case, he knew what the answer would be: she would get up, walk out of the door, and their friendship of fifteen years would be over. Laney would never look back.

"Forget about it, Laney. This is my problem and should remain so. I'm going to go check on dinner and when I return we will act like this never happened. Deal?" Sir Hanley sat on the edge of his chair awaiting her answer.

Elizabeth searched Richard's face for a hint of what he was hiding and then decided that it was better not to know. She had known him long enough to know that whatever it was it was serious and job related. He had no problem discussing his marriage so it had to be job related. She stood up and walked over to the bar.

"It's a deal. Now, don't burn our dinner because I'm hungry."

CHAPTER 33

Henry turned left and entered the A12 highway. After dealing with the tram in The Hague for one week, Henry had walked into the BMW dealership and leased a car. He never regretted that decision. He had been tired of the morning and afternoon rush hours with people pushing him from left to right while entering the tram. He could understand women and the elderly running to get a seat on the tram, but he couldn't understand why the men were running against the women and elderly to get a seat or why the capable wouldn't give their seats up to handicapped or elderly people. He had decided that it was better to enjoy the comforts of his own vehicle, even if it meant a second car note. At least he could keep some of his sanity.

"Henry, I'm honored that you are giving me a ride to the airport." Karim looked outside.

"It's my pleasure, Karim, and thanks for coming to testify for your brother. I know that it must have been a difficult decision under the circumstances." Henry put the blinker on and moved the car to the left into the fast lane.

"What do you mean, Henry? As you Americans always say, 'blood is thicker than water' am I correct? I was just helping my brother." Karim didn't understand what Henry was inferring.

"You mean the brother that tried to assassinate you back in 1980? In this instance we would say that water is thicker than blood, Karim. I have

125

to give it to you. I wouldn't testify for my brother if he tried to kill me and your brother missed killing you, but he did succeed in killing your family, which leads me to my next question. Why did you come to The Hague to testify for your brother?" Henry glanced at Karim and turned his focus back to the road.

"What do you mean, Henry? I just wanted to help my brother. Shouldn't everyone get a second chance?" Karim asked.

Henry was tired of the cat and mouse game or was this a fool's act? He wasn't quite sure, but decided to quicken the pace a bit and decided to show the sketch to Karim. Henry handed the envelope that had been hidden in the sun visor. "We know that you had dinner with this man two nights before your testimony began. We also know who he is and that he's been talking to our other witnesses. Now, I want to know why you were having dinner with him two nights ago." Henry turned into the entrance leading to Schipol Airport.

He was right about quickening the pace a bit because the real Karim appeared and the act disappeared. "Henry, you pretend to understand what's going on, but believe me when I say that you don't. I believe that you really want to help Joseph and in some idealistic cause. That is honorable of you, but you must trust me when I tell you that you don't want to get involved and you don't know who you're dealing with." Karim looked forward towards the airport.

"With all due respect, Karim, it is not your business to tell me what I do or do not want to know. I am trying to defend your brother as best as I can, but I need to know what may be standing in my way. I don't like it when others get in my way of winning a case." He was grasping the steering wheel with both hands as a surrogate for what he really wanted to do, which was knock some sense into Karim so that Karim would begin talking.

Karim lost his patience and glared back at Henry. Henry parked at the departure drop off location. Karim just wanted to escape into the anonymity of the airport. "Mr. Boome, my patience with you has disappeared. I have given you a warning yet you do not want to listen. I have my reasons for testifying and you have your reasons for defending my brother. Let us leave it at that. I warn you for the final time. Stop looking into something that does not concern you. Concentrate on your job which is to free my brother. The rest will take care of itself."

Karim opened the passenger side door and stepped out onto the curb. "Good luck with the rest of the trial, Mr. Boome."

Karim walked towards the sliding doors and Henry was left alone to contemplate his next move. He was awakened by a frustrated taxi cab driver sitting behind him waiting for the parking space. Henry took one last look at the sliding door and then drove away. He knew one thing for sure and that was that Karim didn't testify out of love for his brother. Why was he testifying then? What was the real reason? Did he want revenge? If that was so, then he knew that Joseph wouldn't live long outside of the detention center. He dialed Max's number using the car's integrated telephone system.

CHAPTER 34

Edwards was sitting in a café terrace drinking coffee and enjoying the seaside view. It was ten-o'clock and the city was still sleeping with the sea gulls and a couple being the only visitors on the beach. Edwards watched the couple walking below hand in hand and thought of his wife. It would have been their fifth wedding anniversary that coming Saturday if she hadn't of died in the car crash. Edwards turned his eyes onto the lovely skyline. The mountain on his left was carved stone while the water striking the bottom of the mountain was a clear green color. In two hours the temperature would reach ninety degrees and the beach would be full of tourists and locals enjoying the cool sea water while perfecting their tans. Edwards sat back to enjoy the quiet of the moment and wait for his appointment to arrive.

Karim Kimbala walked up behind Edwards and took a seat opposite him. "Good morning, my friend. I see that you are enjoying the weather?" Karim motioned for the waiter to approach.

"Good morning Karim, it is a beautiful day today, don't you think." Edwards shook Karim's hand. "How are Nancy and the little toddler doing?"

Nancy was Karim's second wife. Edwards had to admit that he actually liked Karim and didn't ask about Karim's family out of politeness. He actually wanted to know. This was against company policy. He was not supposed to cross the imaginary border and have feelings for his contacts, but he had been dealing with the Kimbalas for years and it was difficult to maintain a comfortable distance.

"Nancy and little Samuel are doing well. They want you to come over for dinner if you have time. Nancy is complaining that she hasn't seen you in a while and would like to see how you're doing. She doesn't believe me if I say that you look fine. She needs to judge for herself." Karim laughed and picked up his drink to take a sip.

"I'm only here for two days, but I will see if I can make it over tomorrow before leaving. I have a tight schedule and cannot stay any longer, but I will see if I can. How does it feel to be back home?" Edwards looked inquisitively towards Karim.

"It always feels good to be here even though it's not my real home. Part of me wishes that I was living back in Kilambèa, but then I remember that that part of me is dead along with my wife and children. My brother took my life away from me. I cannot go back so I make the most out of my second life here in South Africa. At least I have Nancy and little Samuel. They really help me to get through the days here and South Africa is beautiful, now that apartheid has seen its last days. I can go wherever I want and not have to wonder if it's permitted."

"But, that's why you waited until 1995 to relocate, correct?" Edwards asked.

"Yes, my friend that is correct. The government took me with open arms in 1995 and I have been able to live a good life since then." Karim looked out over the bright green sea and Edwards could tell that he was thinking of the past.

"How was The Hague, Karim? Did everything go as planned?" Edwards had read the transcript that he had pulled off the internet, but wanted to hear Karim's assessment.

"The testimony went as planned, but Boome drove me to the airport afterwards," Karim shared with Edwards.

"Is it a problem that Boome drove you to the airport?" Edwards questioned.

"It could be. He knew that we had dinner before I testified. He also told me that he knew who you were and that you had met with some of his other witnesses. He was very curious." Karim took another sip of his iced tea.

"You must be very specific, Karim. Tell me everything that Boome told you. This is important for both of us."

Scott and Rachel were sitting at a table not too far from that of Edwards and Karim's table. They were staying as a couple in one of the hotel room's located above the restaurant and had just visited the breakfast buffet included in the room's rate. Rachel peered through her sunglasses at the sea and sipped on her orange juice while Scott glanced through one of the travel guides lying on their table.

Scott placed a forkful of scrambled eggs in his mouth before talking to Rachel. "Do you want to tail Kimbala when he leaves or should I?"

Rachel looked over and grabbed the tour guide, "It doesn't matter, I'll do it. What do you think they're talking about over there?" Rachel pointed to a picture in the tour guide.

"Oh, I imagine that they're talking about the good old times when the Kimbalas used to supply Edwards with one of the girls or how the Kimbalas massacred their own people." Scott took another bite of his scrambled eggs before starting on a sausage.

"Well, I'm bored sitting here. I hope they finish their catch-up talk and Kimbala gets moving."

"Hey, we have all the time in the world as long as they provide us with the information we need. Why don't you sit back and enjoy the view while they're yappin' away? I'm going to order some coffee. Do you want some?" Scott began to stand up.

"Yeah, sure, I could use a cup of coffee. Who knows how long I'll be out today once he does finally get up and leave." Rachel smiled towards Scott.

"That's more like it. I'll be right back." Scott attempted an intimate gesture by placing his hand on her shoulder before he walked away to find the waiter.

"Henry, I just spoke to Scott. He saw Edwards speaking to Karim. Scott and Rachel sat at a table close by in a restaurant. Rachel tailed Karim after that meeting, but came up with nothing. He went about his usual day. Scott followed Edwards and the same thing happened. Edwards acted as a tourist, but then both Rachel and Scott tailed Edwards the following day and ended up at Karim's residence. They couldn't get close, but it looked as if Edwards is close with the family and he stayed for dinner. Scott and

Rachel then followed him back to the hotel. What do you want them to do now? Do you want them to come back or stay with Edwards or Karim or both?" Max waited for an answer.

"Thanks for this update, Max. Tell them to stay with Edwards, even if he boards a plane. I want to know what he's up to or even stay a few paces ahead if possible." Henry made a few notes on his note pad.

"I'll tell them that. Do you still want me to talk to my friend?" Max wanted to know if he would be booking a plane ticket or not.

"Yes, I haven't changed my mind on that one. Let me know how that turns out." Henry hung the phone up and turned to his notes.

CHAPTER 35

Max landed at Gatwick Airport and headed for the Hertz Rent A Car desk. He preferred Gold status, but wanted to make sure that a navigation system was placed in his rental before he left. He only had two locations to visit, Surrey and his hotel, but he didn't have time to waste on getting lost.

Max drove up to a cottage located in an isolated part of Surrey. Tom lived in a beautiful location, but Max didn't know if he could do the same. Tom owned about twenty acres of farmland encased by a lovely stone wall that came up to Max's waist. Max wanted to think that the stone wall was built to keep the cows and chickens in, but he knew better than that. Tom's first priority when he bought this cottage was to secure it against intruders, British or foreign. To the untrained eye, this was a simple stone wall that circled the property and was easy on the eyes, but Max knew that a motion detector was built into the stone wall.

Tom would know in an instant if anyone climbed over the wall and could look at the monitors to see who the intruder was. He had hidden cameras located in the tall trees and the flower pots positioned strategically around the property. It was a beautiful place and no one would know that it was actually a fortress.

Max and Tom had become friends twenty years ago when Tom was working for MI6. They had remained friends after Tom's unhappy divorce from his job. Tom distrusted MI6's work practices, but kept up with a few of his ex-colleagues and kept his ear to the ground in the spy network. Max knew that he could not only get the information that he needed, but that it would also be reliable. The front gate opened and Max drove through over the gravel towards the cottage. He parked the car as Tom exited the house and came over to greet his old friend.

"Max, my old friend, I'm glad that you're here even if it's to pick my brain." Tom gave Max a pat on the back.

"Come inside, old lad and have a drink. Do you still drink sherry? I picked some up especially for you." Tom showed the way into the house.

"Have a seat and I'll fix us some drinks." Tom motioned to a chair in the living room. "And, tell me what's going on. Your phone call sounded urgent." Tom poured the sherry into two glasses, walked over and then sat down opposite Max.

Max in the meantime had been petting Tom's black Labrador, Jimmy. He gave him one last pat and took his sherry glass from Tom.

"Tom, I need some information from you, discreetly as always. You know that my firm is handling the Kimbala case at the International Tribunal. We know that the British Government had dealings with the Kimbalas, but we're learning that its involvement is deeper than what we thought. A man named Edwards has been talking to a few of our witnesses and has close contact of course with Joseph's brother, Karim. A couple of my men tracked him to South Africa where he met Karim Kimbala. We know that this Edwards works for MI6 and that he had a lot of dealings with the Kilambèan government and the Kimbalas in the past. We're just not sure how much the British are involved in his dealings, but we're pretty sure that the government wasn't involved in his eliciting sex from the teenage girls that the Kimbalas held in the sex brothels during their time in power. I need to know what information you have on this Edwards fellow."

Max looked earnestly at Tom. "Any information is helpful, Tom. I don't want you to rat anyone from your own organization out, but I have the feeling that this Edwards is a loose cannon and not always following the correct procedure. You may have your vices with MI6, but I know that you are a stickler for sticking to the code of arms and if this guy is a loose cannon, then he's also trouble for MI6." Max swallowed the last bit of sherry from his glass and watched Tom come towards him to take the glass away. Tom went to the bar to refill their glasses.

Tom came back with two full glasses of sherry and sat down. "His full name is Tim Edwards and he has worked for MI6 for thirty-two years now. Kilambèa was Edwards first and only mission. He started out with Karim. You see, at that time MI6 believed that Kilambèa was not a threat because they were our former colony. If anyone had known the skeletons in Kilambèa's closet, then who would have been the best to have known them but us. We didn't think that it called for an experienced agent because they were part of us. Edwards watched over our interests, mediated between MI6 and the Kimbalas, but basically wrote a lot of memos or so we thought. We found out two years ago that he was actually a tarnish to the organization and did more than writing memos and facilitating. He helped the Kimbalas to control the black market in Kilambèa and any reserves, such as the copper and diamond mines in Kilambèa. Well, Edwards helped the Kimbalas sell the fortunes to foreigners on the black market and robbed the locals in doing so. The darker side includes his involvement in the sex brothels. He was able to pick out any girl he wanted whenever he visited the country and the girls mostly ranged from thirteen to fifteen years old, but you already knew that. What you probably don't know is that Edwards helped, indirectly, with the assassination attempt of Karim Kimbala. Karim doesn't even know that and that's probably why Edwards spends so much time talking and helping Karim. He's helping out of guilt. The thing is that Karim doesn't even know that Edwards had a part in the assassination attempt that took his family from him."

"You mean to tell me that Edwards wanted him killed at one time and that Karim doesn't know that," Max interrupted him.

"That is correct. Joseph Kimbala was seen as the stronger brother and Edwards, along with everyone else, knew that if Joseph wanted to take over the government that he would do so. Karim would not be able to stop him because his popularity with the people had dwindled to nothing and he didn't have the military backing, but Joseph did. Edwards knew that if he wanted to keep everything that he gained in Kilambèa that he would have to side with Joseph, but he did so in the background. Hence, Karim's ignorance of the truth." Tom took a sip of his sherry.

"Okay, so that explains the past history, but what is going on now? Why is Edwards talking to our witnesses and why not leave Karim alone now?" Max was intrigued by the story he was hearing.

"Why my old friend, does anyone do anything in this sort of business? He's following the money." Tom made a flittering motion with his hand.

CHAPTER 36

Max was sitting on the terrace of a café in the center of Beaune savoring a local red wine. Beaune is a quaint little town in the middle of rural France and known worldwide for its premier wines. Café's, bars, and restaurants lined every street and tourists and locals alike filled the terraces for something cool to drink. It was a warm day and the water fountain, surrounded by colorful flowers and plants, in the middle of the square relieved some of the heat. Max watched the laughing children running their hands through the falling water in the fountain, along with tourists walking proudly with bags of recently purchased wines and keepsakes to help them remember their trip to the Burgundy region. Some of the tourists were walking towards the Hotel Dieu, now a museum, or towards the tourist information office to catch the last tour of the famous vineyards. Max was content watching the tourists walk by who were contented with living someone else's life for a few days, a life without bills, stress, hardship, and long unappreciative work days.

The local tourist bus rode past Max's café and was full of men, women, and children dressed in vacation clothes with cameras in hand. He could hear the automated voice coming over the loud speaker explaining the history of the square. Max looked beyond the bus to find Edwards walking towards the bank. Max nodded to Scott who was sitting at another café drinking a cappuccino and reading the local paper. Edwards walked into the

Bank followed by Rachel. Max ordered another drink and waited patiently for Edwards to exit the Bank.

Edwards walked over towards a man and shook his hand. Rachel walked over to a table in the middle of the lobby and began to fill out a deposit slip.

"Good afternoon, Mr. Edwards. It's nice to see you again," the bank manager smiled enthusiastically.

"Good afternoon, Francois. It's good to be back in Beaune. This is the only place where I can find decent wine." Edwards put his briefcase down.

Francois laughed. "Then I am glad that you have returned. Mr. Edwards, I am pleased to tell you that we were able to complete your request. Would you like to follow me downstairs?" Francois motioned with his hand the way to the vault.

"I'm pleased to hear that, Francois. Yes, let's go downstairs." Edwards followed Francois to the vault leaving Rachel behind.

Francois led the way down the stairs to the vault. The exterior of the bank was modest in form. The curb separated the bank from the street with the water fountain directly in front of the bank. Green ivy decorated the front light grey cemented wall and an archway formed the entrance to the bank. The name of the bank, Agricole International, had been placed in gold lettering over the top of the archway. A wooden door stood in the archway and was open the entire day during opening hours. A glass sliding door stood just behind the wooden door and opened automatically when a person wanted to enter or exit the bank.

Rachel took in the interior ambiance of the bank while she waited for Edwards to return with Francois. She was taken in immediately by the beautiful interior. Roman pillars lined the center of the bank leading up to the three teller stations. In between each pillar stood a large green plant while colorful flower arrangements adorned the surrounding walls. Two desks lined the wall on the left while one desk stood alone on the right side.

The manager's office was to the right of the third teller station and enclosed with glass walls. Rachel also noticed that cameras had been placed in strategic areas around the bank. She didn't see a security officer, but knew that one couldn't be too far away. Rachel returned to her deposit slip.

"We received Mr. Kimbala's authorization two days ago and began working on the requests immediately, and I must add discreetly. I understand that this is a delicate situation and want you to know that you can always count on us to provide you high quality service. We will enter this room here. Now, two of your requests have been completed. Three million euro has been transferred to an account in the Cayman Islands. I talked with a reliable estate agent in Cannes and he has an accommodation that he promises you will like. The last request is more difficult. I have still been unable to find a buyer for the diamonds that you have to sell. This will take more time, I'm afraid."

"Why is this difficult? Did you explain that these diamonds are real and where they came from?" Edwards interrupted becoming annoyed.

"I did, Monsieur, but people in this trade are very, how do you say... skeptical. They want to make sure that they are getting real quality and that they are legitimate. Europol has been coming down hard on illegal diamond sales and traders are becoming fearful of being placed on Europol's radar screen. I'm doing my best, Mr. Edwards." Francois handed the paperwork for the wire transfer over to Edwards.

"Do more than your best, Francois. I'm paying you a handsome fee for it." Edwards looked over the paperwork and then shoved it into his briefcase.

"When will your real estate agent have portfolios for me to look at?" Edwards knew that he didn't have much time left.

"They arrive tomorrow afternoon. Can you come back the day after tomorrow? Then I will have the portfolios ready for you to review." Francois looked at Edwards for an answer.

"I will come back then, in the morning, but I must return to England that afternoon so we can't delay this much longer."

Francois led them back to the entrance of the bank. "Mr. Edwards, thank you very much for your service and I will see you in two days. Everything will be ready for you by then. Have a nice evening and I hope that you enjoy some of our marvelous wine tonight with your dinner."

CHAPTER 37

Alex picked up the phone. "Good morning, Alex speaking."

"Alex, it's Max." Max sounded serious.

"Hey, Max. How is France? Is everything okay?" Alex talked into the phone.

"Yeah, everything is going fine. It's just that things are getting complicated here. We knew that we were defending a not so innocent person, but didn't know what else we were getting into. Can you let Henry know that Edwards visited a bank today and conducted some business affairs? We don't know exactly what affairs they were, but he's going back in two days to finalize. We're staying here to watch over him. I have a gut feeling that he's up to no good. How's the court process going?"

"We're in recess right now, but still in direct examination. The witness is doing well so far and things seem to be going according to plan. Of course the prosecution is objecting to all of the evidence we want to tender, but Sam is doing a pretty good job at getting most of it admitted. Henry and Sam are sitting in the other room going through the testimony thus far to see if they need to fill any gaps that Sam may have missed. I'm drafting a motion for protective measures because our next witness just came out of the blue saying that they want it, and Martie is proofing them, going through the evidence and the testimony they will be giving starting tomorrow afternoon. As you can guess, we're pretty busy here. Do you want to talk with Henry?"

Alex turned towards her laptop. She really had to finish this draft for Martie's approval and only had thirty minutes left to tweak any problem areas.

"Nope, can you just give the information that I told you over to him? He knows how to reach me if need be. Hey, good luck with the next witness. If it's who I think it is, then you have your hands full." Max hung the phone up.

"I had Frank tap into the bank's records and it looks like Edwards had a large sum of money transferred to another bank in the Cayman Islands, around three million euro. He also traced the bank manager's phone calls and he's been in contact with a real estate agent and a few diamond brokers. Edwards is planning on disappearing." Rachel grabbed a piece of pizza.

"We know now how he accumulated this wealth, but what is he planning on doing and how do the Kimbalas fit into this picture? Sometimes I wish that I could walk up to our targets and ask them plain and simple what are you doing and why? Things would be simpler that way!" Max took a sip of his beer while he contemplated their next move.

"Scott, you're going back to South Africa. I want to know firsthand if Karim Kimbala is making any strange movements. Rachel, you're staying with me here in Beaune. We're going to taste some more fantastic wine while waiting for Edwards to return to the bank."

CHAPTER 38

"Alex speaking," Alex was not in the mood to handle telephone calls. Their next witness, who happened to be an international witness, had decided to play the stereotypical role and was making everyone's lives difficult, which frustrated everyone including Alex.

"Alex, it's Max." Max was now sitting in a hotel in Geneva.

"I'm sorry Max. The next witness, James Booth, is giving everyone a hard time. He's been here for five days. I can't believe this. The man's witness statement is wonderful and he seemed like a nice modest guy in the beginning, but we've seen him change little by little as he approaches his testifying date. At first we attributed the changes to nerves, but now we're not sure, and to top it off the man told us this morning that he's having doubts about testifying. He's becoming a real prima donna."

"I think I know why he's pulling out, Alex. That's why I'm calling you. Is Henry there?"

"Yeah, we're all here. I'll go get them." Alex threw the phone down and rushed into the other room.

"Max, are you still there? You're on speaker phone. Henry, Sam, and Martie are here listening." Alex motioned to the trial team forgetting that Max couldn't see them.

"Max, Henry here. Alex says that you have some information on Booth."

Can you shed any light on why this guy has turned on us?" Henry was anxious to know what else he was up against besides the British government.

"The Edwards trail took me to Geneva and led me straight to Booth..."

"What? Booth is linked to Edwards? How?" Henry could feel his blood pressure rising. He knew that his health was deteriorating along with this case.

"Booth works for the World Health and Food organization, which is something that everyone knows. He organized the humanitarian aid shipped to Kilambèa and therefore had close ties to the Kimbalas. I'm guessing that he believed this was the only way if the aide was to make it to its destination. Anyway, he did a good job for the first few years. He made friends with the Kimbalas, the aide trucks and employees made it through the rebel held areas safely, and made it to the people that needed it. This continued until the Kimbalas realized that money could be made by selling the aide on the black market. The Kimbalas made a deal with Booth – they would take seventy percent of the aide while thirty percent would go straight to the people. Booth didn't see any way around it. He would have to be satisfied with getting something to the people instead of nothing. The Kimbalas tested him and after a year when things had been running flawlessly, the Kimbalas blackmailed Booth into helping them smuggle some of the girls from the sex shops to Belgium by using the aide trucks. He's probably afraid of both testifying and not testifying. The Kimbalas have probably put word out that he'll be killed if he doesn't, but he's also worried about the truth coming out." Max took a break to let his words settle in. He knew that this was a time bomb for the trial team.

"When is Booth due to testify?" Max inquired.

Alex spoke for the team. "He begins in two days if he decides to testify."

"Or if we decide to continue to call him," Henry chimed in.

"Is this information completely accurate?" Martie added.

"As accurate as it can be. The source can be trusted. I'm sorry about this, guys. Let me know how you want to proceed," Max replied earnestly.

"Thanks for the great work, Max. You may have saved us from complete disaster. Come back to The Hague with Scott and Rachel. Meanwhile, I'll sit here with Martie and Sam and we'll figure out whether Booth will testify or not. See you soon." Henry pushed the speaker phone button ending the telephone conversation.

It was six-o'clock and Alex was preparing coffee at the kitchen counter top while Sam sat at the table thumbing through one of the proofing binders for James Booth. Carter was out picking up dinner for everyone. The atmosphere was tense and they still had to make a decision on whether or not to call James Booth the following morning.

Henry, Sam, and Martie debated the question for four hours before breaking to collect thoughts, also because Henry was due to meet Booth for dinner. Martie was sitting in her office and had made it clear that she was against Booth testifying. Sam was also against Booth taking the stand, but made the point that the prosecution would object and demand that Booth testify. He had a feeling that if they knew about Booth's history, then the prosecution wasn't too far behind them. Maybe they even knew already and were just waiting for the day that Booth would take the stand.

Henry had taken their arguments into consideration, but said that he wanted to hold off until after the dinner with Booth. Sam had volunteered to join them, but Henry wanted to do this on his own. Alex turned around holding the coffee filter in her hands. "So, what do you think is going to happen tonight between Henry and Booth?"

Sam looked at Alex in awe. She was stunningly beautiful to him, but he not only had to worry about dating his paralegal. He had to worry about dating one of the founding partner's granddaughters who happened to be his paralegal. He didn't know which was worse.

Sam sighed and put his binder down. "I don't know. On the one hand we have the right to take Booth off of the list, but I know that the prosecution is going to object extraneously at such a late stage. I'm not sure that the judges will like us either for pulling a heavy witness the day that they're supposed to testify and what do we say when they ask for the reason? Do we say, yeah your honors we found out a few hours ago that this guy is going to demolish our case so we decided to pull him and hopefully save face? And Booth didn't want to testify anyway which could help us because then it's his problem and not ours, but then will the judges force him to testify, which is also bad for us? And will Henry confront him tonight or try to see if the guy still doesn't want to testify? I really don't know."

Sam looked towards the door as Martie walked in and sat down. "Has

Carter left yet? I'm hungry and yet again I don't see myself getting out of here before ten tonight." Martie slumped down in her chair.

"Yeah, he left about fifteen minutes ago. We were just talking about Henry and his dinner tonight with Booth." Alex finished with the coffee and joined Sam and Martie at the table.

"I hope he comes back and makes the right decision tonight. We have been working our asses off on this case the past few months and I don't want it to go down the drain with this one witness. He better come up with a clever way to get us out of this mess." Martie picked up a cookie from the tray.

Henry and Booth were sitting at a restaurant that Henry had discovered a few days before in Scheveningen. He ordered the entrecote with french fries and mushroom sauce. He realized that the Dutch were obsessed with sauces. If you ordered meat, then you had to order a sauce to accompany it. He also noticed that the meat was dry without the sauce. No wonder you had to add the sauce, Henry thought.

Booth ordered the pork tenderloin with pepper sauce. Both men sipped on red wine while they waited for the food to arrive. Booth had told Henry the previous day that he didn't want to testify and didn't understand why they were having dinner. He thought that this was Henry's attempt to change his mind, but it wasn't going to work. He could lose too much; not only his job, but his dignity and family too.

Henry made small talk with Booth to break the ice and make Booth feel more comfortable. He also wanted to monitor Booth's movements to see if Booth's character fitted Max's story. The food arrived along with bread and garlic butter. Henry began pouring the mushroom sauce over his entrecote and then followed with spreading the garlic butter on a piece of warm bread.

"Did you have a good day today, James? Did you get out of the hotel room and see the town? I haven't had much free time, but I would love to see more of the city."

Booth became a little nervous. He was even more confused over why they were having dinner together. "Well, yes, I did walk around the city a little this afternoon. It's very nice. I visited the parliament building and they have a medieval torture museum across the street from parliament. I couldn't believe that they had a torture museum, but it was very impressive. Have you seen it?"

Henry knew that Booth also had a visitor just before lunch, but decided not to mention it. "I have walked through the outer buildings of the parliament, but I wasn't aware of a torture museum. I'm glad that you had a good time. Were you able to think about your testimony, if you are willing to testify for General Kimbala? It would be helpful for someone of your high standing to testify for him. The case is almost over and someone of your caliber could seal the case for us." Henry began chewing on a piece of entrecote. He was going to enjoy his meal no matter what happened that night.

"I have thought about it today, a lot I must add. I really would like to help you and General Kimbala. He is a very nice man and helped me tremendously. I couldn't have done my job without him, but I had a call from my family and need to return immediately. My daughter has cancer and her health has weakened since I've been here. My wife told me that our daughter was admitted to the hospital this morning. I would really like to help General Kimbala, but my daughter comes first. I need to leave tomorrow morning at the latest." Booth nervously jabbed a forkful of pork into his mouth.

Henry knew that Booth's visitor was a friend of Karim Kimbala. This family liked to have others do their dirty work. In a way this helped him in Joseph's case because the prosecution's case was mostly circumstantial evidence, which made it easier for Henry and his team to poke holes and widen the gaps in the prosecution's case.

Henry looked sympathetically towards Booth. "I'm really sorry to hear that, James. I didn't know that. I'm sure that General Kimbala will understand the circumstances with your daughter. What is her name?" Henry knew that Booth didn't have a daughter.

"Her name is Suzy and she's eleven years old. She's our only child. I'm sure that you can understand why I need to get back."

"I do understand and we'll work together to get you back home as soon as possible. First, we need to alert the court of the circumstances and the fact that you will not be able to testify, but it should be okay." Henry was glad that Booth had provided an out for them.

CHAPTER 39

Director Henley sat in his plush black leather chair hunched over his desk. He was holding a document in both hands and reading intently. Agent Scott sat opposite Henley in silence. Scott crossed his legs, looked out of the window, and slowly drank his red wine. It was seven-o'clock and the street lights gave an additional energy to the city life flowing below them. He was due for dinner with his girlfriend of the moment and wanted Henley to fasten the pace, but he knew that this was part of the protocol.

Any agent knew that being summoned to Henley's private office meant that you would also be waiting in silence for at least ten minutes while Henley himself meditated, on what no one knew.

Henley broke the silence. "Stop looking so bored Scott. I am sitting in the same room with you. Is there anything else to report on Edwards' movement?" Henley wanted to know where Edwards had spent the day.

"He visited a bank in France and it looks as if he's about to do a runner. We've also ascertained that investigators from the Kimbala defense team are shadowing him. They know about Edwards's less than good behavior in Kilambèa. The defense also seems to know what Edwards is up to in France and that he's been talking to their witnesses."

Henley interrupted Scott. "I don't care about their witnesses right now. Are you telling me that they know everything about Edwards and his relations with the Kimbalas?" Henley asked.

"It seems to be so."

"And what about Sir Hanley? Have they figured that piece of the puzzle out yet?" Henley inquired.

"No, it seems that they are still unaware of Sir Hanley's background and Edwards's connection," Scott replied taking another sip of wine.

Meetings in Henley's office were always monotonous, but at least he offered high quality wines. Scott accepted this as Henley's personal way of apologizing for putting his agents through this scrutinizing process sometimes too frequently.

"So, our problem has not worsened at least. Is our agent still in France?" Henley asked putting the piece of paper to the side and picking up his whiskey glass.

"Yes, Sir. She's still there," Scott replied.

"Good, then I want you to do two things discreetly. First, Edwards is to be eliminated immediately. He has damaged the country and the company's integrity and security. Second, I think that it's time for Sir Hanley to retire to a quiet life here in England. I want this message to be sent by tomorrow afternoon. He is to announce his retirement, due to family or health reasons, by the end of this week. Tell him that he can choose the reason." Henley looked sternly at Scott. "Edwards betrayed me and that is unacceptable. You can tell him that before he's eliminated. Go and enjoy your dinner." Henley returned to his paperwork.

Scott stood up and placed his wine glass on the side table. It never ceased to amaze him how Henley knew of his movements. He gave up a long time ago figuring out how Henley knew so much about their lives. Scott walked out of the office and walked to his own office down the hall. He was already too late for his dinner date and would have to make this quick. Scott summoned Blake and Wiley into his office for a quick briefing.

"Do not make yourselves too comfortable. This will be a quick meeting." Scott sat on the edge of his desk while Blake and Wiley sat down in the two black leather chairs facing Scott's desk.

"Which one are you seeing tonight? Is it Linda or what was the name of the other one?" Blake looked at Wiley for help.

"I think it was Sarah, mate," Wiley replied in admiration.

"You're both wrong. I'm meeting Amy tonight. Now, shut up about my private life and listen up. You both know the situation that we have with

Edwards and Sir Hanley. Director Henley has informed me that we are to commence with Operation Wading Bird and Operation Bordeaux. Blake, you'll be the point man for Wading Bird while Wiley and I will take care of Bordeaux. Both missions are to be completed within one week. Any questions?" Scott asked.

"No," Blake and Wiley responded simultaneously.

"Good, then I'm off for my dinner date. Wiley, let's meet tomorrow morning around ten-o'clock for coffee," Scott stated in a rush as he picked-up his coat from the coat rack and walked out of the office to meet his date.

Blake walked into Sir Hanley's office and shook Sir Hanley's hand before sitting down. "Good afternoon, Sir Hanley. My name is Timothy Blake and I work in the interior office."

"Good afternoon, Mr. Blake. Your office said that there was an urgent matter, but I don't understand how I can be of help. But, of course I am always here for my country. Please tell me what the problem is and how I can help."

Timothy crossed his legs, cleared his throat and began speaking. He was told to hand the situation delicately and discreetly. "Sir Hanley, you have honorably represented The United Kingdom here at the Tribunal for the past five years and your country is grateful for this. In return for your hard work, we would like to offer you a professorship back in the UK. You will be given your own house, car, and of course a handsome salary. You will need to resign from the Tribunal immediately, but we're sure that your new job will provide the same, if not more, pleasure as your current job here as president of the court."

"Oh, I'm sorry I thought that this was a matter of national security, but you're only here offering me a different job. Don't get me wrong, I am relieved that it is not more serious, but I am taken a bit aback. As you are already aware, I have dreamt of teaching at the end of my professional career, but I don't believe that I'm ready to leave my current post. I'm very happy with my daily duties, the interactions with the different people and cultures. It's very invigorating and therefore, I believe that I am going to have to decline the offer for now." Sir Hanley was very relieved that this meeting only concerned a job offer.

Timothy was warned that gaining Sir Hanley's acceptance would be tough. He shifted in his seat and then took a different approach. "Sir Hanley, I understand that this is a difficult decision for you to make. Working at this acclaimed Tribunal in your position must be an amazing experience, one that only a few in our lifetime will experience. We understand that such an experience and post is hard to give up, but your country would like to have you back where you can enrich young minds. I must stress that you seriously contemplate this offer, Sir Hanley."

Sir Hanley didn't understand why this Blake fellow wasn't taking no for an answer. It is his choice to make and if he says no then he means no. Sir Hanley furrowed his brow. "Is there something else that you need to discuss with me, Mr. Blake?"

Timothy sighed. He was getting tired of beating around the bush. "Sir Hanley, you were visited by a Mr. Edwards, is that correct."

Sir Hanley went pale. "Uhm, yes I had a visit from a man named Edwards. Why do you ask?"

"Furthermore, we understand that Edwards wanted information on the Kimbala case and threatened to publicize your online activities." Timothy stared at Sir Hanley and waited for his response.

"Why yes, he did make a few rushed assumptions. I sent him on his way," Sir Hanley said nervously to Timothy.

"Yes, well we don't want these rushed assumptions to become public do we? Your government is asking you politely to return," Timothy added.

"And when do you expect me to resign and what reason do I give for leaving?" Sir Hanley stood up and began pacing from one end of the office to the other.

Timothy watched him as he paced back and forth. "I have been given instructions that you are to resign this week and return to the UK within two weeks. As for the reason, you are free to choose between health and family."

"And what will happen if I say no and continue working here?" Sir Hanley wanted to know.

"I don't believe that you will like the consequences then, Sir Hanley. In order to help you I have two different resignation letters for you to choose from." Timothy opened his briefcase and placed the two letters on Sir Hanley's desk.

Sir Hanley read the letters. One letter claimed serious health problems, cancer to be precise. The other letter claimed that his wife was seriously ill and that he would be returning due to his wife's wishes.

Sir Hanley held onto one letter and handed the other back to Timothy. "I don't want my wife to be involved at this level. How do I explain this to her? I don't have cancer…" Sir Hanley wondered.

"Don't worry, Sir Hanley, remissions happen every day." Timothy placed the unused letter back into his briefcase and rose to leave.

Sir Hanley watched Timothy silently walk out of the office. Sir Hanley reached over to open the lower left drawer of his desk. He pulled out his secret stash of whisky and a drinking glass. The slow trickling sound of the whisky pouring into the glass was the only sound filling the room. Sir Hanley placed the bottle nearby on his desk and didn't bother to put the cap back on. He knew that he would be filling his glass again within the next five minutes, if not faster.

Sir Hanley picked up the resignation letter and stared at its contents. Multiple questions entered his head all at the same time. What would he tell his wife? Was this going to get back to his children? He cared about his peers at the Tribunal, but his family and friends were more important to him. How could I have let them down? Richard thought to himself. Sir Hanley turned his computer on and began to write what would become the most painful email in his entire life.

Carter walked into Alex's office. "Did you see the email?" Carter asked anxiously.

Alex looked up from her paperwork. "What email? I haven't checked emails since we got back."

Alex turned to her laptop and pulled her email up. "What, this one from the Registry?" Alex began reading the email, but couldn't believe the content. Alex looked up at Carter who was about to burst with anticipation, something that he did when it came to gossip.

"I can't believe that Sir Hanley has resigned from his post. Did anyone know that he was sick? And so sick that he has to resign. It must be terrible to resign from a job that you love. Do the others know about this?"

"I don't think so. The gossip on the grape vine tells me that there's more to this story then him having pancreatic cancer. I heard that he was forced to resign, but no one knows by whom," Carter replied in his usual gossipy tone.

Alex gave a curious look at Carter. "Are you serious? And how do you know all of this?"

Carter waved his finger in front of Alex. "You know that I don't tell my sources. Just remember that my sources are always trustful." Carter walked out of Alex's office.

CHAPTER 40

Adam walked into Jan Paul's office with a folder under his arm. "I have some great information for you and possibly the key information you've been looking for," Adam put the folder on Jan Paul's desk.

"The defense's next witness is James Booth, correct? Well, I just found out that he's even closer to the Kimbalas then we thought. It turns out that he made a deal with the Kimbalas and helped most of the aide shipment to get to the black market; aide that was supposed to be for the people of Kilambèa. I also found out that he helped the Kimbalas to ship girls from the sex shops in Kilambèa to the brothels in Belgium. According to his witness statement, he's an ordinary aid worker, but this information is definitely putting a new twist to his story." Adam sat back in his chair and smiled.

Jan Paul sat forward in his seat and began looking at the documents in the folder that Adam placed on his desk. "Are you serious? How accurate is this information?"

"This is extremely accurate information."

"This could help save the case. Great work, Adam. We only have one problem and that is we have to wait and see if this guy will actually testify. Do you think that the defense knows this information also?"

Adam hunched his shoulders. "I think they're reckless to call someone like this if they know about his background."

"I wonder what their motive is. Let's see if they call him. Meanwhile, I'll go through this folder and let you know if I need anything else. Once again, great work," Jan Paul began happily thumbing through the documents.

CHAPTER 41

Nine fifteen the next morning

The usher escorted Booth to the witness stand and then sat down.

"Good morning, Mr. Booth. I am Judge Theonus Atkinson, to my left is Judge Adrienne Reinhold, and to my right is Judge Jeremy Robinson. Mr. Boome informed us this morning that you are unwilling to testify in this case. General Kimbala has been accused of the gravest crimes imaginable, and therefore it is important that he receives a fair and complete trial. As you can imagine, we are disappointed in the fact that Mr. Boome told us this morning that one of the defense's key international witnesses, meaning you, does not want to testify. It would be an understatement if I said that this was short notice. Mr. Boome, as I have just mentioned, gave the reasons for why you do not want to testify, but now we would like to hear them from you. See, you must understand that this trial is nearing to a close and the prosecution and defense have been preparing for your testimony for at least two weeks now if not longer. You are a substantial witness and it is not fair to anyone if you suddenly drop off of the witness list. That is unheard of and there must be exceptional reasons for this to happen." Judge Atkinson motioned for Booth to begin after turning his microphone off. Everyone could sense that Atkinson was irritated. Judge Atkinson turned his microphone back on.

"Mr. Booth, before you begin I must underscore that we are taking this trial very seriously. You have been summoned to appear as a witness before us in an international war crimes trial. If we do not like your reason, then we have the right to penalize you. According to the Rules of this Tribunal, we can impose one of the following penalties. We can order that you testify and without delay. Another option that we can use is to issue a fine of 3,000 euro. The last available option, under the Rules, is that we can order you to spend one week in the detention center. I hope that you understand what I'm saying to you." Judge Atkinson turned his microphone off and motioned once again for Booth to begin.

Booth sat up and talked nervously into the microphone. "I'm sorry your honors for disturbing the trial process. It is not my intention to do so. I received word from my wife that our daughter, who has cancer, has been admitted into the hospital. She is in the last stage and I'm afraid that her condition has worsened. I talked to my wife this morning before coming here and the doctors do not believe that she has much longer to live. I'm really sorry, but I need to return to my family." Booth sat back in his chair.

Judges Atkinson, Robinson, and Reinhold huddled together to discuss whether or not Booth should testify. Henry looked across at Jan Paul only to find Jan Paul staring back at him. In an instant Henry knew that the prosecution was aware of Booth's background. No wonder the prosecution had objected strenuously this morning. He knew that the decision was now up to the judges and he hoped that they would decide against Booth testifying.

The judges assumed their official positions and Judge Atkinson turned his microphone on. "Mr. Booth, I consulted with my colleagues and we offer our deepest sympathies to you and your family. General Kimbala is accused of grave crimes, but we also acknowledge the importance of family and therefore understand your drive to return to your wife and ailing daughter. With that said, we, the court, will not interfere with your returning home as soon as possible. In other words, we will not force you to testify. You are free to leave."

Jan Paul rose hastily to his feet. "Your honor, I must put my objections on the record. As you stated, Mr. Booth is a very important witness in this case. I understand that he is a defense witness. However, the prosecution also has questions for him to answer. Mr. Booth has stated that his daughter is currently in the hospital. I think that the right course of action right now would be for Mr. Booth to provide medical records as confirmation…"

Booth frantically turned his microphone on. "Mr. De Loon, my daughter is critically ill. She may not live beyond this week. What you are asking from me is absurd. Now, I understand that this is an important trial, but my daughter is more important to me. I'm sorry for you, but I need to get back to her. I need to spend as much time as possible with her right now."

Jan Paul hesitated for a minute before responding. He turned the microphone on before responding in a faint voice. "I understand what you have said, Mr. Booth, but unfortunately I also have a prosecution case to complete." Jan Paul turned to Judge Atkinson. "Your honor, I understand that you will let Mr. Booth leave without testifying. I request at this time that he be ordered to produce his daughter's medical records within two weeks." Jan Paul turned the microphone off and sat down.

"We will take your request into consideration, Mr. De Loon. Once again, Mr. Booth you are free to go," Judge Aktinson stated.

Booth showed immense relief. "Thank you your honors. May I extend my apologies to you, the defense and prosecution? I really am sorry, but as I have said my daughter is priority for me right now."

Henry loosened the grip on his pen. This trial wasn't over yet.

CHAPTER 42

Edwards was sitting in his vacation cottage enjoying a cup of coffee and listening to Mozart playing in the background. He had bought the cottage two years before after falling in love with the French countryside. At first, Edwards had looked at houses around the Beaune area seeing how he would be in the middle of the world's famous vineyards, but then had decided that the French Alps was a better choice. The luscious green landscaped hills were beautiful with small farm villages scattered every few kilometers.

A peaceful feeling overcame Edwards as he opened his balcony door every morning and breathed in the morning countryside air. Every house reminded him of Switzerland with their brown wooden covering adorned with colorful flowers. Cows wearing silver bell collars roaming the fields signaled that they were located near the Swiss border. Edwards knew that the rolling mountains and hills between Beaune and his village were covered with corn and sunflower fields, deer, butterflies, and farms filled with chickens, horses, and pigs. This was countryside full of nature, peace, and calm. Edwards wished that he could stay here forever in oblivion, but he had an appointment in Lausanne that he couldn't miss. His banker in Beaune had followed through and Edwards was pleased. He was almost finished and could disappear from the world, but he would have to visit Switzerland this one time. Then he promised himself a quiet life in his French cottage. He envisioned days of pruning his flowers in the garden, visiting the local baker every morning standing in line to buy his daily bread, and chatting merrily with his neighbors. This was going to become his world soon and Edwards couldn't have asked for a better life; a life that he had control over and no one else.

Edwards looked at his watch and stood up. He turned the stereo player off and locked up the cottage. Edwards opened the door to his little Citroën C1, got in and started the motor. He switched the radio on, opened the windows, and began driving towards Switzerland. The wind carried the sound of cow bells as he drove past his neighbor's farm. He turned left and drove through the village's center consisting of one street. He not only picked this village because of its beauty and remoteness, but also for the size. It was easy to spot strangers in this small town. The town consisted of one restaurant and hotel, two bakeries, one flower shop, one grocery store, one real estate agent, one clothing shop, a gasoline station, hardware store, and one bank. You had to visit the next biggest city for all other needs. As far as Edwards was concerned, he had everything that he needed and would know instantly if any strangers infiltrated the village. The locals loved to gossip about the strange tourists.

Edwards exited the city and continued straight towards Switzerland. The trip to the border would last about forty-five minutes, but the sky was clear and the sun was shining. Edwards turned the volume of the radio up higher. There were no other cars in sight, something that Edwards was used to. He pressed the gas pedal down and felt the wind tickle his neck. Farmers were tilling their lands in the far distance unaware of Edwards's existence. White cows were grazing in the fields close by the roadway and Edwards drove on the winding roads in style. At first, Edwards had had trouble maintaining high speeds while maneuvering those winding roads, but now he was an expert. He wanted to enjoy the open space knowing that soon he would be sharing winding roads while driving down mountains with other cars, trucks and motorcycles. He decided to press down even harder on the gas pedal. The wind brushed harshly over his forehead and his brown hair whipped uncontrollably around his head.

Edwards reached the mountain and began his decent. Maybe he would stop at Starbucks before his appointment. He wouldn't be visiting Switzerland, much less anywhere else outside his newly adopted village, in the near future so he should take this opportunity for some Starbuck's coffee. Edwards looked behind him and saw a person riding a motorcycle coming up. It looked like a man dressed in a blue and silver leather outfit with a black helmet. The black and silver motorcycle was impressive. Edwards remembered the time that he had wanted a motorcycle too. Maybe he should put that on his list of to dos even though he would have to visit the nearby city to take lessons. He would have to think seriously about that, if it was worth the hassle.

The motorcycle passed Edwards on the left. Edwards also wondered if solo motorcyclists were always on their own or if their travelling mates were somewhere in the area. All of a sudden another motorcycle passed Edwards and joined the one already driving in front. He finally had his answer. Edwards and the motorcyclists drove a few kilometers in harmony and Edwards fantasized over what the motorcyclists were doing here on this open road. Were they tourists travelling around Europe for three months? Were they locals from the area travelling to Switzerland for some fun?

A truck appeared behind Edwards's car. Edwards looked in his rear view mirror and saw the truck. He was happy that the truck was behind his car instead of in front. He remembered the countless times that he's had to patiently drive behind trucks attempting to tackle the huge mountains' winding roads, although this one seemed to be going faster than other trucks that he'd encountered in the past. The truck began to pick up speed. Edwards attempted to pass the motorcyclists with no success. A car was coming from the other direction. Edwards knew that he wouldn't have time to pass the motorcyclists before the oncoming car reached them. The truck sped faster and Edwards began to wonder if the truck driver had lost control. He honked his horn to alert the motorcyclists, but they didn't seem to hear his horn. He began to shout towards the motorcyclists and continued to honk his horn while constantly looking into his rear and side mirrors. The last thing that Edwards felt was a jerk from the car. The truck banged into the back of Edwards's car with great force.

Because of Edwards's car's age, it only took one ramming from the truck for Edwards to lose control of his car. The motorcyclists sped up at that moment and Edwards's car sped out of control and continued to the other lane flying over the mountain. The truck came to a stop and the driver got out and walked to the edge of the mountain's side. The motorcyclists returned at the same time that the oncoming car stopped. They joined the truck driver in time to see Edwards's car burst into flames.

"Was Edwards alone?" Scott asked.

The truck driver looked over towards Scott. "Yes, the bastard was alone and he didn't get out before the blast."

"Good, good job boys. I'm going to report this back to headquarters. I'll see you back in London," Scott walked back to his car leaving the three to discuss how well they had orchestrated the attack before exiting the scene well in advance of any onlookers or emergency assistance people showing up and questions needing to be answered.

Max looked down beyond the fir trees below at the burning car and the group of men standing and talking at the edge. Unbeknownst to the men, Max had followed Edwards making sure to maintain a large distance and avoid detection. He had seen the truck appear behind Edwards during his descent and had decided to stop on the side of the mountain and watch. Something was strange about the motorcycles and truck, but he couldn't figure it out until the car was driven off the cliff and the men had gathered at the edge for pats on the back and chit chat. He only recognized Scott, but that was enough. It was enough for Max to know that this was an inside job.

They didn't want Edwards to make it to Switzerland. They also wanted to give a sign to any other agents that disloyalty would not be tolerated, at any level. Max waited for the team of agents to leave before returning to his car. He knew that turning around on such a steep and whining road was suicide, but he also didn't feel like driving past the pack. They could get edgy and think that a witness was passing by. A witness was the last thing that these guys wanted.

CHAPTER 43

Alex was standing at the white board updating the sequence of witnesses, along with the examining attorney information, and key issues, exhibits and evidence that needed to be dealt with during each witness's testimony. She sent the updates to everyone on the team via email, but also liked to keep a hard copy on the bulletin board on the wall left of her desk and the war room, the most used space in their office dwelling.

Henry and Sam walked in and sat down at the round conference table. Alex briefly glanced over her shoulder and then continued with her work. She wanted to finish this as quickly as possible. She had too much work to do and wanted to leave no later than six thirty tonight. Alex had dinner plans with Carter and wanted to freshen up and relax a little before meeting him. She definitely didn't want to go straight from work having the smell of work follow her the entire evening. Tonight, Alex was going to relax completely and forget about this place, the people, and the work.

Sam placed his coffee cup on the table and sat back in the chair. "Are you serious? Edwards was killed in a car crash?"

Alex turned around in silence with a marker poised in one hand and a piece of paper in the other. All of a sudden the sequence list wasn't so important anymore.

"Max saw it happen. He was following Edwards down a mountain top. It looks as if Edwards was travelling to Switzerland. Max said that he kept a large distance between his and Edwards's car, but arrived just in time to see two motorcycles riding in front of Edwards and a truck ramming into the back of Edwards's car. The truck only had to ram once for Edwards's car to veer off the road and off the cliff," Henry sighed. He didn't know if he could take any more surprises in this case.

Sam was very curious. "But how does Max know that this wasn't some stupid accident? It must be difficult for truck drivers to maneuver the mountain roads and if they go fast, then it must be near impossible."

"Unfortunately, Max recognized one of the guys and said that he's a secret agent from Britain. They wanted Edwards out of the way." Henry placed his elbows on the table and began to massage his forehead.

Alex walked into the restaurant and could feel the eyes following her to the table. She felt beautiful tonight after leaving work on time, taking a hot shower, pulling the hair up, adding a touch of make-up and wearing her favorite dress. Alex loved the fact that her clear cappuccino skin didn't need much make-up. Carter was already sitting at the table browsing the menu when Alex walked in. He looked up and his breath was taken away. She looked different for some reason tonight. This was definitely different then the worn out daily Alex that he was getting used to.

Carter stood up to greet Alex with a European hug kissing her twice. "You look gorgeous tonight! Where have you been hiding this side of yourself?"

Alex kissed Carter back blushing. "I decided that I was going to relax and have fun tonight. I'm not going to talk or think about work, and this includes gossip. Do we have a deal?" Alex put her hand forward in an attempt at a handshake.

Carter furrowed his brow. "I'm with you about work, but no gossip?"

"Come on, Carter. I think that you can live without gossip for one night if I can live without talking about work. Do we have a deal or what?" Alex's hand remained poised in the air.

A smile slowly appeared on Carter's face. "You know what? Seeing how this is the first time that I'm seeing you outside the office where you won't talk about work I'm going to seal the deal. Okay, no gossip tonight; just fun and laughs."

"That sounds like a perfect evening!" Alex laughed.

They turned their attention and conversation to the menu.

After dinner, Carter and Alex walked into Deluca's restaurant for a cappuccino and dessert. They were looking over the menu when a tall dark handsome man walked in the front door. He was wearing a dark green suit from Zegna, cream crisp shirt with the top two buttons open. The suit matched his green eyes and hazel smooth skin. He was clean shaven with a close cut haircut. His manicured hands pulled a chair out two tables away from Alex and Carter. He purposefully sat diagonally across from Alex. Carter caught a glimpse of the hunk and how he looked at Alex.

My, my, this should be interesting, Carter thought. He looked at Alex who hadn't even realized that the man even existed let alone had just sat down. How could she not notice when Carter could even smell the man's Hugo Boss cologne?

Alex was enjoying her last bite of cappuccino ice cream while Carter had finished his Crème Brule ten minutes before. He was sipping on a double espresso while simultaneously talking to Alex and keeping an eye on the fine gentleman sitting on their right. Carter saw how the man couldn't seem to take his eyes off of her.

Carter couldn't take it anymore. "Uhm, Alex what do you think about this restaurant. I know that you haven't been here before."

Alex looked up from her ice cream. She wanted to savor every delicious bite. "Hmm, oh, it's really nice. I can see coming back here again. Not too many people, which is nice. We've been able to talk and not scream over the other people or the music. How was your Crème Brule?" Alex smiled.

Carter looked incredulous at her. "How is my Crème Brule? My dear, a 'lekker ding' is sitting not too far from us and may I say, because you haven't been paying attention, that he's been eyeing you all night."

Alex cocked her head to the side and looked at Carter. "What is 'lekker ding'? And who are you talking about?"

Carter shook his head. This case had made Alex's social life non-existent. "Look over to your left nonchalantly and tell me that you're not interested."

Alex looked over the rim of her coffee mug while she perused the room and locked eyes with the man sitting diagonally across from her. She had to admit that he was handsome and he returned her smile. Alex blushed and turned back to Carter.

Carter could see that love was in the air. "You better get his phone number before we leave."

Alex smiled and sipped on her cappuccino. He was handsome, but she always expected the man to make the first move. Call her a feminist, but she wanted to be chased and not the other way around. Carter and Alex went Dutch and paid after dessert, two cappuccinos, and two lattes. Alex stood up and put on her coat. Carter followed behind her until their movements were interrupted by the man who had been sitting two tables away from them.

"You're leaving so soon," he smiled up at Alex.

The man stood up to greet Alex. Alex was taken aback. She wanted him to say something, but thought he wouldn't. "Uhm, yes, we're heading out." Alex smiled at this stranger.

The man stuck his hand out. "Please let me introduce myself before you do. My name is William Turner."

Alex put her hand out waiting for a handshake and gasped when he brushed his lips gently on her hand. What a gentlemen, she thought. Carter was impressed. He didn't know who this man was, but the guy was impressive. William then shook Carter's hand. Carter thought that Alex and William were moving slow and decided to speed things up a little.

"Well, William we were just headed to a club around the corner. Do you want to join us?"

Alex looked at Carter in shock. She thought that they were ending the night and going home, but decided to play along. She wanted to spend some time with this William character.

William smiled showing his perfect teeth and looked at Alex. "Sure, I'd love to."

The three walked out of the restaurant and headed around the corner to the club. The club was situated in between a host of bars. The smell of beer lingered on the streets and a mixture of laughter and music bounced out of the bars and club. Alex, Carter, and William sat at a table at the back of the club next to the bar. The club would have been pitch black if tea candles didn't adorn every table and around the bar. Color lights danced around the ceiling, walls, and dance floor. The dance floor was full of people dancing to the rhythm of the music and the bar was also busy. Alex sipped on her Martini while talking to the guys.

Alex looked around the dance floor and found a mixture of guys dancing with girls, but also guys with guys and vice versa. It had been a long time since Alex had been to a club and wondered if she still had it. All of a sudden, Alex started to move her body gently from side to side.

William looking at her took the hint. "Would you like to dance?"

Alex put her Martini on the table. "Definitely."

She had promised herself a great time tonight and didn't want to spoil it. Carter decided that he no longer had to babysit and also got up from the table. Maybe he could also find himself a 'lekker ding' tonight.

Alex and William were dancing in the middle of the crowded dance floor, but from the looks of them they were the only ones on the dance floor. Alex and William couldn't take their eyes off of each other. They swayed to the beat of the music. Alex wrapped her arms around William's neck while William rested the palms of his hands on Alex's lower back. It was awkward dancing so close with a stranger, but what could you do when the DJ was playing slow music? The music changed to a faster rhythm and everyone on the dance floor followed suit, including Alex and William. Alex was happy because she could lose some of the stocked up energy and tension. She worked out three days a week back in Baltimore, but hadn't had the time to find a gym in The Hague. Alex started running in the mornings to replace the gym, but dancing also helped. They danced for two more hours before ending the night.

"Good morning, sunshine. Do I see a glow on your face?" Carter walked into Alex's office with a bright smile.

Alex turned around and looked at Carter. "Hey good morning, sweetie. Where did you go last night? I was searching for you, but couldn't find you anywhere." Alex sounded concerned.

Carter looked at her in disbelief. "I don't believe you. You were so into Mr. Chocolate that you don't even remember me coming up to you? I told you that I was leaving and the only response I got was 'okay'."

Alex blushed. "Are you serious? I don't remember you doing that."

"My point exactly. So, how and who is Mr. Wonderful? And more importantly did you see anymore of him last night?"

Alex couldn't help from laughing. Carter was naturally curious and Alex knew that he was dying inside for some inside information. "He's from

Jamaica and works at an international political think tank in The Hague. He's been working here for the past three months and is getting used to the job and the Netherlands. He doesn't have many friends here yet and has been hanging out with his colleagues most of the time. So, he was happy to have met us last night."

"You mean he was happy to meet you. Is he married, does he have a girlfriend? What does he do at this think tank?" Carter's questions rolled out one after another.

"That I know of he doesn't have a wife or girlfriend. He's a political analyst at the think tank, and no I did not see any more than you did last night. But, I am seeing him again this weekend." Alex smiled at Carter.

"Finally! You finally have a social life." "I need some coffee. You want some?" Carter screamed as he was walking to the kitchen.

CHAPTER 44

Lizette was walking down the street to meet her friends. She had just finished a day of shopping and didn't have time to stow her bags away in the car. She didn't want to be late. Lizette pushed her way past through the stream of shoppers slowly walking down the street. She knew that she had replaced her husband's lack of attention with shopping, but she didn't know what else to do. Her husband's obsession with doing a good job had taken him further away from her and their children. His emotional absence created Lizette's overflowing closet and unnecessary house gadgets. She hadn't even noticed that their oldest child, Lucas, was having trouble in school. The teacher had pulled Lizette aside the day before and told her that Lucas was having trouble with taking direction. He was also fighting with the other children.

Lizette turned the corner and began thinking about her relationship with Jan Paul. She remembered how happy they were together before coming to The Hague. Jan Paul's personality had changed slowly over the past couple of years so much that Lizette barely saw the man that she had fallen in love with. She looked into a restaurant window where couples were happily drinking wine and reading over menus. She could see fresh love in the air, something that she hadn't seen or felt in years. Lizette roamed over the faces and settled on one table. Jan Paul told her that he would be working late again tonight. This was something that Lizette had become accustomed to. Her bags dropped as she lost the feeling in her hands. Jan Paul was sitting at a table with a young woman. They were holding hands and looking into each other's eyes, just like the other happy couples sitting around them in the restaurant. Lizette couldn't move and she began to tremble all over. This was a nightmare. It wasn't true. Jan Paul was sitting behind his desk at this moment working late.

Jan Paul looked towards the window to find his wife frozen in shock. The look of innocent disbelief in her eyes was devastating. The color disappeared from his face as he removed his hand from Analise's. Analise looked in the same direction as Jan Paul to see a trembling Lizette. Analise could swear that she saw a single tear trail down Lizette's cheek. Analise smiled innocently at Lizette. Jan Paul's seat screeched as he quickly rose from the table. His wine glass fell to the floor along with his utensils. Jan Paul looked briefly to the table and floor to see what had happened. Lizette was gone when he looked back up.

"Love, what's wrong? Are you okay?" Analise smiled calmly at Jan Paul.

Jan Paul slowly sat back down. He felt as if the floor was moving and that it was going to open up any moment and swallow him up. At least that is what he hoped for. "That was my wife."

"Maybe you should have something to drink?"Analise offered a glass of water to Jan Paul.

Jan Paul took the glass of water in his trembling hand and swallowed the contents in one gulp. He could feel the sweat pouring down his temples. What was he doing? What was he going to do? Jan Paul thought.

"So, that was Lizette?" Analise asked. She took a sip of her red wine.

"Yes, that was Lizette. What am I doing here?" Jan Paul looked around with a blank stare.

"What are you doing here, my love? You're having a bit of fun with me, remember? Listen, let's have our dinner. It looks as if Lizette needs time to cool down. You also need to collect yourself. You look awful." Analise removed the sweat from Jan Paul's temples with the restaurant's napkin.

"Maybe you're right. I need some time to think about this and figure out what to do."

"Don't worry, love. I'll take care of you," Analise smiled.

The curious stares from the other restaurant patrons began to disappear and Jan Paul and Analise finished their dinners. Analise made sure that they both ordered three courses to make the time go by more slowly. She had hoped that she could persuade him to return to her apartment with her for after dinner drinks.

"Dinner was lovely, wasn't it?" Analise sipped on her cappuccino.

"It was okay," Jan Paul responded blankly.

"You've been a delight. I thought you were over Lizette. That's why you spend so much time with me, right?" Analise placed her cup down on the saucer.

Jan Paul looked into Analise's eyes and sighed. "Of course, I'm having a great time with you, but I'm also married to Lizette and we have kids together. This has become too complicated."

"This? You mean our relationship? Jan Paul, I love you. Don't you love me?" Analise reached over to hold Jan Paul's hand.

"I owe it to Lizette to go and talk with her. Do you understand that?"

Analise could tell that she was losing the battle, but she had no intentions of losing her man. "Go ahead and talk with her, but don't forget to come back to me."

"Thanks." Jan Paul squeezed her hand. He paid the bill and walked out of the restaurant to face his wife.

Jan Paul entered their bedroom door and found Lizette hysterically throwing his dress shirts and pants into a suit case. One suitcase, filled with underpants and casual clothes, was already strewn on the pavement outside. Jan Paul looked at Lizette in shock. Tears streamed down Lizette's face as she crossed the room from the closet to the drawer in panic.

"Lizette..." Jan Paul managed to utter before stopping again.

Lizette continued to pack his clothes wiping away the tears with the back of her hands. No matter how much she wiped away, the tears continued to come.

Jan Paul began again. "Lizette, please stop. We need to talk."

Lizette turned slowly in Jan Paul's direction. Her eyes said it all. She loathed Jan Paul at this moment. How could he do this to her? They were supposed to be happily married. They had three small children together. She had given up her career for him. She stayed home, watched over their children, cleaned the house, and made dinner for her husband and children. Everything that Lizette did was for Jan Paul and their children.

Lizette spoke in coldness. "You want to talk? About what, Jan Paul? Do you want to talk now about how you have been coming home late? How I thought that you were spending all of your time at the office working hard to prosecute a criminal, but instead were fucking your paralegal? Shouldn't we have 'talked' before you started cheating on us? How could you do this to me?"

Lizette held one of Jan Paul's dress shirts in her left hand as she walked towards Jan Paul, still standing in the door way. She pointed her finger in Jan Paul's face. "How could you do this to your children?"

Lizette looked at Jan Paul. Rage rushed through Lizette's body as the visual of Jan Paul and Analise flashed in front of her eyes. Jan Paul's cheek stung from the slap on his face.

Jan Paul massaged his left cheek and looked in despair at his wife. How could he have done this to her? "Lizette, where are the children?"

Lizette continued with the packing as she tried to control her sobbing. "The kids are at my mothers. I didn't know if you would be coming here tonight, but I didn't want my children to see this."

Jan Paul looked at Lizette and felt as if he had lost control of his home. "Lizette, I'm sorry. Can we please talk about this?"

Jan Paul held his arms out in an attempt to calm her down. Lizette closed the suitcase, walked over to the window, and threw the suitcase out of the window. She then brushed past Jan Paul and ran downstairs to the kitchen. Jan Paul followed only to find her picking up the lighter that they used to start a fire on the stove top. Jan Paul didn't know what to expect. Maybe he had driven Lizette over the edge.

"Lizette, what are you doing?"

Lizette didn't answer. She walked out the front door and into the small patch of garden that they owned.

Lizette turned to Jan Paul waving the lighter in front of him. "You want to know what I'm doing, Jan Paul? I read in one of my American novels... oh, I'm sorry you don't know that I've been reading at night while waiting for you. Well, I read in one of the novels that to get rid of your problems, you should put them into a fire and release them. Supposedly, it helps you to feel better."

Lizette turned towards the suitcases and strewn out clothes. "I actually think that it's a wonderful idea."

Jan Paul watched as his clothes went up in flames. Lizette turned around, walked past Jan Paul into the house, and closed the door behind her. She walked to the living room where Jan Paul wouldn't be able to see her and collapsed on the floor. Lizette sobbed until she fell asleep on the floor in the middle of the living room.

CHAPTER 45

Max walked towards the back of Tom's cottage. Tom told him that he would be pruning the back garden when Max arrived. Max turned the corner and found Tom admiring his rose bushes. He was dressed in gardening clothes, thick gloves, and was holding a hand hoe in his right arm while touching the roses with his left.

Tom looked up at the sound of footsteps approaching. "Ah, Max you made it. Be a good lad and hand me that bottle over there." Tom pointed to a water bottle standing on the table next to Max.

Max handed the water bottle to Tom. "How are things going?"

Tom took the water bottle from Max and continued with his gardening. "Everything is fine. I can't complain. How are things with you?"

Max hesitantly walked forward. Tom was his friend, but he knew that business was business. Tom would never put friendship over the company and protocol. Max chose his words carefully. "I was travelling through France the other day on my way to Switzerland."

Tom looked up. "Really, well did you enjoy yourself?"

Max continued to watch his words. "The landscape was beautiful, but unfortunately I saw a terrible car accident. A car went over the edge. Did it reach the papers here?"

Tom contemplated Max's words. "When did this accident occur?"

"Three days ago. I thought that you may have heard something." Max stared at Tom.

"I did hear something about that. Yes, it was a terrible accident, but I also heard that it was properly cleaned up." Tom moved onto his vegetable garden. He was making a tomato soup for dinner and needed to pick some tomatoes.

"Oh, so the cleaners cleared the way. Do they need to do anything else or have they covered the entire area?"

"I heard that everything was cleaned up, but you can never be one hundred percent certain. Why do you ask?" Tom began picking his tomatoes.

Max was tired of talking around the issue. "Look, Tom, do we have anything to worry about? I'm worried about innocent people getting hurt here."

Tom stood up with a basket full of tomatoes and zucchini. "We always cover our tracks. You're defending one brother, but you've taken your eyes off of the other one. Have you ever wondered why he would come and testify for a brother that attempted to take his life? What does he have to gain from this? If you know their background, then you know that they aren't saints. He didn't come to testify out of the goodness of his heart." Tom began walking to the backdoor of the house.

Max followed behind him. "Then what are you not telling me?"

Tom turned around and looked sympathetically at Max. "My dear friend, I can't help you with this one. You will need to figure the puzzle out on your own. What I will tell you is to be careful. Your defense team isn't the only player in this game. Good luck." Tom turned his back on Max and walked into his house closing the door behind him.

CHAPTER 46

Alex and William were walking through the courtyard of the Binnenhof, Holland's parliament building in The Hague. It was a brisk night and they had just returned from having dinner in Rotterdam. It was a brisk evening, but Alex and William decided to walk from Central Station, where the train stopped, to the center of town. It was such a nice evening that they decided to prolong their goodbye ritual and have coffee at a nearby bar. Alex could hear the click of her heels on the stone walkway as she watched the tourists taking pictures of the parliament building. She had to admit that Binnenhof was beautiful, especially at night. It looked like a miniature castle from the medieval era. The yellow lights shining from below and cascading the walls, and the little attached tower and moot added an extra touch.

William opened the bar door for Alex. He picked that bar especially because it was quiet and he could talk without interruption with Alex. William wanted to learn more about her. He was fascinated with her and thought that she was beautiful. Alex ordered a cup of tea and William a coke. He wouldn't have minded a beer, but decided to follow suit and order something non-alcoholic.

William looked at Alex as the waiter turned around to walk away. "Do you have a busy day tomorrow?"

Alex looked up at William. She had never been to this bar and was studying the menu when William began to speak. She put the menu down and smiled at William. "Yes, I have a busy day tomorrow, but that's nothing new. How about you?"

"I have to travel to a conference in Amsterdam, but should be back by dinner time. I wouldn't mind sharing dinner with you tomorrow, if you're willing." William stared at Alex waiting for a reply.

"Sorry, William. I would love to, but I have court until six-o'clock and then we have a team meeting afterwards," Alex sighed.

William looked disappointed. "You're having a team meeting that late in the evening? Can I ask what you're working on or is that confidential? I don't know how the legal process works or trials for that matter."

Alex smiled at William. He was fresh and didn't act like he knew everything already. "It's okay. It's nice to see that you're interested in what I'm doing. I'm working on the Joseph Kimbala case. Do you know who he is?"

A flicker of recognition passed over William's eyes. "I've heard of him in the news. He was the former president of Kilambèa. From the news, it sounds like he's not an angel. Don't you work for the defense? Are you okay with defending this man?" William looked troubled and concerned at the same time.

Alex laughed before answering William. "Remember that you can't always trust the news. Really, General Kimbala is just like any other human being on this planet and he deserves, just like anyone else, good representation."

William interrupted Alex. "You mean as long as he can pay for good representation?"

"Okay, okay I see where you're going with this, but he really does deserve to be represented and we're doing that with the best of our ability."

William looked into Alex's eyes. "Do you believe that he's innocent? You are correct that my knowledge comes from the newspapers, but you know more. Do you think that he's innocent and are you okay with defending him even if he's not innocent?"

Alex searched William's eyes for any hidden words or feelings. "William, I'm here to do my job, which is to help defend General Kimbala. It doesn't matter if he's guilty or innocent or if I think one way or the other. What matters is that I do my job effectively and to the best of my abilities."

William sat back in his chair and looked across the table at his date.

"I'm sorry, Alex. I don't want to offend or judge you. It's just that you have a really interesting job and I would be lying if I said that I wasn't curious and wanted to know more about what you do."

"It's fine. Please ask me anything you like. If I can't answer, then I will tell you. Do we have a deal?" Alex looked questioningly towards William.

"Deal. How about we enjoy the rest of this evening without shop talk though?" William smiled.

Alex gasped. "Now, wait a minute. This isn't fair. I'm also curious about what you do for a living. I want to ask one question tonight and then we can talk about other things. How does that sound?"

This time it was William's turn to laugh. "Shoot away!"

Alex stood up and took a seat next to William. "I'm a little embarrassed to ask this. I know that you work for a think tank, but what does that really mean?" Alex blushed.

William laughed and kissed Alex on the cheek. "It's okay. I work for Casing's, which is a conservative economic think tank. We track the economies of various countries around the world, conduct research and studies. We also write papers, give presentations, and produce a quarterly publication. Casing's is well known and our publications and studies are used as a reference by universities, companies and other organizations. Have any other questions?"

"Hmm, I'm sorry. I was stuck on the word 'conservative.' I didn't know that I was dating a stiff white collar," Alex giggled.

"What? I'm offended. You're supposed to be in absolute awe right now and grateful to be in my presence." William smiled.

"Oh, well I am grateful to be in your presence because you're so cute. Does that count?" Alex moved closer to William and gave him a kiss.

"Well, that's a start, but you're going to have to do more if you want to make it up to me. You really hurt my ego." William pouted while looking at Alex.

Alex smiled. "I think I can make the pain go away." She inched closer to William and wrapped her hands around his neck before giving him a long passionate kiss.

"I feel much better now. Thanks. Do you have any more questions for me?"

Alex took a moment to think of a follow-up question. "Do you like spending time with me?" Alex blushed again.

"Now, that has nothing to do with my job." William teased Alex.

"Now my ego is hurt," Alex said. She moved away from William. Alex knew that she had just taken a huge gamble asking that question.

William put his arms around Alex and moved her closer to him. "You're not getting away that easily." He hugged Alex and moved his head until his lips brushed against Alex's right ear. "Of course I do, Alex."

Alex collapsed in William's arms. She put her hands around his neck again and wished that she could hold on forever.

CHAPTER 47

Analise was happy. It had been a month since Jan Paul had separated from his wife. At first Jan Paul had wanted to reserve a hotel room, but Analise had talked him into staying at her place. She enjoyed spending more time with him and waking up to a warm body sleeping next to her in the morning. Their love life had improved since the hasty nights had disappeared. She knew that Jan Paul was worried about his colleagues and what people were thinking. She had to admit that she was also a bit worried. Many people were nice to her, but she did feel a cold front from a few of the team members and others in the building. Thanks to Greta, Analise also knew some of the rumors and jokes circulating around the office. Analise didn't pay it any mind as she walked through the corridors and worked with her colleagues. She smiled gingerly and equally with everyone. She didn't care what everyone thought as long as she got what she wanted and Jan Paul, and the status he carried, was what she wanted. Analise's contract was up at the end of the Kimbala case, but she had grown accustomed to the work at the Tribunal and wanted to stay. No, she thought not only stay, but climb higher on the ranks. Jan Paul was her ticket and no one was going to take that away.

Analise was going to the British Embassy for a party, but couldn't persuade Jan Paul to join her. She knew that attending the parties at the Embassy were important for networking, but Jan Paul didn't think that it was important to attend these gatherings. Instead, Jan Paul had decided to work in his office. She would stop by the office on her way home and persuade him to join her. She didn't want to sleep alone tonight.

Jan Paul sat in his office looking at the dossier for the following defense witness. He had decided to cross-examine the witness and wanted to be prepared seeing how the witness was going to begin in two days. He also wanted some time alone to think about his current situation. Jan Paul knew that he had made a mess of things. He was also aware of the rumors spreading around the office and he had to admit that being called into the Prosecutor's office that morning wasn't a plus.

The Prosecutor was known for being direct and she didn't spare Jan Paul either. She wanted to know what was going on and if the rumors were correct. She expected her lead counsel to be above reproach when it came to ethics and loyalty. She reminded Jan Paul of her feelings and that she wouldn't tolerate her married lead counsel having affairs around the office. Jan Paul was to take care of his mess immediately and she expected an update within the week. The Prosecutor stopped before giving Jan Paul the correct solution, but she did say that she expected him to choose correctly before dismissing him entirely.

Jan Paul put his paperwork down on the desk and then sat back in his chair. His last meeting with Lizette hadn't gone well. He still remembered his shopping spree the following day to replace his torched clothes. That was an expensive day. It had been a month since that night and Lizette was still scathing towards him, but neither of them had demanded a divorce. Maybe Lizette wanted to make him miserable instead? She changed the locks on the doors of their house and he also hadn't been allowed to see his kids. Lizette lied and told them that Jan Paul was on a mission for his work. If that wasn't bad enough, Lizette's mother knew the truth, which was like having two women scorned. However, Jan Paul had a bigger problem. Jan Paul's problem was that he loved two women or did he? He loved Lizette. Lizette was the woman that he decided to marry and have children with.

Analise was refreshing, impulsive, and new. He enjoyed being with her, but didn't know if it was love or lust. And, if it's lust, then when will they tire of each other? He also didn't know what Analise felt for him. He wasn't sure if Analise liked him for who he was or for his status and position.

At least Jan Paul knew that Lizette loved him for who he was. He had to make a decision and the Prosecutor wasn't giving him enough time, but he knew that his job was on the line if he didn't follow the Prosecutor's orders. Not only was his job in jeopardy, but his standing back home. He couldn't disappoint his country or family back in Belgium, not now.

---------------- CHAPTER 48 ----------------

The defense team sat in the war room. They were more than halfway through the defense case, but their minds were focused on the activities arising outside of the legal proceedings. Max and Scott were also sitting in the war room. Henry wanted them to give a report on Max's visit to London along with any follow-up information that they may have found. Henry put his cup of coffee on the table. It was a Friday night and they had just finished eating Chinese take away. Everyone agreed that the Chinese food tasted differently, but no one could agree on whether the Chinese food was better in Holland or Baltimore. Many of the team members were looking forward to going out later and hoped that Henry would release them before ten-o'clock.

Henry looked over towards Max. "How did your meeting with Tom go?"

Max wiped his mouth with a napkin and picked up his cup of tea before speaking. "It wasn't as easy as I thought it would be. They are hiding something and Tom was very secretive about it. He did confirm, indirectly, that Edwards was disposed of, but he wouldn't give me any other information. He did tell me that we needed to look into Karim Kimbala. He wondered why Karim would testify for someone who had tried to kill him."

Henry twitched and moved forward in his seat. "Wasn't that my question? I understand that they are brothers, but why would Karim do that and I still remember the odd conversation that I had with Karim when I dropped him off at the airport. Did Tom say anything else?"

Max shook his head. "I tried to get more information out of him, but he stopped me and said that we're on our own."

Henry looked at Max and the others. "We're missing a clue here. We need to figure out what's going on and what Karim Kimbala has to do with all of this. Max, I want you to travel back to South Africa along with your team. Figure out what Karim is up to now. Alex, I want you to research Karim's past and review the files on Joseph Kimbala and their activities. We'll meet tomorrow and I'll let you know exactly what I want. I want a full report by Tuesday afternoon. Now, I know that some of you had plans tonight. Go, have fun, and I'll see you tomorrow."

Alex rushed home to get ready for the night. She, along with Carter, Martie and Scott were going to meet William at a club in Amsterdam. Carter was the only experienced partygoer on the team. It was Alex, Martie and Scott's first club experience in Amsterdam and Alex couldn't wait. She also couldn't wait to see William. He had been away for the past couple of days travelling to Germany for his job and Alex missed him. They had slowly become closer over the past two months and Alex was beginning to share things with him, bring him more into her life. She began thinking of him as her boyfriend even though they hadn't talked about it yet. Somehow she thought that he felt the same even though they hadn't made a formal commitment to each other. Alex pulled her jeans up over her thin legs, added a casual come hither shirt and put sandals on to compliment the outfit. She then freshened her make-up, added some deodorant and perfume and headed for the door.

They were all meeting at Central Station and taking the train to Amsterdam, and she didn't want to be late. She liked the idea of taking the train because then everyone could drink and not worry about one person staying sober and driving everyone else around. She decided to start the night by ordering beers and wine on the train. They would roll into Amsterdam relaxed and ready for a night of clubbing.

Sam stayed behind with Henry. He walked back into the war room with two beers and sat down, "Do you really think that Karim Kimbala is the key? We're putting all of these resources and time into following a blind trail instead of focusing on the case at hand in the courtroom. Are you sure that we're not going to collapse at the end and lose the case too? I'm sorry for saying this Henry, but I'm just wondering if we're making the right decisions."

"I know, Sam, and I wonder the same, but my gut feeling is that we'll lose if we don't figure out what's going on outside of the courtroom. I also wonder if our client has told us the truth. Too many things have happened in this case. We have to figure out what's going on. More importantly, why aren't you out with the others? I hear they're going to Amsterdam." Henry took a swig of his beer.

Sam looked at Henry. "What do you mean? Who's going to stay and keep you company if I don't."

Henry sighed. "Are you staying here because William will be there?"

Sam stood up from his chair with beer in hand. "I don't know what you're talking about. I'm going to get some work down."

He was exiting the room when Henry made his last attempt. "She won't know how you feel if you don't tell her, you idiot."

Sam stopped for a moment and then continued walking to his office where he would have some peace.

Alex, Martie, Carter and Scott were waiting for William in a bar near the Amsterdam train station. They had started the evening on the train ride from The Hague to Amsterdam toasting the night with beers and white wine. Carter was at the bar ordering drinks while the others found seats nearby. It was ten-o'clock and the bars were still sleeping. Everyone would start moving like cockroaches around twelve midnight. It would be impossible to find a seat let alone stand freely without bumping elbows with complete strangers. The team wanted to start the night off slowly plus some of them were meeting William for the first time. Alex wanted Martie and Scott to have some talk time with William before they moved onto the club.

Carter came back with a round of drinks and appetizers to start the night off. Alex looked at the variety of appetizers. Fried cheese balls, chicken nuggets, and Dutch bitterballen covered the plate along with different sauces for dipping.

Alex couldn't believe her eyes. "Uhm, Carter we just ate Chinese at the office. What are you trying to do? Kill us?"

Carter looked defiantly at Alex. "We have a long drinking night ahead of us and we don't want hangovers in the morning seeing how Mr. Boome has ordered us back in the office tomorrow – on a Saturday!" Carter put the appetizers in the middle of the table and began handing drinks around.

Scott always drank beer and had become accustomed to drinking Grolsch when he visited the office in The Hague. Martie had moved onto a gin and tonic while Carter handed Alex the Dutch version of a Piña Colada. Carter was drinking beer from the tap. William walked into the bar and made his way over to the group.

Martie leaned over to Alex. "Is this the man that you've been talking about?"

Alex smiled back at Martie and nodded her head. Martie gave an approving look back. "Well done. Can you find one just like him for me?"

Alex and Martie giggled as William arrived at the table. "Hi everyone. What's so funny?" William looked confused as if he had walked in the middle of a joke.

Scott shook his head and stuck his hand out to shake William's hand. "They're just a little drunk. You must be William. I'm Scott, one of the investigators working with Alex."

Martie interjected. "A little drunk? This is our second drink."

"Exactly, ladies. How are you doing William?" Carter replied.

William shook Carter's hand while responding. "I'm great. It's good to see you again. Hey, I'll be right back. I'm going to get something to drink from the bar. Does anyone want anything?" William looked around.

Alex stood up. "I'll go with you."

"Ah, young love...." Carter smiled at the couple.

Alex was blushing as she told Carter to shut up. William stole a kiss while they were waiting in line at the bar. He wrapped his arms around her middle and swung her gently from side to side. "How's my girl doing?"

Alex looked up playfully into William's eyes. "Oh, I'm your girl? I don't remember us going onto the next level?"

"What do you mean the next level?"

"I mean boyfriend, girlfriend."

William kissed Alex gently on her neck and brushed his lips across her ear before softly whispering. "I didn't think that we had to question that." William gently kissed Alex on the lips before giving her a hug. Alex couldn't hide her happiness kissing William back. They walked back to the group holding hands.

-------------------- CHAPTER 49 --------------------

Alex walked down the tree lined street towards the office. It was a bright Sunday morning and the wind brushed gently over Alex's cheeks and legs causing a wave effect with Alex's trench coat. The leaves cascaded across the street and over Alex's feet as she walked. Alex thought back to her meeting with Henry the day before. She decided to walk this morning instead of taking the bike in order to clear her mind and organize her thoughts.

She walked all day yesterday on cloud nine after leaving a sleeping William in her bed. It was their first night together and Alex had decided not to wake him. She silently hoped that he would still be there when she returned. She began thinking back to two nights ago when their relationship became formal. Alex never thought that she would involve herself with any man while working in Holland let alone have a serious relationship. She felt that her personal life was placed on hold until she finished the Kimbala case and moved back home. It was a small personal sacrifice when building a career, Alex thought. But, now she was in a relationship with a gorgeous man. She would worry about the practical matters of different nationalities and a possible long distance relationship when the time came. Alex decided to enjoy the present for as long as she could.

She had to admit that William was becoming a distraction. Some of her colleagues, Martie for one, thought that it was a good distraction. Carter also thought that it was a good distraction. He administered Alex's billable hours and shared his worries about her long work hours. She was working more than fifty hours of overtime per month. As far as Alex was concerned, fifty hours was the same as twenty hours. She only cared that the work was done. Alex was halfway when she turned her thoughts to her current urgent project. She had about five other urgent projects coming from all three attorneys, but Henry made a point yesterday that this project was to take top priority. Alex had called the Baltimore office to make sure that her assistants also came to work today. She would need them to compile and log documents onto the system so that Alex could pick them up tomorrow. It was eight-o'clock in The Hague making it two-o'clock in Baltimore. Alex made a mental note to call the Baltimore office at three thirty this afternoon. Her assistants would arrive at nine-o'clock. If she called at three thirty her time, then it would give them a half hour to organize themselves and get a cup of coffee.

Alex turned the corner and breathed in the fresh morning air. The streets were quiet and everyone was either still sleeping or getting ready for church. Henry had told Alex that he wanted her to pull any and all factual information on Karim Kimbala. He wanted to know everything about the man. She needed to liaise with Max and his investigation in South Africa. She also needed to conduct general research by combing past and present newspaper articles mentioning Karim Kimbala. She also needed to search the legal databases to see if Karim was involved in any court cases. Henry basically wanted a biography from Karim's birth to now.

She was also tasked with creating a diagram showing Karim's government along with his allies, enemies and common alliances, acquaintances, and friends with his brother Joseph. Henry wanted to know every detail including the place of Karim's birth mark and by Tuesday afternoon. Although the team had a few files on Karim Kimbala, Alex knew that she couldn't finish this project alone. She would need to lean on her assistants and Carter who was also coming into the office. Carter was not going to be a happy man being asked to come in on a Sunday morning, but Alex needed him if her project was going to be successful. Alex walked up the stairs and unlocked the front door. She entered and was greeted with silence. She hung her coat up in the foyer, placed her briefcase in her office, and then walked straight to the kitchen to make the first pot of coffee for the day. The first pot of coffee would transform the odorless empty space into an aromatic lively work space. Alex inhaled the coffee bean smell as the beans poured into the coffee machine. She poured water into the reservoir and then turned to arranging the breakfast pastries on a plate when the front door cranked open. Alex listened for the first sound of a voice and then it came.

"I'm here," Carter said in a gruff voice.

Alex smiled. It was just the voice she wanted to hear. "Good morning, sunshine. Come in the kitchen. I have breakfast ready. We can sit down and eat first, then get to work."

Carter stood in the doorway and leaned against the door frame. "I know that you don't expect me to be cheery on a freakin' Sunday morning? Where's Mr. Boome? He should be sitting down with us for coffee this morning. Where's the rest of the gang? They don't expect us to be the only ones working today?" Carter sauntered over to the table and sat down.

Alex turned around and noticed that his sunglasses were still on. "Look, they're coming in soon and you know that..." Alex stopped at the sound of the front door opening.

She looked at Carter with a raised eyebrow. "See, I told you so. Now, how about some coffee?"

Martie walked into the kitchen and took her mug out of the cabinet for a cup of coffee. She turned to Carter and then Alex. "Good morning everyone. How is everybody doing?"

She filled her coffee mug, picked up a pastry and sat down at the kitchen table. Carter grunted hello and continued munching on his pastry while Alex chimed in with a smile.

"Good morning, Martie. I placed the witness sequence list on your desk. We have a problem with witness number five, one of our insiders. The witness unit called last night saying that the witness refused to enter the plane and doesn't want to testify. They also told me that the witness that's here now, Mr. Cross, is also now refusing to testify. I left the information on your desk and told the witness unit that you would call them back today with instructions."

Martie rose from the table. "Thanks, Alex. There goes my peaceful morning out the door. I'll be at my desk if you need me." Martie picked up her coffee and walked out of the room.

------------------ CHAPTER 50 ------------------

Sam was camped out in the defense war room. Ten binders containing materials on Karim Kimbala lay sprawled across the long table. Sam was impressed with Alex's work and felt as if Karim Kimbala's entire life up until now covered the pages on the table. Sam had begun four hours earlier reading the short summary on Karim Kimbala. He then had moved onto Karim's teenage years and now he was deep into Karim Kimbala's rise to presidency. He read the articles about the militia group that Karim belonged to in his late teens and early twenties. He began browsing over the militia photos before taking a swig of his Heineken beer. He studied the photos carefully one by one, hoping to uncover a secret. He then moved onto the file containing information on Karim's successful coup attack. Sam was halfway through the pile of documents and articles about Karim's presidency when he decided to join the group in the kitchen for dinner. Seven straight hours of reading made him famished and Italian food was going to hit the spot.

Sam returned to the war room after dinner. Henry expected a report the following afternoon and Sam had yet to find anything to report. All trails were leading to Karim Kimbala, but Sam felt as if they were invisible trails. He didn't know what he was looking for and felt helpless. What was he missing? Sam read through to Joseph's successful rise to presidency, Karim's demise, and then began to read every document again from the beginning. He hoped to find a clue the second time around.

Alex walked into the war room to pick up an upcoming witness file when she saw Sam hunched over one of the binders deep in thought. She hesitated before saying "How's it going? Can you find what you need?"

Alex knew that Sam had been putting in a lot of hours at work lately and was worried about him. Sam was known to be a dedicated worker, but this was even a new level of devotion for him. Sam looked up realizing for the first time that another person was in the room.

He smiled at Alex and turned the page. "I haven't been able to find anything that would help us yet." Sam sat back in the chair and threw his pen across the table. "I've read everything so far, but I'm hoping that I've missed something. So, I'm going through it a second time." Sam shook his head and rolled his sleeves up.

Alex could tell that Sam wasn't going to give up until he found something. Maybe this even meant another office sleep over. Alex thought back to the home office and how Sam always came over as a self-confident man; as if he could accomplish anything he set his mind to and with ease. Alex knew that it was all an illusion especially now that she'd been able to spend so much time with Sam and the others too. They slowly transformed into regular human beings before her eyes. They were self-confident on the outside to their colleagues and enemies, but vulnerable to their friends and the people that took time out to actually see them as people.

Alex looked at her watch. William was coming by to say good-bye before leaving for Belgium for a business trip. Alex looked back at Sam while pointing to five green binders at the end of the table. "Have you looked through those binders yet?"

Sam looked over to where Alex had pointed. "No, I haven't looked at those yet." He stood up and walked over to pick up one of the binders. He then looked at the spine labels of the other two. "These are the financial records for Karim and Joseph Kimbala."

Alex looked at Sam. "Were you planning on reading through them?"

Sam looked a little confused at Alex's question. "Actually no, but maybe I should."

Alex was surprised. "Sam, you know that the Kimbalas completed a lot of financial transactions during their prime time, right? Some transactions were done together and others not. There is some interesting information in there and I thought that you might find something that we can use."

Sam sighed and sunk back down in his chair. "You're right, Alex. I can't believe that I didn't think of this myself." Sam put his head down onto the table, "I'm so tired. That must be it." He raised his head and massaged his temples with his fingers. Alex felt sorry for him.

William walked through the door. "Good evening, everyone." He looked first at Alex and then Sam. "Is this a bad time?" William looked concerned looking first at his girlfriend and then towards Sam.

Alex walked towards William and gave him a hug. "No, you just walked in to a regular day on the job. We're trying to find the key to our case and Sam is having a little bit of a difficulty. But, I'm glad that you're here because I can introduce you now to Sam."

Sam stood up to shake hands with William. "Hi, William. It's nice to meet you finally. I've heard a lot about you."

William looked familiar to Sam, but he couldn't figure out why. He looked like someone that Sam had met before, but couldn't place where.

William smiled back and shook Sam's hands. "Same here. Alex has told me many nice things about you. Actually, she's told me many nice things about everyone that she works with."

Alex interrupted him. "Now, you don't have to share everything that I've told you. Sam, how about I help you with these binders? I know what's in them and it'll be faster if I guide you through the materials. Do you want me to help?"

"At this point, Alex, I wouldn't say no. I think that I need an extra pair of eyes right now."

"Good, I'm going to see William out and then we can start."

Sam stood up looking a little embarrassed. "I'm sorry, William. Where are my manners? I've spent the last seven hours reading this material." Sam gestured to the sprawled out documents and open binders that camouflaged the desk. "Would you like a beer?"

"Sure, that would be great," William smiled.

"Are you sure? When do you need to be at the airport," Alex inquired.

"It's fine. I'm taking the red-eye flight. I can stay for a little bit and then I'll take a taxi to the airport."

"Wonderful, you can try and find an empty seat in this mess. I'll go get some beers." Sam walked out of the room.

Alex quickly gave William a kiss on his cheek. "Take your coat off. I'll help him with the drinks and get some chips too. I'm glad that I'll get to spend some more time with you even if a colleague is sharing that time." Alex winked and walked out of the room to join Sam in the kitchen.

Sam and Alex returned a few minutes later with drinks and snacks. "So, what do you think of our little war room?" Sam asked.

William took a swig of his Heineken beer and looked around the room. Binders were stacked neatly on the six bookshelves that flanked the room. A typed written label adorned each binder spine. Any organizing freak would have admired the work that was put into organizing the book shelves.

William settled his focus once again on the table situated in the center of the room, where they were sitting. The table was a stark contrast to the bookshelves and screamed chaos. William sat back in his chair and accidentally bumped his elbow against one of the binders that was stacked on an adjoining chair. The binder fell unceremoniously to the floor causing an avalanche of photos and various documents to spread out umbrella style on the floor.

William bent down and began gathering the sprawled documents and photos. He quietly slipped one photo into his jacket pocket before sitting up again. "Well, it looks like you guys are really busy."

"The room usually doesn't look this bad. Alex organized the room and likes to keep it tidy. I think she's being lenient with me because of a project that I've been assigned to by Henry."

"It must be a big project and important too."

"It is actually. Our defense case hasn't been going well lately. So, we had to look at our options. Sorry, do you know anything about this case?"

"Not a lot. I mean I know the basics. Alex doesn't like to talk about her work too much, but I'm interested in what goes on here. It's not every day that a person can see what goes on behind the scenes in an international war crimes case."

"That's a good idea not to talk about work outside of the office."

"Exactly. I already work so many hours and take work home with me. It's good to have a break and talk about other things. How about we compromise? I'll give you a tour of the building instead?"

"I was actually serious about learning more, but I understand how you feel." William looked over at Sam. "Maybe we can get together once I'm back and you can tell me more about the case?" William asked.

"That sounds like a great idea, William. I'm looking forward to it." Sam shook hands with William.

Alex was happy that she wouldn't have to talk about the case. "And now for the tour. As you have been told, this is our war room. All of the documentation that we have been using in the case is filed here so that everyone has access. Any motion that has been filed in the case can be found here in this room. That also goes for witness documentation and copies of exhibits that have been tendered in the case. Follow me and I'll show you the rest of the office space."

Alex walked out hand in hand with William. Sam felt a stabbing pain watching the two leave the room.

"You've seen my office already. Martie's office is down the hall opposite Sam's office. Henry's office is right next to Sam's office. We don't have a lot of space so the secretaries share a common room next to my office." Alex stepped into the common room with William following behind her.

"This room is huge," William let out a gasp.

"I know. They have the most space. I like what they've done with the décor adding the green plants and flowers. It almost looks as if they're working in a park instead of an office space."

"It is nice. They should come and decorate my office," William said.

Alex laughed. "I have a feeling that Carter would come over if you asked him nicely." Alex walked over to the light switch and turned the lights off. "We're going into the kitchen now."

"How big is this place?" William asked.

"We have two floors. Another business has the third floor. They have an entrance at the back of the building. Now, this is our popular kitchen. It is probably the second most used space in this office."

"What's the first most used space?"

"Follow me and I'll show you." Alex walked out of the kitchen and walked up the adjoining stairs to the second floor. She turned left once she reached the top of the stairs and entered a large lounge area. "This is the most used space in this office."

William looked around. A television hung above the fireplace. A large couch faced the television while two love seats had been placed on either side of the couch forming a u-shape. Large green potted plants were placed strategically around the room providing a calming effect.

"I really need to see if Carter will come to my office." William looked around in awe.

Alex giggled. "I'll show you the last room on the tour."

They walked out of the common room and strolled down the hallway to the last door on the right. Alex opened the door. "This is our storage room. Not the most luxurious room, but it works."

"Well, you have to put things somewhere." William sighed.

"That is quite true," Alex said.

"Thanks for the tour, baby. I hate to say this, but I need to leave for my trip."

Alex escorted William downstairs and gave him a hug and kiss. William picked up his luggage and walked outside to find a taxi.

Alex walked back into the room with a cup of tea and a cookie. She sat down next to Sam and opened one of the binders. Sam watched Alex's every move and was tempted to reach his hand out and brush her hair back behind her ear.

Sam sat back instead and attempted a joke. "Where's my cookie?"

Alex looked up and offered her cookie. "I'm sorry. Do you want mine?"

"No, that's okay. I'm just kidding. What are you looking at there?" Sam gestured towards the binder.

Alex became excited. She liked talking about her work. "These binders include summaries and detailed information of the Kimbala's financial histories. Their financial histories cover the period between pre-coup period and Joseph Kimbala's fall. This binder here covers the first years or pre-coup era. We have their bank statements and information on their black market ventures. The second and third binders continue with more of the same, but also include information on their government activities. That's also the time when the brothers began to actively use off-shore accounts and the stock markets. The fourth binder is skinnier because of the instability of the government and Joseph Kimbala's coup attempt. The fifth binder contains information mostly on Joseph Kimbala's finances seeing how Karim was, by then, living in exile. Where do you want to start?" Alex looked at Sam with a twinkle of excitement in her eyes.

Sam shrugged his shoulders and sighed. "I guess we'll begin at the beginning."

Henry sat at the table in the war room while Sam and Alex stood before him. They had spent most of the night at the office poring over the documents until the Kimbala's financial history took shape. They had finally finished at two-o'clock, closed the door, and cycled home half asleep. Henry sat back and crossed his legs. He was curious to find out what the two had come up with especially after Sam's call at six-o'clock. Sam only disturbed him before eight o'clock if he had found a gold mine and Henry was anxious to find out what the gold mine was this time around.

Sam took a sip of his Coca Cola and then began. "Henry, Alex and I reviewed all of the financial documents last night and pieced the Kimbala's financial history together. Now, we know that the Kimbalas have kosher and some non-kosher dealings financially. The Kimbalas both have normal, legal bank accounts including savings. They also have shares in stock markets, both together and separate. It looks as if the shared stock options are valued at five hundred thousand at today's rate. We dug deeper and learned that the Kimbala's black market dealings range from weapons deals with neighboring countries and forced prostitution including human trafficking. Of course we don't have an estimate on the black market sales, but I'm sure they didn't do it for fun. We also found out, well Max did, that both brothers embezzled funds from the government."

Sam looked at Henry. He knew that this information wasn't interesting to Henry. He knew that Henry would already know this part of the story so he decided to peak Henry's interest. "The funny thing is that the Kimbala's both embezzled money during their presidencies. We've all heard the rumors about them embezzling, but never thought that they would have conspired together during Joseph's presidency…"

Henry sat up and interrupted Sam. "What do you mean?"

Alex took over the conversation. "What we're saying is that Joseph and Karim Kimbala had contact with each other even after Joseph attempted to kill Karim. They have an off-shore account that was created shortly after Joseph took over the presidency. Money was placed in the account every month until Joseph landed in The Hague. The account has been valued at seven million dollars."

Henry shook his head. "Why would the two of them have a joint account? One brother tried to kill the other. More than that, Joseph took over Karim's job, killed Karim's family, and made Karim flee the country. This has got to be the strangest family relationship that I've seen so far."

"We thought that this information would interest you. Alex called Max this morning and he's travelling to Kilambèa this afternoon to find out more information."

CHAPTER 51

"The defense has less than ten witnesses left and we still have a lot of work to do. Meredith is taking the next two crime based witnesses. Henry is taking the third witness, which is also a small witness. You're taking the expert witness after that, and I'll take the following two. And then we'll only have one witness left to deal with. We need to talk about the closing brief, Jan Paul." Gabriel shifted in his seat.

Jan Paul had caused him a lot of stress in the past few months and his blood pressure rose every time he was summoned to Jan Paul's office. He also heard all of the rumors streaming through the office about Jan Paul and Analise. He saw a few signs, but decided to ignore them. If the rumors were correct, then Gabriel was going to lose all respect for Jan Paul, but at least he would understand what part Jan Paul was thinking with. Gabriel only knew one thing for sure: he would make sure that Jan Paul regretted the day he stepped over the line. Jan Paul needed to realize that he was playing with all of their careers and not just his own.

Jan Paul looked over his desk at Gabriel. He could tell that Gabriel was anxious to leave the office. Their relationship had deteriorated gradually over the past two weeks and Gabriel's patience had become short when talking with Jan Paul. Jan Paul also noticed that Gabriel had disrespected him a few times during the team meetings, but Jan Paul had ignored it. His mind was on other things. He had talked with Analise last week and made it clear that he had to stop their relationship. She hadn't taken it well. In fact, she had told him that she didn't believe him and that he should stop making jokes. She had even stopped by his hotel room last night wearing only a coat. He had meant to turn her away, but ended up following her to bed. Jan Paul was losing control; not only in his personal life, but also at work.

"You've been edgy and distant lately, Gabriel. Is there something wrong?" Jan Paul knew that there were no secrets in this building. He didn't share his marital problems with anyone at work, but he was sure that everyone knew. He also knew that everyone must know about his affair with Analise by know. They always knew.

Gabriel stared back at Jan Paul. He felt uncomfortable, but rage made him speak. "Are you having an affair with Analise, our paralegal?"

Jan Paul sat back and sighed. "Well, there goes the distant part. I didn't expect you to be so blunt, Gabriel. What does my personal life have to do with you?"

Gabriel sat straight up in his chair; his frustration and anger turning into agitation. "What does your personal life have to do with me? Your personal life is affecting this entire case yet alone all of us. What do you mean with 'what does my personal life have to do with you?' We already have to deal with your mediocre talent as lead counsel, but you're screwing all of our careers at the same time…"

"This tone is unacceptable, Gabriel. I won't have you talk to me this way." Jan Paul's face turned red from shock and anger.

Gabriel rose from his chair and walked to the door. He put his hand on the door knob before turning back to Jan Paul. "Wake up, Jan Paul. We're hanging on a thread here and our so-called leader is lost in our paralegal's panties. All of us have made sacrifices for this case. We've worked long and hard hours to pull things together without a leader at the top. We've basically put our lives on hold. Sabrina hasn't seen her kid for more than three hours at a stretch for the past year. Suzanne is threatening to leave me and move back home. We're not the only ones suffering here, but I'll be damned if we also lose this case. You better wake up and get back into the game or I'm going to the prosecutor and demand that you be taken off of this case." Gabriel opened the door and stormed out of Jan Paul's office.

Jan Paul remained behind his desk and whispered. "Don't worry my friend, the prosecutor already knows."

CHAPTER 52

Max, Henry and Sam gathered in the war room. Max had just returned from South Africa with new intel and Henry wanted a debriefing before the end of the morning. Alex and Martie were in court examining their current witness and Henry promised to join them later if necessary. Max was busy pinning pictures of Karim Kimbala's known associates on the cork board. Sam and Henry were drinking coffee and sharing details of their sleepless nights. They both agreed that stress was the cause and moved onto the cookies that Carter had brought especially for morning coffees in the office. Max finished pinning the last picture on the cork board and then turned around facing both Henry and Sam.

Max picked up his cup of coffee and began talking. "The first picture is Edwards and Karim sitting at the restaurant in South Africa. We all know this one. Scott and I were sitting not too far from them when this picture was taken. The next picture is an old associate of both Karim and Joseph Kimbala. His name is Kevin Cray and he used to be the brother's middle man on their international financial matters. Cray tracked their stocks and kept their bank accounts in order. He recently visited Karim in South Africa. Scott did a background check on Cray and I bought the report with me." Max handed copies of a detailed report on Cray to both Henry and Sam.

"He's from New Orleans which made it easier for us to track him. He's a certified accountant in New Orleans, but handles accounts for various persons around the world. Most of his clients are criminals and the Feds have also placed him on their radar once or twice. He came into contact with the brothers during Karim's presidency when Karim invited him to visit Kilambèa. Cray only takes on new clients through references made by his regular clients. He started out by creating off-shore accounts for the brothers. He then increased his business with the brothers over the years until he became their main accountant. This man is holding many secrets that we want to know. He continued to do business with Joseph once Joseph took control of Kilambèa. The odd thing is that Scott was able to track transactions that Cray made on behalf of Karim at the same time. What's even worse is that some of the transactions were made in both of the brother's names. We all believed that Karim and Joseph cut ties after Joseph attempted to kill Karim, but the paperwork trail is saying something else. We just don't know why. I have Scott working full-time along with the others on this puzzle and of course Alex is informed and maintaining a duplicate set of whatever we find here."

"How long do you think it will take before you know more about the brother's financial transactions?" Sam wondered if this task was going to be finished before the end of the trial.

"I know you're worried that we'll finish our investigation after the trial, which will be too late, but we're working as fast as possible." Max looked at Sam and then Henry.

Henry focused intently at each picture, but said nothing. Max wasn't worried though with Henry's reactions. He knew that Henry was absorbing all of the information so that he could make a decision on what the team needed to do next.

Max pointed at the last picture. "The last picture is of a man that Karim befriended in South Africa. They met each other shortly after Karim moved there and have, it seems, become very close if not best friends. The man's name is Nicholas Raine and he grew up in South Africa. They used to see each other frequently, but our surveillance shows that the two haven't been seen together the last three months. It looks like these two were good friends, but Scott is going to confirm that after he's finished researching Raine's background and his relationship with Karim."

Sam stood up and walked over to get a better look at the photos. He stopped at the last one. "This guy looks familiar to me. Do you have any other photos? Any photos better than this one?"

Max looked into his briefcase and pulled out a beige folder. He placed a packet of photos on the table. Sam and Max began rifling through the photos until Sam found what he was looking for.

"I have seen this guy before…" Sam looked at Henry. The color faded quickly from his face.

Henry snapped out of his thoughts. "What's wrong, Sam?"

Sam looked at the photo hoping that he was wrong until he looked at the man in the photo and knew that he was correct. "We have a real problem, here. This is Alex's boyfriend, William."

A concerned silence engulfed the war room. If this was true, then they had more to worry about then a rogue boyfriend. This meant that an outsider had infiltrated the team. He had access to the entire office and no one paid close attention to a man that worked at a think tank; a think tank that had no interest in their work. The team would have to worry about what this William or Nicholas had overheard and what documents he may have seen. More importantly, everyone knew how happy Alex was nowadays. She was going to be crushed. Alex was the type of daughter that Henry would have liked to have had.

"Are you sure about this, Sam?" Henry put his hand out to stop Sam from answering. "Let's not beat around the bush here. I want you to honestly think this through. I know that you have feelings for Alex and it hurts to see her with another man, but this accusation, if true, will hurt this team in more than one way. Are you sure that this man in the picture is William?" Henry put his hand down as a sign that it was okay for Sam to speak.

Sam sighed and looked at the photo again. He admitted that he had feelings for Alex, but he also didn't intend on hurting her. Sam looked at Henry. Anguish filled his eyes as he said. "I'm sure Henry. I'm sorry, but I'm sure that this is William. He has a mustache in this photo. That's why I didn't pick up on it earlier. But, do you see this little birth mark here underneath his right eye? William has the same birth mark. What are we going to do?"

"I don't know," is all that Henry could summon to answer.

"We should have completed a security check," Max said.

"Hindsight is always better, but who would have thought that this could happen? We are also juggling too many balls at the same time. Adding security checks for anyone that enters the office would add chaos to the madness," Henry said. "Listen, I just need a little bit of time to think this through."

The front door opened and closed. The guys could hear Alex and Martie's voices as they entered the office premises.

Max walked over and closed the door to the war room. "Whatever you decide, Henry, it should be fast. If this Nicholas guy is Alex's boyfriend, then we have a real problem. We still haven't figured out the connection between this Nicholas and Karim. We were thinking that they were just good friends, but if William is Nicholas, then we know that something else may be going on. We can't place Alex in danger knowingly. Also, remember that there may still be a connection between the brothers. We have too many unanswered questions and not enough time to find answers."

"I know that, Max, but thanks for the clarity of the situation. We're all concerned here for Alex's safety, but we have to think this through for her sake too. Max, see what else your team can figure out. Has Alex seen any of these photos?"

"No, this was her set for the file here."

"Okay, if she asks, then tell her that you forgot them or decided to have them sent via courier. Sam, go see how the witness did today. Act normal, but don't say anything about this meeting. You can leave the photos with me. I'm going to sit here for a little while. We'll have a plan in motion by tomorrow afternoon."

It was the end of the day and Alex was preparing to leave the office. She put her black trench coat on and then proceeded to turn the computer and lights off. Sam came around the corner and appeared in her office doorway as Alex turned the main light off. Alex's umbrella collided into Sam's leg causing Sam to bend over gasping.

Alex quickly recovered from the shock and put her hand on Sam's shoulder. "Are you okay? Did I hurt you?"

Sam looked up while massaging his right knee. "No worries, I'm okay. Are you about to head out?"

"Yeah, I'm going to meet William in the center. Are you working late?"

Sam took one step backwards staring at Alex. "Oh, no. I was hoping to catch you. I thought that we could have dinner tonight. It's been so hectic the past months that we haven't been able to take time out and just talk." Sam didn't want to give her too many options.

He wanted to keep Alex away from this William person until they knew who he really was and what his intentions with Alex were.

"That's a great idea and I wish that we could have dinner tonight, but I'm meeting William in the center for dinner and he doesn't have his cell phone on him." Alex walked through the doorway towards the front door.

Sam followed her. Alex suddenly turned around and smiled. "Can I take a rain check?"

"Of course you can. We'll do it when you're free. We can talk tomorrow." Sam opened the door and watched as Alex drove her bike down the street and out of eyesight.

-------------------- CHAPTER 53 --------------------

Sabrina sat in Gabriel and Gert's office. They spent the last half hour sharing office gossip and public secrets. All of them understood that the international community was a world of its own and that secrets were hard to keep in such a small community. Analise hadn't worked in the unit for a year yet had made her way into their boss' bed. Not only had she done that, but also helped to distract him from the case. The team was frustrated and morale had hit an all time low. Sabrina was a regular in Gabriel's office, but he had gotten used to having regular traffic nowadays. From their other colleagues, the staff had begun to look at Gabriel for leadership and security. It was a Wednesday evening and most of the team had left the building. Gabriel closed the door and Gert placed wine and liquor glasses on the desk. Gabriel pulled out the red wine and rum and tonic. Gert poured the glasses. This was a weekly gathering and he already knew what Sabrina and Gabriel wanted to drink.

Sabrina looked up at the ceiling and sighed. The court session was finished for the day, but certain parts of the day kept replaying in Sabrina's head. The defense had placed a key expert on the witness stand to testify about events that had occurred in Kilambèa. His testimony would weaken the prosecution's case. The prosecution needed desperately to cast doubt on this witness's testimony. The problem, Sabrina knew, was that Jan Paul was going to cross-examine the witness. Sabrina thought back to a week ago when she sat in this office brainstorming with Gabriel and a couple of others on how to stop Jan Paul from taking this particular witness. Their efforts had been relentless and ended with Jan Paul beginning the cross-examination of the expert witness, Jan Miller, three hours ago. The nervous team members had watched their monitors as the prosecution's case weakened with every question that Jan Paul asked.

Many of the team members had left already for the day. They were unwilling to stay around and help revive the case. Sabrina and Gabriel didn't even call or walk to Jan Paul's office to offer assistance. They had decided that a drink or few was a better way to spend their time. Gert couldn't take it anymore. He was working on a different African case and team altogether, but felt as if he was a part of Gabriel's team with all of the information he knew and advice he gave to others on Gabriel's team. He had been stuck in legal seminars all day and missed the hourly updates from the team members that constantly popped into their office.

He wanted to know what he missed. "So, what's the scoop on what happened today? Did Jan Paul pull it off?"

"Did he pull it off? We're near disaster! We knew that he was not in a state to cross-examine a military expert. The defense found an expert that says that there was chaos in Kilambèa during the indictment period and that Kimbala was president in theory. The NIS acted on their own accord and Kimbala didn't have knowledge of the rogue acts committed by the NIS. Furthermore, they're using this witness to show that the NIS was forging Kimbala's signature on key orders and that Kimbala would have stopped the NIS if he had known that they were committing these heinous acts. I don't know which was worse – swallowing what the defense was trying to pull or Jan Paul's performance. We have three days more of torture." Gabriel reached for his rum and tonic.

He wished that he was somewhere else. This case was becoming a jail sentence for him and he hoped that the sentence would run out before his sanity did.

"Most of the team is gone. We were watching the monitors in the team room and couldn't believe what we were watching. I tell you, Gabriel, the morale in the team has fallen to an all time low. Adam actually turned the monitors off halfway through the cross-examination and walked out. I haven't seen him since and no one knows where he went." Sabrina looked beaten and tired.

Gabriel looked at her and thought that if anyone had the most to lose emotionally with this case, then it was Sabrina. She was fighting for justice for her family and her homeland. She must feel it a mockery that this idiot was placed in charge of something that changed the course of her life, he thought.

"What did he do today to cause Adam's walking out? Adam doesn't lose it this easily?" Gert felt as if he'd missed a lot that day. He hated attending those seminars because he missed a lot at work.

"The question is what he didn't do. He didn't object during the examination in chief so a lot of evidence went into the record without a fight. Now he's doing the cross-examination and doesn't ask the pertinent questions. We spent the past three days helping Jan Paul to prep for cross examination and he didn't take our advice at all. I don't even know why he asked for our help in the first place."

"How many more hours does he have for cross?"

"He has to finish by the end of tomorrow's session. Then the witness is free to go and we have to move onto the next witness."

"Well, if this witness is so important to you, then maybe you need to go and see what Jan Paul is doing right now."

Gabriel swallowed a large gulp of his drink. "He's probably lost in our paralegal's underpants right now. He's definitely not spending time on this case or at home with his wife and kids."

Sabrina looked earnestly towards Gabriel. "What are we going to do, Gabriel?"

Gabriel looked back at Sabrina and shrugged his shoulders. "I don't know, Sabrina. I'm so sorry that this is happening to you. That this idiot is in charge of this case."

CHAPTER 54

Alex climbed out of bed and walked towards the bathroom. Her nipples were hard and she could still feel the wetness dripping down her legs. She wished that she could crawl back into bed, sprawl her legs over William, waking him up by rubbing herself gently over William's penis before pushing his manhood into her, but she needed to get to work. William turned over onto his side and watched as Alex walked towards the bathroom. He felt himself getting harder with every step she took. Alex turned the shower on and stepped inside. She reached for her bath sponge and favorite perfume wash gel. The shower door opened as Alex began washing her legs. She turned around slightly to see William's hard penis and stood up as William entered the shower and closed the door. He kissed her passionately before turning her around and taking the bath sponge. He began cleaning her back by softly moving the bath sponge in circular motion across her back. He used his other hand to play with her nipples before moving down to her vagina. Alex balanced herself by pressing one hand up against the shower wall. She then felt her way with her other hand to William's penis. She loved touching his masculinity. She released his penis and pressed her other hand against the shower wall completely releasing control over to William.

William dropped the sponge and cupped Alex's breast with both hands and kissed her neck. He then moved in closer until his chest was touching

Alex's back. Alex shivered with pleasure tilting her head back onto William's shoulder. It was six-o'clock in the morning and court wasn't due to start for three hours. Alex thought that work could wait. She moved her hand down William's stomach to his penis. William groaned and turned Alex around. They looked caringly at each other and smiled not noticing the warm water trickling down their bodies. William bent down and kissed Alex while pulling her up with both arms. He lifted her up against the shower wall and then thrust himself inside. Alex closed her eyes and forgot about work and her worries.

It was eight-o'clock when Alex walked through the front door. She rushed to her office to pick up a folder that she needed for court.

She turned around and Henry was standing in the door way. "Oh, good morning Henry. I know that I'm running late, but I just came to pick up this folder. I'm heading over to the courtroom now. Do you want me to take anything for you?" Alex was walking to the doorway wondering why Henry wasn't making way for her to pass through.

"There's no court today, Alex. It's been cancelled."

"But, that doesn't make sense. Our expert witness is still on the stand. The prosecution is supposed to finish with their cross-examination this morning and then Martie is going to ask a few questions on re-direct."

Alex realized that the office was silent. People were usually roaming around checking their messages, fixing coffee, their breakfast, and recapping on what had happened the night before.

She couldn't hear anyone at this moment. "What's going on Henry?"

"Put the folder down and follow me." Henry turned around and walked back to his office. Alex put her folder down and followed him.

Henry sat on the couch in his office and summoned Alex to sit next to him. A thin folder sat on the coffee table that stood directly in front of the couch. This was unusual for Henry. He normally sat behind his desk while others sat on the other side with an uncomfortable distance in between.

"Our expert witness is in the hospital. He's been diagnosed with an extreme case of salmonella poisoning and is too weak to do anything let alone testify in this case. The prosecution has already taken initiative to see if they can strike his entire evidence because they were not able to finish their cross-examination."

Alex interrupted him. "But their cross was weak. They wouldn't have gained anything anyway."

"I know and that's why they're taking this opportunity to have it excluded. The trial chamber has asked for written motions to be submitted by both parties and Martie's going to start working on it today. She needs your help to complete the motion and it needs to be filed within two days. Then it's up to the trial chamber to decide."

"Sure, I'm always willing to help. I'm sorry about this Henry. We were doing so well and now to have this happen. I'll go see Martie now and figure out what she needs me to do."

Alex began to rise, but Henry motioned for her to stay seated. "That's not all, Alex. I need to talk to you about something else."

Henry picked up the thin folder that was sitting on the coffee table and handed it to Alex. Alex opened the folder and saw that it contained black and white photos. These looked like the type of photos that Max had been sending to her for the files.

"Are these from Max?" Alex began sifting through the photos until one captured her eye.

William was staring back at her. He was smiling. His appearance and dress were immaculate as ever and she could tell that this picture was taken a few years ago. This was a younger man, but it was William. Alex looked at the other people in the photo. They were sitting at a table enjoying a meal. Alex couldn't tell if it was dinner or lunch. They were dressed in casual clothing and looked relaxed. Alex looked over the faces and moved the photo closer to her face. This couldn't be true. She looked up at Henry for a sign that this couldn't be true, but he didn't live up to her hopes. Alex could feel the room closing in and reached out to grasp the arm of the couch. Henry held onto her shoulder.

"What is going on, Henry. Why is my boyfriend sharing a meal with Karim Kimbala?"

Henry wished that he could have taken the last five minutes away. Alex was like a daughter to him and he felt uncomfortable seeing her so distraught.

He shifted his position on the couch and moved closer towards Alex. "Alex, Max came across these photos while investigating Karim Kimbala. He brought them here and showed them to myself and Sam. Sam is the one that picked William out of the photo."

Alex turned towards Henry. "When did this happen? Max was here three days ago and I remember him meeting with the two of you. Did it happen then? I asked Max if he had any additional materials for the files, but he said no."

"Yes, we met with Max three days ago, Alex."

"Did he give you these photos at the meeting?" Alex looked at Henry.

He knew where she was leading this conversation and he realized that his silence over the past couple of days may guarantee a permanent distance between him and Alex. Henry sighed before answering. "Yes, he showed the photos to us then."

Alex's confusion slowly turned into anger. "You thought that my boyfriend had relations with this Karim Kimbala three days ago and are telling me just now? How am I supposed to take this news? What am I supposed to do now?"

"I'm sorry Alex. I wanted to make sure before coming to you. You have become very close to him and I didn't want to bring this to your attention if I couldn't be absolutely certain. Max was able to ascertain that William's real name is Nicholas Raine and he is good friends with both Joseph and Karim. I'm sorry, Alex. I'm really sorry." Henry moved to the edge of his chair uncertain as to whether or not he should give Alex a hug.

Alex rose clutching the photo in her hands. She gathered her balance not realizing that tears streamed down her face. She walked out of Henry's office and continued walking until she stood on the front step outside of the building. She could hear Henry calling after her as she continued walking down the street, still clutching the photo of William and Karim Kimbala.

Alex woke up to find herself engulfed in silent darkness. She searched for the light switch, but then remembered her talk with Henry and decided to keep the lights off. She also remembered pulling the phone cord out of the outlet not wanting anyone, especially William, to contact her. She needed to sort out what was happening and get the truth. If anything, Alex knew that she wouldn't get the truth in her current state of mind. She also knew that she didn't want any condolences or well wishes right now. Why did the team wait so long to share this information with her? How could they do this to her? Wasn't she important to them? She thought that they cared about her. Alex didn't only have to worry about who her boyfriend might be. She also needed to worry who her team mates really were.

Carter and Martie stood at Alex's front door. They had been standing there for the past ten minutes hoping that Alex would open the door for them.

Carter banged on the door while Martie tried the phone again. "There's no answer on her phone."

"I know she's in there. I can hear her walking around."

Carter raised his voice loud enough for Alex to hear them. "Alex, we're not leaving so open the door. We will stay here and continue to bang on the door and call you until the neighbors wake up…"

The door opened and Carter saw a distraught Alex staring back at them. Her hair was uncombed and she held a tissue in one hand. Her mascara and eyeliner streaked down her face. Carter had the feeling that she was still wearing the same clothes from the morning before. Alex stepped back in silence and Carter and Martie walked in and closed the door behind them. The apartment was dimly lit. Carter saw the unplugged phone and drew Martie's attention to it. Martie nodded knowingly.

Alex sat down on her couch. She felt exhausted and the last people she wanted to see were work colleagues.

"What are you doing here?"

Carter sat on one side of Alex while Martie took the free spot on the other side.

"We're here for you, sweetie. We heard what happened this morning and have been trying to reach you all day on the telephone, but now I see that it was futile."

"What do you mean? You knew about this before, but didn't mention anything to me."

"Huh? Alex, Sam took us all out this morning for breakfast. He said that you were coming in later and wouldn't be joining us. We found out what was really going on when we got back from breakfast. Henry sat us all down and told us about William."

"You mean you didn't know about this before?"

"Of course not. The man wouldn't have been able to get within thirty feet of you if I had known about it."

Martie chimed in. "I didn't know either, Alex. And to be honest, Henry and Sam didn't want to say anything until they were sure about William. They both know how you feel about him and didn't want to hurt you or your relationship if it wasn't true. Henry told us that he had a full investigation started once he and Sam saw the pictures of William and Karim Kimbala together. Henry, well we all see you as family and he wanted to protect you. Do you understand?"

"I don't know. I'm so tired and I've been crying the whole day. I don't know what to think anymore. I was angry at William, Henry, and Sam…."

Alex began crying again. Carter pulled her to him and held her close. "Don't worry. We're here for you. Like Martie said, we're all family. You can count on us. You haven't eaten anything have you?"

Carter looked around. "At least you stayed off the booze too."

Alex laughed. "You know how to make me laugh."

Carter looked at Martie and smiled. Seeing Alex he knew that Alex was going to be okay. "Hey, boss you know that we're living in a parallel world right now, don't you? We're living in a closed off community full of internationals. We work together. We socialize together. We find our best friends in this community and sometimes we even sleep together and find our partners in this community. A lot of weird things happen here because people aren't worried that their family and friends back home will find out. Unfortunately, you've been bitten and hurt by this insane community, but at least you know that it's temporary living. We'll be going back home soon to the real world and you can leave this all behind you."

She rested her head on his chest. Alex needed to find comfort and security somewhere. "Thank you, Carter. I really appreciate that you're trying to protect me, but my heart can be broken back home in Baltimore too. Granted it won't be broken in this way, but it can happen all the same." Alex sighed and reached for a tissue.

Carter had an idea. "Listen, how about we order in some food and watch some movies. You need to get your mind off of you for awhile and watch other people's misery. What do you say? And remember that no is not an option. I'm not leaving you tonight."

"Maybe I do need some company."

"Okay, let's start by putting the phone cord back into the wall." Carter winked at Alex before rising to make the food order.

CHAPTER 55

Gabriel and Meredith sat in the prosecutor's office. The prosecutor sat down behind her desk and faced the two attorneys who had requested a private meeting with her.

She failed to hide her annoyance when she finally spoke to them, "I have a meeting in ten minutes. My secretary was generous enough to put you on my schedule. My advice would be that you don't make her day any tougher by wasting my time. Now, why are we meeting?"

Meredith was taken aback. She had heard the rumors circulating the office about the prosecutor, but didn't think that the rumors would be confirmed so quickly in her first meeting with the prosecutor. Gabriel knew the prosecutor's tendency to talk bluntly and began to fill the silence. Meredith had to admit that she was impressed with how Gabriel was handling the situation.

"Madame Prosecutor. We understand that your time is very valuable and we don't want to take too much of it so we will keep this short. We are experiencing problems with Jan Paul on the Kimbala case and we wanted to bring it to your attention seeing how the case is about to close..."

The prosecutor interrupted Gabriel. "What problems are you experiencing?"

"The defense put their last expert witness on the stand and Jan Paul cross-examined him. The expert witness was crucial because he could seriously injure our case. Jan Paul decided to cross-examine the witness against our advice. He delivered a weak cross-examination and lost crucial evidence. He's also experiencing personal problems that we believe may be hindering his concentration and taking his mind off of the case. In short, we have lost confidence in our lead counsel and are coming to you for help. In actuality, the entire team has lost confidence in Jan Paul."

"When did you begin to lose confidence or notice problems with Jan Paul and or the case?"

"Approximately three months ago, Madame."

The prosecutor took a moment to read Gabriel and Meredith's faces and posture before speaking. "And it took you three months to come to me? What do you expect me to do?"

"Madame Prosecutor, with all due respect we have tried to settle this on our own without having to involve you, but the case is almost finished and the team is pulling together to finish well in spite of our lead counsel. Unfortunately..."

The prosecutor let out a large sigh. "Young man you have less than one minute to come to the point."

Gabriel shifted in his seat. "We would like you to either remove Jan Paul from the case or have him step aside and have his decisions run by you first."

"Do you have anything to add to this?" Madame Prosecutor looked towards Meredith.

"Only that I agree completely with Gabriel, Madame."

"I have to get ready for my next appointment. Let me think about what you have said." Madame Prosecutor dismissed them silently as she picked up her pen and began making notes on a document lying on her desk.

CHAPTER 56

Alex walked into Henry's office and sat down. Sam and Henry had just concluded their meeting when Alex walked in. It was Alex's first day back and they wanted to make it as easy as possible. Henry picked up his telephone and asked Max to join them.

"Welcome back, Alex. It's good to see you. How are you feeling?"

Alex was dreading this moment. She always hated it when someone asked her how she was doing especially when it was completely obvious. Henry was smiling at her, but she could tell that he was uncomfortable in this situation. She knew that Henry was at his best in the courtroom and telling people what to do. Alex looked up at the ceiling and sighed.

"It is okay, Alex. We know that this is hard for you so take your time. We're here for you, okay?" Sam reached over and touched her arm lightly.

Alex looked over at Sam and then Henry. "Then why did it take you so long to tell me what was going on?" Alex whispered. Sam pulled his hand away and sat back in his seat.

"Alex, look that was my call. Sam recognized William in a photo, but I wanted to make sure that we could confirm that it was him before getting you involved. I wanted to protect you from harm if possible and I didn't want to cause confusion or hurt your relationship if we were wrong. Please understand that I did this with your best interest in mind." Henry wished that he could take the pain away.

Alex sat back in her seat defeated. "I don't know who to be angry at. Should I be angry with William for not telling me? Should I be angry with you for not telling me sooner?" Alex looked at Henry. "Are you sure that you're right about this? I mean completely one hundred percent sure?"

"Yes, we're sure. Are you ready to hear what we've learned?" Henry picked up a manila folder containing documents and photos.

Alex stared at the folder before answering faintly. "Yes."

CHAPTER 57

Jan Paul sat across from the prosecutor. He waited patiently while the prosecutor finished red lining a submission for the court. He understood that this was a form of intimidation and control, but he was tired of the act. He figured that he had lost ten minutes of his day waiting on the prosecutor whenever he was called into her office for a meeting. He was about to say something when the prosecutor looked up and put her pen down.

She picked the receiver up and spoke into the phone. "Lucy, come and get this submission please." Lucy, her secretary, walked into the room and collected the submission.

"Close the door on your way out, please. Oh, and no phone calls."

The prosecutor sat back in her chair and studied Jan Paul. "Jan Paul, two of your staff attorneys visited me the other day. They have some concerns about your performance." She stopped and stared at Jan Paul.

Jan Paul was surprised. He wasn't aware that anyone from his team had spoken to her. His confidence was slowly fading away and nervousness took its place.

Jan Paul stuttered as he spoke. "Who may I ask came to speak with you? And what concerns do they have?"

"Gabriel and Meredith visited me. It worries me that two of your top people are concerned about your work product and emotional well being. That's why I'm taking this seriously. They also know about your affair with Analise, which tells me that things are out of hand. Should I feel that way?"

"Of course not, Madame Prosecutor. I have everything under control. I really don't understand why they came to you and not me." Jan Paul began to sweat. He could feel his shirt dampen with every passing second.

"Jan Paul, cut the crap. You've lost control. Don't treat me like an idiot in the process. The Kimbala trial is almost over and that's why I'm not going to step in directly. I shouldn't have to. That's why we hire competent lawyers to handle the cases. What I am going to do is put Oliver from appeals on the case. You will still be seen by the public as the lead counsel, but Oliver makes the decisions from now on. Do you understand me?"

Silence filled the room. Jan Paul grasped the armrest of the chair to stop the room from spinning. His world was crashing and he didn't know how to save the little bit of dignity that he had left. All he could do was answer with a muddled, "Yes."

"Jan Paul, I expect a letter of resignation to cross my desk within a week of the trial's closing date. I will not condone shoddy work and mindless affairs by any staff member from this office. You may go."

Jan Paul gathered himself and then walked out of the office. The prosecutor had already turned her concentration to her next meeting and didn't notice Jan Paul's departure.

----------------- CHAPTER 58 -----------------

"I went back to Kimbala and South Africa with Scott to do some research and find out more about Nicholas Raine. In the beginning, we weren't sure if Nicholas met Karim Kimbala recently in South Africa and became friends without knowing about his past. We also wanted to make sure that Nicholas didn't have ties to the Kimbalas back in Kilambèa. If he was attached to the Kimbalas during their reign, then we knew that we would have problems. Not only would you be in danger Alex, but the case and the rest of the team also. We needed to assess the situation before any of us could go further."

"Max, I understand that all of you were doing your best. Please show me what information you've found out about William...I mean Nicholas."

Max began a recount of the intel he had gathered over the last few days. "I'm really sorry about this Alex. Nicholas met Karim, when he was twelve years old, in a Botswana boarding school on the border of South Africa. They hit it off and have been best friends ever since. Nicolas also met Joseph while visiting the Kimbalas on holiday in Kilambèa. They became friends, but he's closer to Karim. We wondered why Karim wanted to live in South Africa. According to our records, Karim didn't have any known relatives or close ties in South Africa. Now, we know that Nicholas stayed under the radar. They meet constantly in South Africa and Nicolas is also close with Karim's family. We were able to trace Nicolas' monthly travels and he visits South Africa once every two months. Other times he's travelling to countries within Europe and Washington, DC. He works for the Dutch branch of a South African company, which is actually owned by Karim Kimbala. This fact has made it harder to track his activities because they are under the guise of business."

"And what type of business is this South African company?"

"What no one likes to hear: they're into exports and imports."

Alex looked around the room. "And what do we do now? What do I do? William, I mean Nicholas, is out of the country on business, but he returns in three days."

Max answered. "Nicholas is currently in South Africa. I have Scott watching him."

Alex began to shiver. She remembered William telling her that he had a business trip in Belgium, "Well, it seems that you still haven't been able to answer the key question. What is Karim Kimbala up to?"

Henry chimed in this time. "Alex, we were hoping that you would help us out with that."

Sam couldn't believe what he was hearing. Henry hadn't mentioned this to him at all. "What do you mean? You want to put Alex in danger?"

Alex put her hand up as if to silence the room. "What do you want me to do?"

Sam became infuriated. "No Alex. Henry, the trial is almost over. Why can't we just finish, pack our bags, and go home. Shouldn't we let the police handle this? Better yet, we should put Alex on the plane tomorrow."

"First you make decisions about whether or not to tell me about William. I'm sorry Nicholas. Now you want to make the decision on whether or not I participate in finding out what my own boyfriend is doing and why? Sam, you cannot control my life. You never had the permission to do so and I'm not conceding now."

Alex turned to Henry and Max. "Tell me what plans you've made. I know that you have something in mind already."

Alex spent the next two days rehearsing the plan with Henry, Sam, and Max. She was very tired and it took every last bit of energy for her to walk home. It was only six-o'clock, and already dark outside. She could hear the rustle of the tree leaves as she walked down the dimly lit street. Henry told her to go home and get some rest. William was due to arrive the following day and Henry wanted to make sure that she was fully rested and thinking clearly. Alex was rehearsing the plan in her head when a man suddenly appeared quietly behind her.

"Hey fine stranger. How could anyone so beautiful as you be allowed to walk these streets?" William wrapped his arms around Alex's waist and gave her a kiss just below her right ear.

Alex stopped frozen in her tracks as she listened to the voice that once sent thrilling chills down her spine. Alex tried to remain calm and normal while turning around, but she was trembling inside.

Alex gently freed herself from William's grasp. "William, you're back? I thought that you were supposed to arrive tomorrow?" Alex kept a small distance between her and William.

"I couldn't stay away from you any longer. I missed my baby. Why are you so far away from me? Do I get a kiss and a hug? Maybe even an 'I missed you too'?"

Alex hesitated and then moved closer towards William. Sam appeared out of the darkness riding on his bicycle.

"Alex, there you are. I'm on my way to the restaurant. Did you need a lift? William, is that you? We thought that you were still out of the country. How are you?"

Sam shook William's hand smiling. "Alex has missed you so much that a few of us wanted to ease her loneliness by taking her out to dinner tonight. The others are at the restaurant already. Do you want to join us?" Sam didn't want to give William the option of leaving with Alex, alone.

"That was very nice of you to watch over Alex. Well, I am tired. I travelled in today and came straight over here to see her."

William turned towards Alex and then back to Sam. "I missed her too. You go ahead and have dinner and I'll see you tomorrow."

Sam felt relief as the tension flowed from his body. "Are you sure? We can always add another person and I'd hate to separate the two of you tonight?"

"I'm sure. Have a great dinner. Alex, I'll call you tomorrow." William bent down and kissed Alex lightly on the cheek.

Sam walked Alex home. "Are you sure that you don't want to have dinner somewhere tonight?" Sam was walking beside Alex and steering his bicycle at the same time.

Alex yawned. "No, I'm sure. I think that these past few days have been too much of an emotional roller coaster for me. I just want to climb into bed and get some sleep."

They stood in front of Alex's apartment building. "You should eat something. It's not healthy if you go to bed without eating dinner. At least order a pizza."

Alex laughed. "And you're talking about eating healthy?"

She placed her hand on Sam's shoulder. "Thanks for your help and support these last two days. I really appreciate it and I will be looking to you for support in the next coming days, but right now I just want to sleep. Okay?"

Sam backed down and decided to give up. "Okay. Get some rest. You know how to reach me if you need something."

"Thanks, Sam."

Alex turned around and walked inside her apartment building. Neither of them saw William standing in a side alley across the street watching them.

CHAPTER 59

"Ladies and Gentlemen, Welcome to Durban, South Africa. If you look out of your window and below, then you will see the beautiful coastline on our left. Directly below us is the city of Durban. We will arrive at the airport shortly. Please remember to stay seated until we have landed and the fasten seat belt sign is turned off. We hope that you enjoyed your flight with us and we hope to service you again in the near future. If you live here in Durban, South Africa, then we would also like to take this opportunity to welcome you home. For all visitors, we hope that you enjoy your stay. If this is the first leg of your journey, then you will find monitors and a helpful stewardess in the terminal to answer any questions you might have. Have a great day." the head stewardess hung the telephone up and sat down.

Alex looked outside at the busy city below. She felt a mixture of feelings running through her body, but fear and uncertainty grasped her the most. Her body had become one with the chair and the butterflies in her stomach became worse as the plane descended. Alex had no idea what she was going to learn in Durban. Who was the man that she had shared her bed with, Alex thought. Alex knew that she would have to face the truth. She only hoped that the truth would not break her spirit. Alex looked outside the cabin window and did something that she hadn't done in a long time. She said a little prayer as the plane landed in Durban, South Africa. Alex stood up and grabbed her bag as soon as the seatbelt sign was turned off and casually walked off of the airplane. The walk through the airport was surreal and Alex felt as if she was having an outer body experience. She knew where she was, but it was as if her body was on auto pilot. Alex silently continued to follow Max and Scott to the rental car booth. Alex breathed a sigh of relief once she stepped into the rental car. She had made it this far. The adventure had begun.

Alex put her sunglasses on and watched as the scenery flittingly passed by. The sun was shining and the sky was a beautiful landscape of blue with patches of white fluffy clouds. It was a perfect summer's day. A direct contrast to my mood, Alex thought. Streams of men and women walked briskly along the side streets trying to make the most of their lunch break. Max turned right and drove down a side street before driving up to the entrance of the hotel. The valet and concierge greeted them as they stepped out of the car.

Alex walked into her hotel room after a quick check-in and placed her baggage in the closet. She then walked out onto the balcony. She looked around in awe and forgot about her troubles for a moment. The scenery was breathtaking. Alex looked down onto the clear green sea and white sand. The sun was shining, but a slight breeze brushed across her forehead. Alex closed her eyes and breathed in the fresh air. A single tear fell down her face and dropped onto the balcony rail. Alex couldn't believe that this was happening to her. She had finally found the man of her dreams. She had been in heaven not knowing that hell was waiting patiently around the corner. All she wanted at this very moment was to fall apart and separate from the world, at least for awhile until all of the actors had disappeared. Alex had followed Max's orders before leaving and told William that she was travelling back to the office in Baltimore to complete some work during the court recess.

Alex picked up a tissue from the bathroom and sat down on the bed. She stared into the distance and tried to compose herself. She needed to focus and get through this trip. Alex decided to focus her thoughts on her anger. She threw her tissue away and splashed her face with water. Alex looked in the mirror and searched for a sign of strength before walking out the front door to meet the rest of the team for dinner.

Everyone gathered in Max's room after dinner. Max wanted to briefly go over the agenda for their trip. They only had three days and Max wanted to make sure that every item on the list was completed before they left for The Hague. Max began to lay out the agenda for the coming days.

"Tomorrow morning we're going to scope out Karim Kimbala's head office and visit the land records office. We also need to figure out how to get a hold of business records and get Nicholas' financial records dating back ten years. The day after tomorrow we're going to visit all of Nicholas' hang outs and see if anyone will talk to us. Oh, and we'll also walk around the neighborhood where he grew up, which is about five kilometers away from the city. He now owns an apartment here in the city. I've left the last day open for any surprises or unfinished business that needs to be cleared up. Alex, I want you to understand that this could be dangerous. Scott and I are going to talk to all types of people on this trip. We are also going to learn some things about Nicholas that you probably didn't know before and probably would rather not know. You can opt to stay in the hotel during this trip, but I want you to understand that I may order you at times to stay in your hotel room. If you do decide to accompany us, then I may even tell you that you can't travel with us to certain places. I was against you coming here in the first place and Henry knows that. But, now your safety is in my hands and you need to follow whatever I say. Do you understand?"

"I do. I know that you're worried about me, but I really need to see for myself who this man really is. I also wouldn't mind figuring out why this happened. Why did he do this to me?"

"Don't worry, Alex. We'll figure out all of the answers, but be careful when you're also walking around in this hotel. We can't trust anyone here and we're not in a spy movie so watch your movements and the people around you. Carry your cell phone at all times, and if you see anything suspicious, then you need to call one of us immediately."

The following day, Max and Scott sat in a rustic café across the street from Karim Kimbala's head office. Alex decided to stay at the hotel and promised Max that she wouldn't leave the premises. Max and Scott were drinking coca-colas out of the bottle while watching the busy city street life move in front of them. Old cars and mopeds streamed by causing the dust and dirt to create a constant haze. The office was open, but hardly anyone walked in or out. Max contemplated on walking into the office, but then he recognized Karim Kimbala walking down the street and then entering the office's front door. Max and Scott waited patiently for two minutes before Scott rose from the table, casually walked across the street and into the office.

Scott walked up to the receptionist making sure that his back was facing Karim. He shuffled his back pack and looked uncomfortable while quietly saying good morning to the young lady behind the counter. He opened his back pack and took out a tourist guide book. He blushed and confessed that he was lost and wondered if she could point him in the right direction. Meanwhile, Karim Kimbala, oblivious to Scott's entrance, was talking to a well dressed African man. Scott kept his back to Karim, but was able to catch glimpses of the two in the mirror located behind the receptionist desk. He could tell that Karim was not happy and the well dressed man was trying to calm him down.

"Sir, are you listening?" the receptionist looked quizzically at Scott.

"I'm sorry. I don't think that I've seen such a large mirror before in my life and..."

Scott moved forward a little. "The two men behind us don't seem to be too happy either."

"I'm sorry about that, Sir. They have been acting like this all week, but at least you get to walk out of here."

Scott smiled in return. "And I'm sorry that you have to put up with this. Now, about those directions. I promise to pay attention this time."

The receptionist smiled and began illustrating the way to Durban's cultural museum on the map for Scott. Karim Kimbala, still not noticing Scott's existence, ended his conversation and walked out the front door.

Alex was walking back from the fitness room. She had spent the morning exercising on the treadmill and bicycle before taking a swim in the pool and then relaxing for a half hour in the sauna. She had taken a shower in the communal shower room and decided to return to her room and order room service for lunch. She was famished from the morning activities and hoped to find a nice soup and salad combination on the room service menu. Alex slowed her pace as she was moving to the elevator. She had a strange sense that someone was following her, but quickly denounced the idea. She had to admit to herself that travelling to South Africa was a bold move on her part. She should have left this to Max and Scott. She felt safer in Holland and maybe she should have done what she told William she was doing. Maybe

Alex should have gone home to Baltimore, but Alex also knew that if she had travelled home, she probably would have stayed there, for good. She hoped that the guys were okay. Alex walked into the elevator and watched as the double doors closed.

Her hunger pains grew as she opened her room door and walked towards the night stand. Alex stopped in her tracks as soon as she saw William sitting in the chair next to the balcony door. She wanted to turn around and run out of the room screaming for help, but she couldn't will her body to move. It took all of her energy to speak as she felt her body shiver.

"What, what are you doing here?"

William looked at Alex. "I could ask you the same thing, Alex. You told me that you were going home to Baltimore to do some work, but you're here in South Africa instead. What does South Africa have to do with you? And why did you lie to me?"

Alex went from fright and shock to anger. "Why did I lie to you? Lie to you? How did you get into my hotel room? Are you following me?"

Alex began to step back as William held his hands up and motioned her to stop. "I thought that you would be happy to see me. I told them downstairs that I was your fiancé so that I could get in."

"How did you even know that I was here? And why not just call me?" Alex shouted.

"Please calm down. I didn't expect you to be so angry. You're my girlfriend albeit a girlfriend that lied to her boyfriend. Why are you here?" William stood up, but didn't move away from the chair.

"Why should I have to tell you anything William...or is it Nicholas? I've been getting confused a lot lately on what to call my boyfriend," Alex hissed out.

He sat back down in the chair and covered his head with both hands. Silence filled the room and the tension was rising to a breaking point. Alex was thinking about her chances of escape when William spoke again.

"My real name is Nicholas Raine and I grew up in South Africa, actually a few miles outside of Durban, which I'm guessing you already know."

Nicholas searched Alex for any clues that his words were getting through and then continued. "I work for Karim Kimbala, but it's not what you think."

Alex gasped and covered her mouth. She already knew the truth, but it still hurt to hear it directly from him.

She whispered gently. "I don't want to know anymore. I don't know why you're sitting in my hotel room or how you figured out where I am, but I don't want to know. All I want right now is for you to leave my room. Please leave now."

Alex moved out of the way to make room for Nicholas' exit, but noticed that he wasn't moving from his chair. She asked him once again adding more strength to her voice. "Please leave now."

Nicholas stood up and moved slowly towards Alex. He stopped in front of her and attempted to put his hands on her shoulders. Alex stepped backwards and put her hands in front of her assuming a defensive position.

"Don't touch me. Just leave!"

Nicholas put his hands down. "Alex, I don't want to hurt you. I never have. How can you think that I would ever want to hurt you? You are my girlfriend and I love you. We've shared too much for you to think that I would hurt you. I want a chance to explain what's really going on. Can you please let me explain? After all we've been through?" Alex looked up and into Nicholas' eyes. Nicholas could feel the pain resonating from her eyes. He always felt that he could read her soul when he looked into her eyes and it hurt him to see the pain she was in.

"What I want to know, Nicholas, is how you could hurt me like this? You talk about what we've been through? We were a couple. I shared secrets with you. We slept together. I shared my life with you and I didn't even know your real name. How am I supposed to trust anything you say to me now? You say that you don't want to hurt me, Nicholas? Well, I have news for you. You have hurt me. You have hurt me more than you could ever imagine. Don't talk to me about trust."

Alex sat down on the bed and began to cry. She had controlled the tears all morning and thought that she was doing better. How dare this bastard show up in her room?

Nicholas sat down beside Alex, but knew that it would become worse if he touched her. Instead he picked the tissue box up and handed them over to Alex.

Nicholas sighed and confessed. "You're right, Alex. I did hurt you. I see that now. I didn't mean to cause you pain and it hurts me to see you like this. Please believe me that it wasn't my intention to hurt you. I really need to explain everything to you and show you something. Will you let me do that? Please give me a chance. I may be able to alleviate some of the pain. Will you come with me? I promise to bring you back here safe and sound."

Alex looked up with red eyes at Nicholas. "I'm here with Max and Scott. They will wonder where I am."

"I know. I promise to have you back before they return."

"How did you know that I was here?"

"Honestly, I'm not James Bond. I didn't follow you here. I travelled here for business. I know that I told you that I was going to be somewhere else, but I came here and had a meeting in this hotel yesterday. To my amazement, I saw you walk into the lobby and up to the check-in desk with Max and Scott. I finally got the nerve to see you now. I had a feeling that you were here for either Karim or me or both and I wanted to make sure that you received the truth from me first."

CHAPTER 60

Nicholas and Alex stood on a hill top above Nicholas' birth place a half hour later. Alex looked down below and took in the sight of shack houses stacked almost on top of each other. Paved roads didn't exist here and Alex knew that one gust of wind would tear most of the shack houses apart leaving these people with little to nothing. Little girls and boys ran through the mud puddles playing soccer and hide and seek.

Nicholas crossed his arms over his chest and turned to Alex. "This is the village where I was born, where I grew up. When I was eleven years old, my parents were given an opportunity of a lifetime. The South African government wanted to show good will and set aside scholarships for fifty children from shack villages to attend boarding school. I was shipped off at age twelve to the Plum Tree boarding school in Botswana. There were enough boarding schools here, but the government didn't want to pollute its schools with black people. Apartheid was strong back then, but the South African Government was being pressured by the international community. So, I travelled by train to Botswana for my education. It was tough in the beginning because everything was new. I had never ridden on a train before and my education was basic. I had a lot of catching up to do. I had to learn things that the kids in my group were already fluent in, but Karim helped me. He helped me with everything from homework to fitting in with the other kids." Nicholas gestured for Alex to walk down the hill and followed after her.

He continued his story. "Karim and I became best friends in boarding school. If you found one of us, then the other was not too far behind. He came from a middle class family, and I really admired his lifestyle. He wore the latest fashions, had spending money, and travelled home for holidays. The war broke out in Kilambèa during our third year in school and his country deteriorated after that. His family's wealth didn't change, but the poor people of his country suffered the burden. I still remember the summer of our fourth year when he came back from summer vacation in Kilambèa with his family. He had changed a little and became more rebellious."

Nicholas motioned for them to turn left. They were walking on one of the narrow streets between the shacks. People watched as they moved along. It had just rained so Alex and Nicholas were walking through mud puddles as they made their way past the makeshift houses. Alex tried to look at the houses and inhabitants without staring, but she found it difficult.

"He came back with stories about the people of Kilambèa and how the Government was treating them. I had never seen him so excited about common people before. He was nice before that trip, but never spoke about the common man's need. Now, he wanted to do something about it as if he was a born again activist if you can say that. I brought him here once after that summer to see my home and visit my family. He told me that he felt at home here, but thought that people should live in proper houses. I reminded him that this was all we had. He promised that it would be different one day for all of us. We graduated. He went back to Kilambèa and I moved onto college in Oxford, on scholarship."

"But you kept in touch after graduating right?" Alex inquired.

Nicholas knew where Alex was going with this question, but continued with his story. He turned to Alex. "We lost contact for the first four years after high school. I graduated from Oxford with a degree in business. I worked in England for two years, and then came back to Africa. I missed it too much. I didn't return to South Africa in the beginning. I travelled to Namibia, Botswana, and then ended up in Kilambèa. I had heard so many stories about Kilambèa from Karim that I wanted to see it firsthand. That's where I saw Karim again. He was already the president of Kilambèa by then. We talked about old times and I met his brother and family. They treated me like a family too and I stayed on in Kilambèa for a few years. We became business associates and worked well together until Karim began to experience problems. The economy took a turn for the worse and the people were suffering. Karim didn't want to see it, but I did."

Alex and Nicholas continued to walk through the streets. Alex couldn't tell if Nicholas was guiding her to a specific location or if they were walking aimlessly through this little village.

Nicholas read her thoughts. "This is what we call a township. The Government, during apartheid, segregated the country by moving blacks and colored's into distinct areas in order to separate us from the whites. I believe that this was like the Jim Crow laws that you had back in the States? I wanted to walk here and show you where I come from. Please come this way."

Nicholas pointed to the right and they continued walking. "As I was saying, problems were developing in Kilambèa. Karim made a lot of promises to the people, but hardly made good on any of them. It became impossible talking to him about what was going on. He was the powerful leader and I think that such power changed him. I left Kilambèa when I couldn't recognize Karim anymore."

Alex and Nicholas arrived at the township's stream of running water. Alex saw women washing their clothes in the water. Babies were playing nearby.

"We had no contact until Karim showed up here in South Africa. He was a changed man. His brother was president and Karim was a man that had fallen to his lowest and came back for the better. He realized what he did during his presidency and how he had affected his people. He didn't have much financially, but used what he did have to start up the business that I now work for. Our friendship was renewed and we've gotten closer over the years. He's now one of my best friends."

Alex turned to Nicholas. "Did you think that by showing me this township that I would melt in your arms? What do you want from me?"

"I want you to understand who I am and where I come from."

"You lie to me about who you are in the first place and you think that a half hour conversation is going to change what I think about you and this situation?"

"Alex, I'm sorry about this. I should have told you my real name. Do you believe me now?"

Alex turned around. She wanted to find an exit to the township and head back to the hotel. "Nicholas, I still don't know what you want from me. Where will this charade lead?"

Nicholas ran behind Alex. "Alex, please understand. I'm trying to say that I didn't want to hurt you. We needed to know what was going on in The Hague and if the court intended to arrest Karim, but then you and I, well we started getting closer to each other. I didn't mean for this to happen, but I've fallen for you."

Alex turned around in shock and anger. "How dare you. How dare you say this to me? As for your friend, why didn't he just inquire with the prosecution's office as to whether they considered him to be a suspect? Get me out of here now and take me back to my hotel."

Nicholas looked at Alex and knew instantly that his pleading lay on deaf ears. He put his hand out and gestured the way for Alex to walk back to the car.

CHAPTER 61

Alex raced into her hotel room to pick the phone up. She breathed into the phone's headset. "Hello?"

Scott answered on the other end. "Alex, are you okay?"

Alex sat down on the bed exhausted. "Hi Scott. Yes, I am."

She remembered that she was supposed to have been in the hotel all day. "I'm sorry. I was just coming back from the exercise room and heard the phone ringing."

"Oh, I'm sorry. Hey, I just wanted to let you know that we're back. Are you going to join us for dinner at six?"

Alex looked at the clock. It was five-o'clock. "Yes, I'll see you downstairs at six."

"Okay, see you then."

Alex put her purse down and walked towards the bathroom. She turned on the shower and stepped in after undressing. Some people liked to drive or run when they had a lot on their mind, but Alex liked to take long hot showers and enjoy the hard pounding of water on her back. She closed her eyes and let the steam envelop her.

Max and Scott were sitting at the back table when Alex walked in. It was still too early for the South Africans to dine, but Max and Scott thought that the timing was perfect. They were also hungry after a full day of running around the town chasing clues of Nicholas' past life. Max enjoyed this part of the job most. The thrill of uncovering someone's life firsthand was better than watching the Discovery Channel. It was also as close as Max was going to get to his former life chasing one step behind danger. Scott loved watching and learning from Max. The two worked well as a team and depended on the other's instincts more than anything else. Max watched as Alex walked into the room and gradually made her way over to the table.

He'd known Alex long enough to know that she was hiding behind a mask of confidence. Alex was a privileged young lady who had practically grown up with a silver spoon in her mouth. She strove to stand on her own two feet and build her own career, but Max knew that she was lacking some street sense and experience, especially with men. Obtaining this job was a blessing for Alex. She worked in her grandmother's firm and had worked hard for people to accept her for her work product and not see her as the founder's grandchild. Max cared for Alex like a daughter even though he didn't quite understand the sort. Alex was rich, but chose not to be. She could also make the choice not to be, something that most of the world's population couldn't afford to do. Alex sat down at the table and placed the napkin on her lap. A glass of San Pellegrino was already waiting for her. Alex smiled at the thought that these guys remembered to order San Pellegrino for her. After today, she really wanted something that would add more punch, but picked up the glass of water instead.

Max decided to skip over the pleasantries. He already knew how she felt. "We already ordered a sampler for the appetizers and the waiter is coming over soon to take our entrée orders. Do you want to hear what we've learned today or shall we start with yours instead?"

Alex perked up. What had he meant with my day, she thought. "My day was boring. Tell me more about yours."

"We spent the day scouting Karim Kimbala's office and visiting city hall. We found some pretty interesting things out about Kimbala's business. Scott walked into the office this morning and witnessed a confrontation between Karim Kimbala and his account manager Simon Black. Karim wasn't happy from the looks of it and stormed out soon after Scott walked in. We've also found out some things that Henry needs to know about. The South African government and Interpol have been watching Karim Kimbala and his business activities. It looks as if Karim has been using the business as a front for many reasons, money laundering being one of them.

I'm going to visit Interpol tomorrow while Scott is going to visit locations that concern Nicholas."

"What do you mean by money laundering?" Alex wanted to know.

"I won't know the details until tomorrow, but you're free to come with me. I asked them to run Nicholas' name in the computers to see if something comes up. This may be interesting for you. So, what did you do today?" The food had arrived and Max began eating.

"I relaxed a lot and took advantage of the exercise room and sauna today. Nothing exciting really," Alex decided to follow suit and picked up her fork before taking the first bite of her meal.

-------------------- CHAPTER 62 --------------------

Max and Alex were escorted to the conference room at Interpol's regional office in South Africa. Timothy Bernhardt was waiting for them. "Good afternoon. My name is Tim and I'm the lead investigator on the Kimbala case. I hear that you are here in South Africa investigating Karim Kimbala's financial activities."

"That's correct. My name is Max Kayhorn and this is Alexandra Cayhill. Our firm is defending Joseph Kimbala in The Hague and we're chasing some leads."

"How is tracking Karim Kimbala's financial business history going to help you with Joseph Kimbala's trial?"

"I'm sorry, but that information is confidential due to the nature of the trial. We would be grateful for any information that you can tell us."

"Okay, I understand, but can you both please sign this document? It's an agreement that you will not divulge any information shared today outside of your team." Max signed the agreement and then handed the document over to Alex for her signature.

"Great. Thank you." Tim pulled a thick file out of a large pile of documents sitting on the conference table.

"We have been tracking Karim Kimbala's movements ever since he moved here. We were aware of his history in Kilambèa and wanted to make sure that he was monitored. He opened his business within six months of moving here, which sent alarm bells up the chain at my office because no one knew where he obtained the money from. His tax documents for that year show that he used a mixture of savings, salary, and loans from friends. The business also being export/import raised alarm bells. Karim's business, Export in Harmony LLC, grossed fifty thousand in the first year. It has steadily increased over the years although you hardly see customers walking in or out of the office. Over the years, we have also seen Karim's business activities become even more diverse.

We understand that Karim, during his time in Kilambèa, was involved in many criminal activities including embezzlement. We're gathering evidence that will prove that Karim is conducting illegal business transactions through Export in Harmony. As you know this type of world is hard to infiltrate and the paperwork is sometimes non-existent, but our intelligence shows that Kimbala is involved in human trafficking and money laundering. There is also an unaccounted sum of four million dollars missing from the Government of Kilambèa's Treasury Department. We haven't been able to track that sum down, but we have a feeling that it's tied up in Export in Harmony."

Max leaned forward. "Can you tell us more about the human trafficking and money laundering?"

"Sure, I can." Tim sorted through the pile of paperwork before finding what he needed.

"Ah, here we are."

Max stole a look towards Alex before turning back to Tim. They were getting the missing information that they needed and Max didn't want to miss anything.

Tim began again. "South Africa has been a hot bed for human trafficking. Men, women, and children are trafficked in from other African countries, Asia, and Eastern Europe. The men are trafficked in mostly to perform forced agricultural labor while the women are forced to become prostitutes here in South Africa or trafficked further to Western Europe. There is a lot of money to be made in this business. We believe that Karim Kimbala has a strong underground network here in South Africa and abroad in Belgium. The money that he makes from trafficking is then laundered through Export in Harmony. He's kept his staff and business associates close and he doesn't trust outsiders easily which has made it difficult to infiltrate his network. We were able to find a few of the women that were trafficked in to this country and also abroad in Brussels, but every girl stuck with the same story. They smuggled themselves into the country to find work.

"The Kimbala brothers are not innocents and have practically committed almost every sin known to man. Our main priority is to shut down Export in Harmony, but we need to trace all of Karim Kimbala's activities before doing so. I have a feeling that there is more to uncover when I read through the files. Karim Kimbala is greedy. He has a lot of money, but always wants more. I'm hoping that this will also be his downfall."

"How long do you think this will take? Are you closer to finding out more about Karim Kimbala's business affairs? I'm asking because we're wondering if there has been any connection between the two brothers in the past few years. Actually, we're interested in whether or not the brothers remained in contact while Joseph was in office and their financial history and business transactions may answer this."

Tim smiled and pulled out a file with a sticker labeled '1983.' Max had the feeling that Tim could recite the entire pile of documents by heart, but wanted to confirm that the agency had factual documents to back everything he said.

"Joseph Kimbala took over the presidency in 1980 as we all know. The brothers didn't have contact that we know of for almost three years. All of a sudden unusual personal business transactions popped up and new bank accounts were opened. We found a trail of correspondence between the brothers that began in early March 1983. There wasn't a lot of correspondence, but just enough for us to follow. Then the brothers resorted to communicating through a third party."

Tim took out a photo and handed it to Max from across the table. "His name is Nicholas Raine. He began organizing business deals for the brothers in late November 1983 and has continued to do so even to today."

Max looked over at Alex to make sure that she was okay. Alex was focused on the picture before her.

She handed the photo back to Tim. "How did this relationship begin between the brothers and Nicholas Raine?" She remembered what Nicholas had told her the day before about boarding school and hoped to hear the same story repeated by Tim.

"Our research has shown us that Nicholas Raine came into the picture through Karim. They went to boarding school together and kept in close contact after graduating. Nicholas went off to university and then lived in Kilambèa for a few years. That's when he began his friendship with Joseph Kimbala. The men's relationship became tighter and both brothers began to rely on Nicholas for his friendship and business skills. This three way relationship weathered through the assassination attempt on Karim Kimbala, Karim's withdrawal from Kilambèa, and Joseph's presidency."

Alex could feel her heartbeat moving faster. "And what sort of business dealings did he set up for the brothers?" She already knew the answer, but needed to hear it from Tim.

"It looks like Nicholas is the all around sort of business man. He set up and still manages clean accounts for the brothers along with secret accounts in the Caribbean. He also has knowledge about the trafficking business, but it looks as if he only handles the financial side of the business and hasn't gotten involved in the transferring of people. He's strictly a money man. The brothers trust him with their lives and this Nicholas fellow has his hand in every financial deal that the Kimbalas are a part of. He even advises them on financial matters. He must know where the unaccounted Kilambèan money is."

"We have information that Nicholas Raine works for a South African think tank that's based in the Netherlands," Max added. He wanted to know if this had any truth to it.

"Ah, yes. On the books, it is seen as a think tank, but it is actually a front for the Kimbala's financial dealings in Europe. Two people are working there as analysts to make it look like they are conducting research. Raine does have an office there, which makes him look more legal and professional, but he makes sure that he conducts any questionable behavior outside of the office."

"Is the Dutch government aware of this? Are they doing anything to monitor his movements?"

"We are talking to the Dutch authorities on a constant basis and they are monitoring the office building. It is more difficult to track Raine's movements because he hasn't committed any crimes. I should correct myself. Raine has been very careful to keep his hands clean as far as we can tell. It is also difficult to track his whereabouts seeing how he travels throughout

Europe and Africa constantly. The financial burden is too large for us to swallow. However, because the Dutch authorities see a potential threat they have been very helpful. Their secret service, the AIVD, is tracking the financial records for the think tank and Raines' travel. Because of the AIVD, we know when Raine enters and exits The Netherlands. Now as for the brothers' business dealings, we rely on information from agencies located in the countries that the brothers are conducting business in. We can't do our job without their cooperation."

"You said that Raine has been the account manager for both brothers. Can you possibly tell us if Raine conducted mutual transactions for the brothers? I mean transactions that have both of the brothers' names on them."

"Like I said before, there was only a three year gap where we couldn't find communication between the brothers, but that doesn't mean that they didn't have some type of contact. Other than that Raine conducted transactions and deals for both of them apart and also together."

"Is there any way that we can get copies of your records?"

"Sure. I can't give you our entire file, but I can give you enough that will help you with your research."

"Thanks, Tim. That would be a great help to us."

Max and Alex walked down the front steps of Interpol's building. Max was carrying a thick envelope and couldn't wait to return to the hotel to see what Tim had given them. He was confident that the answers to their questions were contained in these documents. Finally, Max would understand the connection between the brothers and Raine. He would finally understand why Raine infiltrated their team and disrupted the defense's case. Max only hoped that he would finally be able to see what else might happen in the near future. Alex stopped halfway down the stairs. Max continued walking down until he realized that Alex was no longer walking beside him.

He turned around only to notice that she was standing five steps above him. "Alex, are you okay?"

Max furrowed his brow. He didn't understand why Alex wasn't walking. He hoped that the meeting with Tim hadn't cause a setback for her emotionally.

"Max, I have something to tell you, but I don't want you to be upset with me."

"Why would I be upset with you?" Max began walking back up the five steps to hear Alex better.

"Because I have something to tell you about yesterday. I only told you part of the truth of what I did yesterday." Max waited for Alex to continue.

"I saw William yesterday..."

Max interrupted her. "His name isn't William, Alex. His name is Nicholas and what do you mean when you say that you saw him?"

Alex heard a trickle of anger in Max's voice. She began hesitantly to tell the truth. "I did go to the gym yesterday and even spent time in the sauna. William, I mean Nicholas, was waiting for me in my hotel room when I returned."

"How did he get into your hotel room?"

"I don't know, but he was there. I tried to get out of the room, but couldn't move. Seeing him again hurt too much. I didn't know what to do. I hope that you understand."

Max sighed and took Alex's arm. He led her down the stairs and out to the car. "Alex, I can honestly tell you that I don't understand. We're going back to the hotel and you're going to tell me everything that happened yesterday. I want to hear every detail and you better not leave anything out. Then we're going to go through this paperwork that Tim kindly handed over to us. Do you understand what we're dealing with now after meeting Tim?"

Max stopped and turned Alex towards him. "Do you understand?" Max gripped Alex's upper arms and stared into her eyes.

Alex looked scared and began to tremble. "Yes, I understand. I'm really sorry, Max. I really am."

Max put his arms around Alex and let her cry on his shoulder. He had never been in this situation before, but it was important that he find the answer and get them all back safely to The Hague.

-------------------- CHAPTER 63 --------------------

Karim was pacing back and forth through the small living room. He remembered his previous glory days as President of Kilambèa. The entryway to the presidential palace was bigger than the living room that he occupied now. His wife had taken the kids to the park so that he could have a private conversation with Nicholas. Nicholas sat patiently in the old red armchair waiting for Karim to release some of the built up tension. He could tell that Karim was not happy with Nicholas' news. He had gotten used to Karim's temperament over the years and knew that Karim's pacing was his way of thinking things through and solving obstacles in his path.

It was annoying sometimes going through this long process. Nicholas liked to dwell on the problem for maybe two minutes before turning to problem solving, but he preferred to have Karim pace back and forth instead of becoming physical. Karim finally stopped at the window and gazed down below at the traffic. Nicholas used this time to take in the surrounding furniture and family possessions. Karim lived a modest life compared to when he was president. Nicholas didn't understand why Karim lived so modestly, but knew that Karim dreamt of returning to a higher social level in life and recapturing what his brother had stolen from him.

"I spoke with Reginald yesterday at the Belgium office. The police raided one of our boats in Brussels and took the girls into custody along with the captain and help. The police impounded the boat too and are questioning everyone including seeking records. Things were finally looking up and now this happens."

Karim walked towards Nicholas and sat down. "My lawyers are taking care of things in Brussels, but I'm worried that our plans are going to be affected, especially if they dig any further and if Interpol gets involved, which they're sure to do. How's it going in The Hague?"

Nicholas looked over at Karim and saw frustration in Karim's face. This was a new Karim for him. Karim had lost big once in his life and he wasn't going to let it happen a second time. Nicholas had practiced what he was going to say ever since seeing Alex here in South Africa.

He began in a measured tone. "Things are not going so well. Alex is here in South Africa. They know that you and I are friends. She's not alone. Two investigators from Joseph's defense team are with her. I don't know what they're doing here exactly, but it's not good."

"What do you mean, you don't know?"

"I saw her arrive two days ago and decided to approach her yesterday to see why she was here."

"You knew two days ago that the defense team was here and you didn't tell me?" Karim stood up and began pacing back and forth again.

The temperature in the room was rising and Nicholas was becoming nervous. "Look Karim, I wanted to see what was going on first before telling you. She arrived two days ago with these two guys. She confronted me about my friendship with you and told me that she didn't trust me anymore. I took her to a small shack town and preyed on her good side. I told her about my humble beginnings and that my friendship with you was above board. I don't know if she believes it or not, but I thought that it was better to try while she was here and gain any information that I could before she left."

Karim stopped in mid-pace. "You didn't come from humble surroundings, especially not a shack town. She's more naïve than we thought if she believes that one. So, why are they here then?" Karim placed his arms on the back of his chair and stared at Nicholas waiting for an answer.

"I'm guessing that they're here checking into our friendship. She thinks that my relationship with her was a scam to get inside information for you about Joseph's trial. Now that we're talking, why did you go to The Hague to testify for Joseph? You never told me the reason?"

Karim lifted himself off of the chair and walked over to the window again. "I went to The Hague to speak with Joseph. Testifying for him was a plus point for me. I wanted to talk to him about some of our financial matters, matters that you don't even know about."

Karim turned around to see the shocked look on Nicholas' face. "I'm sorry, but there were some deals that we made together shortly before Joseph tried to kill me. He had some information that I needed. He told me that I could have it on one condition, if I testified for him. I agreed to do so and got my information. The sorry bastard is more stupid than I thought. The prosecution made sure that the judges knew about my past and I doubt that they will see my testimony as credible."

Nicolas couldn't wait anymore. "What financial deals are you talking about?"

Karim sat back down. "We had a few legal and non-legal scams operating back then as you already know, but there are two that you never knew about. One scam involved people walking the city streets in European countries and America asking for donations to pay for hungry African children. We made a lot of money on that one. Some of the money went to the revolution, but most of it went into a secret bank account that we set up offshore. A part of the money that went into the bank account was reinvested in stocks, but we pulled out when the market was good and ended up accumulating quite a reserve. Then there were a few smaller deals that we made. I was mainly interested in what I just told you. Joseph promised that I could have the money from the scam and stocks if I testified for him. He thinks that my testimony will help them to acquit him, while I hope that I helped to put the last nail in his coffin. Now you have to deal with the girl and figure out what they're up to."

"What about Brussels?"

"Leave Brussels to me. I'll let you know if I need anything."

CHAPTER 64

Henry sat down at the table in the visitor's room and waited for Joseph to arrive. He sat in this tiny room often with Joseph discussing trial strategy, but this was the first time that he was here to confront his client. Any trust that Henry had in Joseph vanished after Max and Alex's return from South Africa. Henry was beyond furious at being used like a puppet.

He could have been sitting in his office back in Baltimore charging more than five hundred dollars per hour instead of sitting here defending Kimbala and now Kimbala has added insult to injury by using him and his team. Henry placed a manila folder on the table showing proof of Joseph's relationship with his brother, Karim, and Nicholas Raine. He wanted to know why Karim agreed to testify and what Nicholas Raine's function was and why Joseph didn't trust him to do his job by bringing Raine's into the picture.

Kimbala was escorted into the room by a security officer. It always amazed Henry how relaxed the security system was there in the detention center. The detainees back home were always in handcuffs and sometimes shackles for minor crimes. He had never seen Joseph Kimbala in handcuffs or shackles here even though he was charged with the most gravest of crimes. Kimbala sat across from Henry and stared at the manila folder.

"Did you bring case work for me to look at?"

Henry took a moment to take in Kimbala's composure before taking the documents and photos out one by one covering the table. He watched Kimbala as he strategically covered the table waiting to recognize any sign of recognition to flicker across Joseph Kimbala's face.

Joseph Kimbala was at first confused at Henry's attitude and watched as his financial paperwork was laid out on the table. Then Henry placed a picture on the table of Joseph, his brother Karim, and Nicholas Raine sitting together at a restaurant table eating dinner. Joseph went back in time. He could clearly remember that day as if it were yesterday. The three were celebrating their first successful financial deal and had decided to celebrate with a dinner at one of the best restaurants in the city.

They were so happy with themselves that Joseph remembered ordering champagne and toasting to a long friendship. Joseph looked up to find Henry staring at him. Henry put a financial document on top of the picture and watched for Joseph's reaction. Joseph picked up the document and read its contents. This was the contract for the very first deal, the deal that they celebrated in the photo. Joseph was still confused, but decided that it was best to stay silent and follow the story that Henry was laying out in front of him. Henry took another photo out of the manila folder and laid it beside the first photo. Joseph recognized his brother having drinks with Nicholas, but he didn't recognize the place or its surroundings.

Henry followed the trail with another document; this time a bill of sale. Joseph could feel his pulse quickening. Henry picked up on the change in Joseph's composure and decided to continue with his picture show. He then placed telephone records and emails between the two brothers on the table laid out like a fan.

Henry broke the wall of silence. "Why did you lie to me?"

Joseph sat back and gazed over the mass of documents and photos. "What do you mean, Henry? I have told you everything that you need to know."

Henry leaned forward and grabbed a handful of documents throwing them in Joseph's direction. "Then tell me what I don't know. You told me that you haven't spoken to your brother since the assassination attempt, but these records say differently. You obviously didn't trust me by putting a mole in my team. I want to know what's going on and I want to know that now! I'm not leaving here until you have told me everything that I want to know."

CHAPTER 65

Meredith sat down at the table in the war room and looked around at her colleagues. Jan Paul was late yet again, but everyone knew that another simple meeting was going to turn into a dragged out two hour meeting with no decisions made. Meredith had to remind herself constantly that this job was temporary. She was tired of hiding behind her boy toys and wanted to exit purgatory. All she had to do was finish this case, and then Meredith was moving back to the UK. She thought about her two prospects and knew that she had to make a decision that week. Meredith smiled when she thought about handing in her resignation letter.

"What are you smiling about? We're sitting here waiting for the two hundredth dreadful meeting to begin." Henri looked at Meredith with a curious look on his face. Meredith didn't have time to respond with Gabriel taking the spotlight once again.

"I can see having countless meetings if we actually made a decision. We practically have three weeks to write our closing brief. We've hardly done anything structurally because we've been too busy catching up because of Jan Paul and now we have to go through this meeting instead of actually planning what we're doing for the next three weeks."

"Our paralegal also came to see me this morning," Meredith began.

"Did she find her way out of Jan Paul's ass? What did she want?"

"She wanted to remind us that the draft brief needed to be done in two weeks so that the revision process could begin."

"Then she's also dreaming right? Let's see what this idiot is going to talk to us about," Gabriel said. Meredith smiled.

"What are you smiling at?" Henri wanted to know.

Meredith looked at her two colleagues with fondness. "I'm going to miss working with the two of you once this case is over. We've been through a lot together and I don't think that I would do it over again, but I have enjoyed working with the two of you."

Jan Paul walked into the war room followed by Oliver Purnell from appeals. Jan Paul registered the looks of shock on their faces as he sat down at the table. Oliver sat next to Jan Paul after greeting everyone.

"I called this meeting because, as all of you know, we received an order this morning with a deadline for our closing brief. We have three weeks to file which isn't a lot of time at all. I've asked Oliver to join us today and help us out with drafting and finalizing of the brief. You're unaware of this, but Oliver and I have been talking the past few days about the case and how the final brief should be structured to favor the strong points of the case. Oliver is indispensable because of his knowledge of appeals and the case history of this Tribunal. He understands, from an outside point of view, our case's strengths and its weaknesses. Oliver will also be taking over the case in the appeals stage so it's a good idea that he steps in now to safeguard as many issues as possible in the appeals stage. We know that at least one of us will appeal after sentencing so Oliver doesn't have to worry about his job."

Jan Paul let out a small laugh before continuing. He passed a skeleton drawing around the table. "Oliver and I drafted a skeleton for the brief incorporating the key issues in the case along with a few suggestions of what we think our strong evidence is for each issue. We also delegated sections to everyone. We want you to take a week to examine your sections and begin drafting your section of the closing brief. Analise is sending you the template to work from. We know that this is going to be a stressful three weeks, but you must use the one template in order to make the formatting easier to handle. If you have any questions, then call Analise."

Oliver decided to add to the conversation. "We delegated areas where you're experts in on this case. If you have any questions about the brief or legal argument, then please come to one of us immediately. Like Jan Paul stated, you only have one week to digest and regurgitate the testimony and evidence from this trial. We expect your submissions by COB Friday afternoon. Analise will combine into one draft and then everyone will take a copy home for the weekend. On Monday morning we'll go over the suggested edits and begin revising the draft. The goal will be to have a final draft product to hand over to Analise by Thursday afternoon. Analise will then take a full four days to proofread and make any structural changes before handing it back to all of us for one last review. The final review will go from Tuesday to Thursday morning. We want to have a final closing brief ready to file by Thursday afternoon in three weeks time."

Jan Paul looked around to find looks of shock and admiration. "Do you have any questions?"

Gabriel shook his head followed by Meredith and Henri. "Great, then we can get to work. You know where to find us if you need help."

Jan Paul rose from the table and walked out of the office. Oliver was a little slower to rise, but soon followed Jan Paul's footsteps and returned to his office. Gabriel, Meredith, and Henri were left in silence to ponder what had just happened.

"This has got to be the most structured meeting that we've ever had and it lasted for less than a half hour and decisions were made. I don't know what just happened to us." Henri looked confused and unsure of himself.

Gabriel looked at Meredith. He knew that something was up if Oliver was involved. "So, why is Oliver on our case all of a sudden?"

Meredith rose from the table and shrugged her shoulders. "You know what? I don't care. If you ask me it's a little too late to have the knight on the white horse come to our rescue. I am glad that we have some structure for the next three weeks, but I'm not feeding into this act, whatever they're up to. I'm going to the cafeteria for a coffee. Anyone want to join me before we get cracking on this?"

She walked out of the war room. Gabriel looked at Henri and shrugged his shoulders. He then got up with every intention of catching up to Meredith. Henri knew them well enough and decided to follow behind them. He couldn't help but think of a line of ducks as he rushed to catch up to Gabriel. Henri was looking forward to a cappuccino.

CHAPTER 66

Alex read the order for the submissions of the final brief. She couldn't believe that they had reached this point. She and Martie spent the entire trial organizing the evidence and legal arguments specifically for this moment. Alex continued to read through the order. The prosecution had three weeks to file their final brief and the defense was ordered to file two weeks after the prosecution's submission was filed, which would give them time to review and answer the prosecution's final brief.

Sam stood in Alex's doorway. "Hey, Alex, Henry wants to meet with us this afternoon about the order. Can you make it at two-o'clock?"

"Of course, I'll be there." Sam turned around and walked back to his office. They began preparing for the two-o'clock meeting.

"The order states that we need to file our final brief three weeks after the prosecution submission date. It also states that we only have an eighty thousand word limit excluding annexes. I called the chief legal officer this morning and no exceptions will be made."

Henry looked towards Martie. "How are we doing with the analysis?"

"Well, thanks to Alex's help we've been able to keep up with the evidence throughout the entire trial and have our strengths and weaknesses laid out for us. I think that our problem will not be reaching the eighty thousand, but making sure that we cut our brief down to fit within the eighty thousand word limit that the court has ordered. We have an idea, from this program that we've been using, where the prosecution believes that their strengths are, and can get an idea of how they will format their final brief."

"Good Martie. The two of you have done a wonderful job throughout this case and now we seem to be in a pretty good state. Okay, I don't want to wait for the prosecution's brief to be filed before we start working on ours. Let's cut up the sections and begin working off what we have already assembled. Once the prosecution's brief has been filed, then we'll be able to see how to fine tune our brief and make changes where appropriate. The deadline for the first draft is one and a half weeks from today. I want our brief to be ready by the time of the prosecution filing so that we can use our time making cosmetic changes. Let's get to work."

CHAPTER 67

Nicholas provided a fake name and identification to the security officer before being escorted into the waiting room. He passed a set of vending machines before turning the corner and entering the first waiting room on the left. Joseph Kimbala walked in a few minutes later and sat down opposite Nicholas. Nicholas stretched across the table to shake hands, but sat back down when Joseph returned his handshake with a cold stare.

"What are you doing here?"

"I'm here to offer friendship and advice." Nicholas placed a manila envelope on the table.

Joseph looked incredulous. "You want to offer friendship and advice after all of these years? Where were you when I needed you? Where is my share of the money? I worked hard for that money too."

Nicholas sat back and sighed. He remembered the days back in Kilambèa with the two brothers and couldn't believe that it had ended up like this. He never expected that he would be visiting Joseph in a detention center located thousands of miles away from Kilambèa. He turned his attention to the problem at hand. He needed to finish his job before leaving the room and Joseph would have to cooperate if he was going to be successful. Nicholas sat up in his chair and opened the manila envelope. He took a small beige envelope out and passed it over to Joseph.

"What is this?" Joseph picked up the envelope and examined the writing on the outside. He recognized the writing as his brother's.

"This is from your brother. I don't know what's inside."

Joseph opened the envelope gently and took out a three page letter. He sat back in his chair and began to read.

Nicholas wished that he had stopped at the vending machine before coming in. He could have used something cold to drink right now. He decided to use the spare time to think about his next job, Alex. He knew that the parties were working on their final brief, but he needed to know what the defense team was doing and if it was going to affect his plans. He just didn't know if Alex was going to speak to him. He had to figure out a way to make her want to talk with him. Joseph put the letter down and looked at Nicholas.

"What is this letter supposed to mean?"

"I haven't read the letter Joseph. I told you that already."

"I'm not an idiot, Nicholas. I don't want to read how you're going to screw me over in a letter. I want to hear it from your lips. What else do you have in that manila envelope?" Joseph gestured towards the envelope that Nicholas was holding onto to.

"What has my brother actually sent you to do?"

"He hasn't sent me to do anything, Joseph. I'm here on my own free will."

Nicholas removed more contents from the envelope and began organizing the documents. "Joseph, I think that we all know that your chance of being acquitted in this trial is slim. They will probably ask for the maximum sentence and at your age, you may not make it out alive."

"Are you playing an attorney nowadays?" Joseph retorted sarcastically.

Nicholas ignored the comment and kept on talking. "It will be more difficult to reach you after conviction and that's why I'm here now. I have a few forms that you need to fill out."

"What type of forms are these?"

Nicholas pushed the paperwork across the table. "They are power of attorney forms and wire transfer authorizations. We need you to sign these documents so that the money will stay safe."

"You mean my money, right? You want to take my money?"

"This is only for safe keeping purposes. We also need to access the money if you die in prison."

"You already know what you can do with these forms and this offer of safe keeping."

Joseph began to rise from the table when Nicholas lifted his hand and motioned Joseph to sit back down. "Joseph we have known each other for a long time, and I wanted to ask you nicely. Please don't make me do this the hard way. We can make you sign these forms, you know that we can. Don't make us use that pressure. We don't want to trouble your family back in Kilambèa or make your life worse in detention."

CHAPTER 68

Henry sat in the same waiting room as his last visit with Joseph. He had received a call the night before. Joseph had wanted to meet him and said that it was urgent. Henry had spent the last three nights in the office working on the final brief and was happy to focus on something else although he knew that he would be itching to return to the office soon. He had no idea what Joseph wanted to talk about, but he couldn't say no to his client even if the client had been lying to him the entire time.

Joseph walked through the door and sat down. Henry noticed the urgency and nervousness right away. He had never seen Joseph this way before. Joseph was always very careful to control his emotions around people and show that he was self confident. Matter of fact, Henry thought, Joseph still acted as if he was still the president of Kilambèa. Henry gave up searching Joseph's face for clues and decided to ask him up front why he requested a meeting.

"Joseph, what are we doing here? I'm trying to finalize the final brief. This is our last chance to fight for an acquittal."

Joseph rubbed his hands together nervously and looked over his shoulder before answering Henry. "Nicholas came to see me yesterday."

Joseph had Henry's attention now. "How did he get in here to see you? His name is on the forbidden list. I requested that myself."

"I don't know, but they can access any area that they want to no matter which country it is. It doesn't matter."

Henry noticed that Joseph was becoming more agitated by the second. "Okay, calm down Joseph. They can't reach you right now. Tell me what happened with Nicholas. What did he want?"

Joseph leaned forward and continued to rub his hands, but Henry could tell that he was becoming calmer. "He wanted me to sign some papers. They were power of attorney forms and wire transfer authorizations. My brother and Nicholas are taking all of my profits from our business dealings."

Henry was shocked and couldn't understand how this could happen when they didn't know if Joseph was going to be sentenced or set free. "But, they don't even know if you're going to be sentenced or released. How can they ask you to sign forms right now? And I thought that Nicholas was a friend of yours too."

Joseph shook his head. Henry obviously didn't understand his world. "Friends don't matter when it comes to money, Henry, plus Nicholas told me that they've been paying someone in chambers to make sure that I'm convicted. They don't want to see me released."

Henry took a moment to take in every word that Joseph uttered. "Joseph, how much money are we talking about?" Henry couldn't believe that Karim and Nicholas would go through this amount of trouble for a few hundred thousand dollars.

Joseph pondered the question before answering. "Twenty million dollars."

Henry stood up out of confusion and disbelief. "Did you just say twenty million dollars?"

He began to walk back and forth on his side of the table. Joseph watched him walk from one end of the room to the other. It didn't take much seeing how the room was as big as a toilet stall, but Henry was using every inch of space that he could find.

Joseph decided that it was better to keep his answer short. "Yes."

Henry sighed and looked up at the ceiling. He couldn't believe that this was happening to him. Joseph looked up from the table at the sound of hysterical laughter. "What are you laughing at? This is a serious life and death matter and you're laughing?" Joseph emphasized his words by gesturing towards Henry's posture and attitude.

Henry collected himself and sat down again. "I'm sorry, Joseph. I began to laugh because of everything that I've encountered in this case. I feel as if I'm a character in a novel and not working a real life case. There have been too many dramatic episodes occurring and now you tell me that not only did you have twenty million dollars that your brother and friend are taking over, but that someone in chambers has been paid to make sure that you receive a guilty judgment." Henry looked at Joseph earnestly. "Look, I'm sorry. I really am. If anyone should be angry or nervous about what's happening it's you. Now, did Nicholas give any ideas of who they were paying in chambers?"

"No. He only said that it was a done deal and that the person was high enough up the ladder to ensure the guilty verdict."

"Did you sign the papers that Nicholas brought for you to sign?"

"Of course I signed. He threatened to hurt my family and promised to reach me in prison if I didn't sign. I had no choice but to sign the documents."

"Okay, I need some time to digest this information and figure out what we should do next. Are you going to be okay on your own here or do I need to talk with the warden and request higher security measures for you?"

"No, I'll be okay. I don't believe that they would try to touch me now, not before the judgment. Anyway, I signed the paperwork. I did what they wanted me to do."

Henry rose from the table and shook Joseph's hand. "In that case I'll leave now. I'll come back tomorrow when I have a plan ready."

Henry turned to walk out, but stopped short of opening the door. He turned around to face the General. "Joseph, my team tried to find the ghost men mentioned in old documentaries before you were arrested. I mean the men that complained about abuses and then it supposedly turned out not to be true. It looked as if the media was trying to falsify the truth or manipulate the realities of Kilambèa." Henry took a breath before asking a question that he didn't want to know the answer to. "Joseph, we never found those men. Did they ever exist?"

Joseph thought about Henry's question. He had already lost what he loved the most. He decided to tell Henry the truth. "Henry, you know the answer to your question."

Henry nodded his head in silence before turning around and walking out of the room.

----------------- CHAPTER 69 -----------------

Henry and Jan Paul were sitting in a pancake house close by the Tribunal eating pancakes and drinking coffee. It had taken Henry some time to get used to having his bacon embedded in the pancake itself, but he enjoyed it. He did miss maple syrup though and wouldn't miss the thick syrup that the Dutch used. Henry picked up his glass of freshly squeezed orange juice and took a few gulps before attacking his pancake again.

"You obviously have gotten used to the Dutch pancake?" Jan Paul smiled while taking a bite of his own.

He loved the opportunity to eat a pancake with strawberries and fresh whipped cream on top. Lizette used to make this for him every Sunday morning before church, but they were just beginning to restore their marriage and Jan Paul knew that Sunday breakfast was a long time away from now.

"So, what's the urgency Henry? Is this your way of trying to screw our final brief up? You know that we're working on it right now. I should be in the office."

Henry took another bite of his pancake before answering. "For all I know you've already finished and are just waiting to file it on the deadline date."

Jan Paul laughed to himself. If only Henry knew the chaotic state he and his team were in, then he would know better than to make ridiculous comments like that.

Henry became serious and put his fork down on his plate. "I met with Joseph yesterday in the detention center and he told me something that I think you should be aware of."

Jan Paul was taking a sip of his coffee and decided to put it down. Henry and Jan Paul had gotten along well during the trial and both played above the belt. He knew that Henry wasn't leading him into a trap. Whatever they had discussed must have been important.

Henry read his mind. "No, my learned colleague, this is not about a plea bargain."

Jan Paul was disappointed, but quickly recovered. "What's going on then?"

"There have been some odd activities happening during the trial, but I didn't mention them to you because I didn't believe that you were affected by them. Now, I think that these activities do affect you and I didn't want to leave you in the dark."

Jan Paul became concerned. He sat up in his chair and listened to Henry intently.

Henry sighed and began again. "What I'm about to say needs to stay between the two of us. I have to have your word that this conversation will stay between the two of us and not be used in the case at all. Can I have your word?"

Jan Paul whispered. "You have my word."

Henry took a deep breath and began his story. "My investigators found out that Joseph and Karim were not estranged after the assassination attempt. In actuality, the assassination attempt was staged by the brothers. They knew that the public was upset with how Karim was running the government and that the people would soon call for a coupe de tat. The brothers then came up with a fake story about how Joseph had fallen out of favor with Karim. The brothers were running a lucrative business and if Karim was going to be taken out of government, then he would rather it be by the person closest to him, his brother. They staged the assassination attempt, but from what I'm told, the killing of Karim's family was intentional. Joseph told me that Karim thought that the people would be more gracious and forgiving if their beloved first lady and children were involved. At the same time, they would fear Joseph and Joseph could take over control with little opposition. It worked. It actually worked too well.

The brothers continued to do business together, through a friend of theirs, Nicholas Raine, and now Karim and this Nicholas Raine are trying to take over Joseph's profits from the businesses over the years, a net worth of around twenty million dollars."

Jan Paul was sipping on his coffee when he heard the amount and began to choke.

Henry patted him on the back. "Are you okay?"

"Am I okay? You just told me that they made twenty million dollars."

"Well, that's not the worst of it. Karim and Nicholas are so keen to get Joseph's money that they hired someone in chambers to ensure a guilty verdict."

"Well, he is guilty. He should be found guilty and sentenced."

"Jan Paul, we both know that you don't have enough evidence to put Joseph away for very long. You have a weak case."

Jan Paul sat back in his seat and played with his fork. "What do you want from me?"

"We need to figure out who the mole is in chambers." Jan Paul looked at Henry as if a crazy person was sitting next to him.

Henry decided to bargain on one last plea. "Jan Paul, if you're more interested in justice and a fair trial and not only in winning, then you have to help me find the mole. They have to base the judgment on the evidence and not because someone's being paid."

-------------------- CHAPTER 70 --------------------

Alex took her place at the defense team's table. She was too nervous to notice the packed audience sitting in the gallery. Joseph's family was sitting in the front row while curious strangers sat around them and news reporters sat a few yards away from them. No one uttered a word and the courtroom remained silent as the judges filed in and took their seats. Judge Atkinson welcomed everyone and reminded them of why they were there.

"Mr. Kimbala, please rise. You have been charged by the prosecution with murder, torture, enforced disappearance of persons, political persecution, and sexual slavery. For the past eight months, we along with the public have heard from forty prosecution witnesses and twenty defense witnesses. We have heard evidence about the notorious NIS, wherein the prosecution presented evidence of the gruesome acts committed by NIS agents allegedly under your direct and indirect orders. We heard from one witness, Ms. Ntanga, about how the NIS terrified the community. We heard from other witnesses that were brutally tortured and terrorized by former NIS agents. One witness in particular, lost her father supposedly at your hand. Nine hundred exhibits have been tendered in the case including thousands of pages of documents, maps, videos, and photos. The parties have left us with two varying stories of what happened under your reign in Kilambèa. The trial chamber has no doubt that these stories that we have heard from most of the prosecution witnesses and seen in the documents are correct, in their own right."

Judge Atkinson turned to the gallery. "Ladies and gentlemen, I am about to do something that is unusual here at this tribunal. Please understand that it is necessary and will last for a short time only. Can we please go into closed session?"

The court deputy closed the session and wondered what was going to happen next. The audience members felt as if they were watching an old movie. They could see Judge Atkinson's mouth moving, but could only hear silence from their headphones.

Judge Atkinson turned to the accused. "Now, Mr. Kimbala, I want to inform you that your charade did not work."

Everyone became confused. They didn't know what Judge Atkinson was talking about. Joseph Kimbala turned to Henry and then looked back at Judge Atkinson. Judge Atkinson resumed, "You attempted to bribe a member of our staff in the hope of affecting our decision. I can tell you that not only were you not affective, but that the staff member in question came to us the first time that your colleague approached her. What you have done is unacceptable and unheard of in this Tribunal. Mr. Boome, I understand that your team had nothing to do with this. I want you to understand that we are not accusing you of any wrong doing. Can we please go back to open session now?"

The court deputy pushed the button and the audience could hear Judge Atkinson once again. "Ladies and gentlemen, thank you very much for your patience. Mr. Kimbala, the trial chamber finds you guilty and sentences you to life imprisonment."

-------------------- CHAPTER 71 --------------------

Alex decided to visit the Starbucks down the street instead of the one located in the lobby of her office. Living in Holland had provided a lasting mark on her life, one that she hoped would continue. She learned the meaning of Dutch 'gezelligheid' and wanted to live every day to its fullest. She wasn't to the point of working to live, but wanted to see how far she could get in order to reach a feeling of content in her life. Alex walked down the street and took a deep breath. She was happy to be home and would never take home for granted again. It was a wonderful feeling being able to understand people as they walked by, read the local newspaper, and buy hair products that she had grown up with. Alex grinned as she reminisced about some embarrassing moments in the Dutch supermarket and restaurants. Alex gave herself an imaginary pat on the back. She was able to organize for trial, deal with Nicholas, get around a foreign language and culture, and come out of it all without too many bruises.

Alex walked into Starbucks and ordered her coffee. She then picked up a Baltimore Sun newspaper while waiting for the coffee and eyed the desserts. She chose a piece of zucchini bread and paid before picking up her coffee. Alex juggled her breakfast while walking towards a table when she bumped into a man passing by. She looked up into Nicholas' eyes and took a few steps back. Alex stared at Nicholas in silence.

"Good morning, Alex. Fancy meeting you here."

Alex quickly composed herself and smiled. "Good morning Nicholas. What are you doing in this neighborhood?"

Alex decided that it would be better if she ate her breakfast back in the office and started walking towards the front door. Thank goodness that the lady behind the counter had bagged her zucchini bread and placed her coffee in a paper cup, Alex thought.

"I thought that you were going to sit down here and eat your breakfast." Nicholas held the door open for Alex.

"Thank you. You know me. I'm a workaholic. I'm going to eat at my desk back at the office. You haven't answered my question, Nicholas. What are you doing here?"

Nicholas fastened his pace and stepped in front of Alex. He motioned for her to stop. "Please give me a few minutes." Alex stopped walking and looked in the direction of her building.

"I'm sure that you know which building I work in. You have until we reach the building." Alex moved around Nicholas and began walking again.

That's my girl, Nicholas thought before beginning again. "You left Holland without saying goodbye. I wanted to come and see how you were doing. Do you know that I'm based in Washington now?"

Alex looked both ways before crossing the street and answering. "Yes, I read that in your letter."

"Then why didn't you call me? You didn't give me a chance to explain face to face back in Holland so I wrote the letter. I explained everything to you and you still didn't call me."

Alex stopped walking and turned to Nicholas. She took her first sip of coffee and briefly felt her senses waking up. She hated having deep conversations before her first morning cup of coffee, but knew that this had to be done now.

"Nicholas, I read your letter and you did explain everything. I want to thank you for that. I would never have known how much you cared for me if you hadn't sent that letter."

"Alex, I haven't stopped caring for you. As a matter of fact, I love you. It hurt me that you left Holland without trying to talk with me to resolve what happened."

Alex took another sip before speaking. "It's great to know that you weren't this dark evil character at all, but were working for the South African secret service. I'm sure that I'm not even supposed to know that."

"Then why didn't you contact me if you think that it's so great?"

Alex stopped just as they reached her building and turned towards Nicholas. "Because our relationship was based on a lie, Nicholas. I didn't even know your real name for the first couple of months."

Nicholas sighed and knew that he was losing this fight. "I never lied to you about my feelings, Alex. Isn't that what counts?"

Alex shook her head. "It's not all that counts, Nicholas. You put me through a lot of pain that I didn't deserve. You also used me to gather information about our case. I trusted you and you threw my trust away. You placed your job above me, above our relationship. How can we build a relationship on a lie?"

Alex looked in the building's lobby and had a sudden urge to run inside. Nicholas knew Alex and it occurred to him that his trip to Baltimore was a waste of time. He had lost Alex some time ago in Holland probably before her trip to South Africa.

"What are you going to do now?"

Alex smiled and a sense of relief ran through her body. "I don't know. I think that I'll take some 'me' time for awhile. I need to figure out what I want for myself. I also want to get to the point where I'll remember the good times when I think about us."

"Do you think that we could ever try again?" Nicholas looked hopeful. He wanted to reach over and touch her, but knew that that would be a mistake.

"Maybe...but probably not. I hope that we can be friends one day though. Hey, I have to go inside now. Take good care of yourself, okay?"

Alex leaned forward and kissed Nicholas on the cheek before she turned around and walked inside. Nicholas watched Alex disappear into the elevator and knew that he would never see her again.

Alex sat down at her desk and thought about her brush encounter with Nicholas. She had cried her last tear a couple of weeks before and had made a promise never to cry over Nicholas Raine again. Alex rose and walked over to the window. She looked below with dry eyes at the moving traffic before turning around at the sound of Carter's voice.

Carter returned her smile. "Good morning sunshine. I see that you got breakfast without me this time."

Alex walked back to her desk wondering if she was going to be drinking iced coffee instead. "I decided to walk down the street instead and catch some fresh air."

"Did you catch anything else? You look radiant this morning."

Alex knew how curious Carter was and loved him for it. "I'm just trying something new. In Holland I was cycling or walking to work and didn't have to use the gym. Here, in Baltimore, I'm driving to work and then spending most of the day behind my desk working. I've decided to change my life a little. I live too far away to walk to work, but I am going to get from behind this desk a few times a day and exercise these legs. More importantly, I'll be getting some fresh air."

Alex sat down and took a sip of coffee before sifting through the morning mail. "Hey Carter, have we received all of our boxes from The Hague? I want to make sure that the assistants have everything inventoried."

"We're still waiting on two boxes, but everything else has arrived. The assistants are working on the inventory now and their report is due at the end of next week. We're hoping that the other two boxes will have arrived by then."

"Thanks, Carter. Why don't you go and get some breakfast? We can talk when you come back. I'm just going to rummage through my pile of mail. We've been back for a week already, but I'm still going through the general mail and office updates. Can you believe that?"

"You've been working on an adrenaline rush the past few months and now the battery is empty. I don't understand why you're here and not on vacation somewhere instead. Your body needs to rejuvenate, Alex."

"I know and that's why I'm taking some time off starting next week. You know that already."

Carter turned around to walk out of the room, but couldn't resist leaving the room without having the last word. "Two weeks off is nothing. You need a month, honey."

Alex heard a shuffling sound and looked up from her mail expecting to see Carter but faced Sam instead.

"Hey good morning, Sam. How are you?"

Sam wished that Alex hadn't heard him standing in the doorway. He wanted to watch her if only for a moment. He knew that Henry was correct. He did love Alex, but didn't think that this was the right time to tell her, especially after Nicholas Raine.

"Good morning Alex," Sam responded walking into Alex's office. "Henry wants to meet with us in an hour about a new case. Can you make it?"

"Yeah, sure. Have any idea what it's about?"

Sam shook his head. "I wish I did, but no I don't know." Sam turned around to walk out of the office, "See you in an hour."

Alex reached for her zucchini bread and returned to her pile of mail.

---------------- CHAPTER 72 ----------------

Jan Paul walked down the hall holding a piece of paper in his left hand. He turned the corner and walked past the prosecutor's secretary and opened the door. The secretary was half way out of her seat when the door closed behind Jan Paul. Jan Paul walked over and threw a piece of paper on her desk right on top of a brief that she was reading. The prosecutor looked up to find Jan Paul standing in front of her desk. She was annoyed with his disrespectful manner, but knew that his days were numbered.

"What is this?"

Jan Paul looked down at the prosecutor and smiled. "You expected my resignation so here it is, Madame Prosecutor."

"And when is your last day."

She expected that he would want her to counter his resignation and hold out, but she was ready to tell him that he had thirty days to clean his office out.

"Madame, this is my last day." Jan Paul turned around and knew that he would savor the prosecutor's shocked look for the rest of his life.

He returned to his office and called his wife. "Hi, love, I did it and you should have seen the look on her face. I'm going to finish packing my boxes, drop my badge off, and then head home. How's the packing coming?"

Lizette felt relieved. She wasn't sure how Jan Paul was going to handle his resignation and now she felt as if the last road block to them moving on was removed.

"It's going fine. The movers are coming tomorrow to pick everything up and our friend down the street, Nadine, agreed to supervise them so that we can leave tonight."

Lizette stood in the kitchen and leaned back onto the empty kitchen counter top. She began to feel a little nervous. She didn't want to force Jan Paul into leaving Holland, but she also didn't see how they could survive as a family without returning home immediately. She looked up to the ceiling and took a deep breath before asking. "Jan Paul, are you sure that you're okay with leaving Holland and returning home?"

Jan Paul felt a stab in his heart. He had hurt Lizette so much in the past few months and couldn't believe that she was giving their marriage another chance. He wasn't going to let her down now.

"Lizette, this is the right decision and I would move to the other side of the world if that's what you wanted to do. I don't want to lose you or our family and I promise that I will do whatever I have to never hurt you again. Listen, I'm not going to stay the entire day here. It's my last day. I'm going to finish packing and walk upstairs to say goodbye to the team. How about we have lunch around noon today and then we can get an early start back home? I'm looking forward to seeing our real home and being in familiar surroundings. What do you say?"

Lizette felt better and wiped a tear from her cheek. "Love, we're waiting for you. We'll go home as soon as you're here."

Jan Paul hung the phone up and picked up his last box to pack. Analise walked into his office with a shocked look on her face. There had been a distance between the two of them the past month, but she hadn't wanted to give up that easily.

"I heard a rumor that you resigned."

Jan Paul placed a book in the box and turned around to face Analise. "Good morning, Analise. That was fast. I just turned my resignation in about twenty minutes ago."

"News travels fast here. Why did you resign?"

Jan Paul sighed and sat down on the corner of his desk. "Analise, this place was killing me personally and professionally. I almost lost my family because of it. Lizette was about to leave me and I couldn't let that happen.

She also opened my eyes to the truth. I was turning into someone that I loathe to see in others."

Analise looked around the room and noticed that it was bare. She hadn't visited his room in the past month. He must have been preparing to leave for awhile. There was no way that he could have packed the contents of this office in one day.

"You've been planning this for awhile haven't you? What about us then, Jan Paul?"

Analise started to move closer to Jan Paul. She wanted to touch him in an effort at intimacy, but Jan Paul rose from the desk and started to pack again. He looked up at Analise. He had thought about their relationship and knew that Analise didn't really care about him. When he thought about it he really didn't care for her either. She had been, temporarily, his stress reliever. It had been his way of avoiding everything in his life when the pressure became too much. Jan Paul made a mental note to look into a stress management course back in Brussels.

"Look Analise, there is no 'us' and there really never was. We enjoyed each other for a little bit and I want to thank you for helping me through a tough time in my life, but now I need to move on and you do too."

Analise couldn't understand what was happening. Her plan was falling apart. How could he leave so unexpectedly?

"I thought that we had something together and now you're leaving, just like that and without saying goodbye? How can you do this to me?"

Jan Paul looked earnestly at Analise. "Analise, I was going to stop by upstairs to say goodbye to everyone."

He thought about closing the door, but didn't want to add to the rumors already circling the building. He decided to keep the door open and stick with the truth. He had been lying for too long now and the truth felt liberating now a days.

"Analise, we both know that you were looking at me for your promotion here at the Tribunal." He could see anger seeping into Analise's eyes and continued. "Please listen to what I'm saying. I know that I'm better off back home working for my government instead of in this place. Your work is really good and I don't know why you feel the need to give yourself up in other ways. If you're not promoted based on your work, then I would hope that you would value yourself enough not to sleep with someone higher in position just for the promotion. Now, I'm going to finish packing and get home to my family." Jan Paul continued packing.

Analise was furious and could hardly contain herself. "The nerve that you have in speaking to me like that," Analise spit out the words. "How dare you speak to me like this. Does your pretty wife know everything about us? What you've said to me in bed? Maybe I should give her a call?" Analise started walking towards the phone.

Jan Paul answered her in a calm voice. "My dear, I told Lizette everything. I came clean with her and am happier for it. You don't have anything damaging to add. I've already done that and she's still willing to take me back, which I'm grateful for."

Analise turned around and walked out of the office. "Pathetic woman. You don't deserve me anyway."

"I think that you're right," Jan Paul mumbled to himself as he watched Analise leave the office. Jan Paul continued with his packing. He had a lunch date with his family and he didn't want to be late.

------------------ CHAPTER 73 ------------------

Alex walked into the restaurant to find her friend, Melanie, already waiting for her. She walked over to the table and Melanie rose for the bear hug. They were still getting used to physically seeing each other instead of email and phone contact. Alex didn't know how much she'd missed her best friend until the ordeal with Nicholas Raine. Melanie did her best remotely and offered to fly over to help, but Alex knew that Melanie was on a strict budget and she couldn't put her friend through that type of financial stress. Alex sat down and put her coat on the back of the chair. The waiter walked over and took their drinks order before handing them menus. Alex enjoyed having quick customer service again too. She would never take it for granted again.

They opened their menus knowing that the waiter would return soon with the drinks and request their dinner order.

"So, have you been able to settle back in at the office?"

Alex took a moment to think about Mel's question before answering. "Yes, it feels good to be back in my own office and familiar surroundings. I also missed you and my family and friends." Alex decided on roast chicken and vegetables for dinner.

Melanie decided that it was safe to ask about Nicholas. "How are you feeling?"

Alex looked over her water glass. "About what?"

"Alex, you know what I mean."

Alex put her water glass down. "I'm actually fine. I'm doing better than I thought I would. He showed up this morning."

Mel was shocked. "Where did you see him? Did he come to the office?"

Alex thought back to her morning. "It's actually a little odd. You know that I normally have breakfast at the office, right? Well, this morning I decided to pick up coffee and some breakfast down the street at Starbucks. I bumped into him on the way out."

"What did you say when you saw him?"

"We talked. He wanted to know if we could start again, but I said no."

"Are you sure about that? He's the first guy that you've ever really cared about. Where is he now?"

"He's in D.C. I didn't just care for him, Mel, I loved him. Our relationship was wonderful before everything fell apart. He was my dream man."

"That's what I'm afraid of. Are you sure that you can walk away from him. You know now that he wasn't this terrible guy doing monstrous things. Maybe you should give him another chance. Alex, I've never seen you as happy as you were with him."

The dinners were placed on the table and they began eating. "Mel, I know that you mean well, but I need some space and personal time right now. I learned a lot about myself in The Hague. I want to change some things in my life and have a lot of decisions to make. I don't need Nicholas to confuse me right now. Maybe we'll cross paths in the future, but for right now I need clarity."

Melanie decided to give in and changed the subject. "So, how did the meeting go? Do you know what you're going to be working on next?"

Alex smiled and opened her menu. "Yes, and I'm happy. I not only know which case I'm working on, but the firm wants to keep us all together as a team and everyone has agreed to stay together. The best thing is that we'll be working out of the home office here in Baltimore. So, I get to keep my office."

Melanie took a sip of her wine before continuing her interrogation. "What's the next case?"

"You would like to know that wouldn't you?" Alex said sheepishly.

"Now, that's just plain rude!" Melanie gasped.

Alex laughed. It had been a long time since she had been this happy. She also had felt as if she was getting stronger every day. "I'm sorry, sweetie. Management has sworn us to secrecy. All I can tell you is that this next case will be just as interesting as the Kimbala case." Alex took a sip of her wine. "I just hope that it will lack the drama of the Kimbala case. I think I've had enough drama to last me for the next few years." Alex rolled her eyes.

"I'll toast to that," Mel said.

The girls lifted their wine glasses in the air. The clinking of their glasses reverberated throughout the restaurant.

Lightning Source UK Ltd.
Milton Keynes UK
UKOW050027300312

189867UK00001B/75/P